T0294459

DEAD MEN'S
SILENCE

A CHRIS BLACK ADVENTURE

The Chris Black Adventure Series

By James Lindholm

———————

JAMES LINDHOLM

DEAD MEN'S SILENCE

A CHRIS BLACK ADVENTURE

CamCat Books

CamCat Publishing, LLC
Brentwood, Tennessee 37027
camcatpublishing.com

This is a work of fiction. Names, characters, places, and incidents are either products of the author's imagination or are used fictitiously.

Hardcover ISBN 9780744300710
Paperback ISBN 9780744301359
Large-Print Paperback ISBN 9780744301472
eBook ISBN 9780744301533
Audiobook ISBN 9780744301823

Library of Congress Control Number: 2020945854

Cover design by Jerry Todd. Book design by Maryann Appel.

5   3   1   2   4

To the Plan A Team—

Kameron, Megan, Paulina, and Tommy
(with some help from Matt
and plenty of moral support from Marisa).

Just in case you guys have any doubts about how much
I've enjoyed working with you.

Previously, in *Blood Cold*,
Chris Black's second adventure. . .

De Klerk was not a good swimmer. If they were going to put him in the water with his hands tied, he might drown.

"Please. Please don't put me in the water. I can't swim! I'll give all the money back! I will do anything. Please." He paused. "At least cut my legs free. Please!"

The blue-eyed man grabbed de Klerk by his two wrists and hefted him up on to the stern gunwale. Momentarily disoriented by the move, it took de Klerk several seconds to get his bearings.

He was seated on the stern with his legs dangling over the back of the gunwale. In front of him, perhaps seventy-five feet away, was a very small island. More like a large rock pile than a proper island. It was covered with what looked like some kind of seals. There were literally thousands of them. The din of sound that earlier had reminded him of a party was their near-continuous vocalizations, kind of a barking yelp. The stench, even at this distance, was overwhelming.

Seals were coming and going from the island; leaping off the rocks into the water and jumping about in small groups. A small huddle of penguins watched from the water's edge.

A new panic erupted in de Klerk, a panic like nothing he'd ever experienced before. He shook violently and tried to rock his way back into the boat. Large hands clasped down on both his shoulders and prevented him from moving.

He knew he was staring out at Seal Island, a small rocky outcrop located a few kilometers offshore in False Bay. It was known to Cape Town residents, as well as much of the TV-watching world, as the home of South Africa's famous "flying" great white sharks.

De Klerk's mind involuntarily reviewed the last nature special he had seen on TV. This was the spot where one-ton sharks literally leapt from the water at 25 mph in pursuit of their Cape fur seal prey, a behavior rarely seen elsewhere in the world. Erupting from the water, the sharks would split the small fur seals in half. They would then thrash about at the surface in a frothy red mix of seal blood and seawater as they finished off the meal. Sea birds would swarm on the kill spot, grabbing loose seal innards and fighting over them in the air above as the shark thrashed about below. Occasionally, an unlucky seabird would stray too close to the gaping maw of the white shark and become dessert to an already satisfying meal.

Perhaps the most disturbing aspect of these predatory attacks was the incredible speed with which they took place. If you sneezed, you missed it.

1

Damien Wood died first. In the dwindling twilight of a Colombian sunset, a pirate cut his throat from ear to ear as he sat at the helm of his father's sixty-foot cabin cruiser *Innovator*. The entire incident took less than twenty seconds. One instant he was leisurely staring out the cruiser's front windshield, smiling as he thought about the last *Game of Thrones* episode he'd watched, the next he was dying. Damien's last conscious act was to look down at the blood pouring over his tanned-but-skinny torso and wonder, "What the hell?"

The *Innovator* had left Newport Beach two months prior and slowly worked its way down the length of Baja California and along the Mexican mainland in four weeks' time. Investment banker Jared Wood had been initially hesitant to loan out the *Innovator* to his son Damian and his friends. He'd only owned the boat for a year and had hardly spent any time on it himself.

Wood had ordered the crew, via satellite phone, to steer clear of Honduras, El Salvador, and Nicaragua for fear that they might run afoul of "bad people." But it was at the last stop the *Innovator* made in Colombia that the boat had caught the attention of four men lurking in a small converted fishing boat at the partying crowd's perimeter. The crew of the *Langosta Espinosa* were nondescript enough to move freely among the boats moored around the island without attracting attention. The boat itself was unremarkable, and the five Hispanic men that operated it could have fit in anywhere along the Central American coast.

If anyone had looked closely, they would have seen that the wooden-hulled boat had not been lobster fishing for some time; with traps irreparably broken and fouled on the back in a way no active fisherman would ever allow. But in a crowd more concerned with merriment than potential dangers, no one gave the boat or the crew a second look. And the lagging Colombian economy had left the already under-funded coast guard with very few assets to patrol the extensive coastline.

Late in the morning, the *Innovator* had crossed into Colombian waters and sought refuge in the first cove the captain could find. The last week of partying had taken its toll on all passengers aboard, and the group required rest. As life-long, unrepentant nerds, Damien and his friend Stephen Long had survived this far with minimal experience in alcohol-fueled merriment. Damien's other friend, Mike Hanson, had done his share of partying during his football days, but these days had been over for years. Though all three guys had warmed quickly to the opportunities for celebration among their international boating community, they'd not had much endurance.

Cracks had begun to form in the façade holding the three young men together. As roommates during freshman and sophomore year at the University of Southern California, Damien and Mike quickly worked out the challenges of living in close quarters together, Stephen had no such training. He'd lived at home in his parent's basement for what little of college he'd attended before departing USC for the glory of the movie business. His career as third assistant to the director had lasted merely six months. The film for which he'd quit school was canceled mid-production due to financial issues. By the time the *Innovator* had reached Colombia, Stephen was complaining more frequently about Mike's nightly snoring. Mike, in turn, noted that Stephen rarely cleaned up after himself, leaving "his shit all over the place" while he played games on his smartphone. Damien had simply been frustrated by how stupid he thought these complaints were as he tried to keep the peace.

As the *Innovator*'s first day in Colombian waters came to a close, the three friends were as far apart as the boat allowed, each lost in his own thoughts. That made them easy targets.

After Damian, Stephen Long died next; and just as quickly. He was stretched out on the *Innovator*'s bow playing a driving game called *Asphalt 8* on his smartphone. Stephen was so immersed in the game that he didn't sense the pirate's presence until his attention was redirected to the handle of the eight-inch ka-bar knife sticking out of his chest.

For every pound that Damien had been missing from his torso, Stephen had made up for on his own. He looked down at his chubbiness for the last time and wondered where his mom and dad were. *Asphalt 8* continued on its own for another two minutes until the phone's battery went as dead as Stephen.

Mike Hanson put up a fight. He was down in the galley, making his second sandwich for the evening when the third pirate came through the main hatch to get to him. At six-foot-four and two-hundred-and-fifty pounds, Mike looked at the smaller man wielding a knife and smiled.

Mike decided to resolve the situation quickly in his favor. Growing up in South Central Los Angeles as the only child of a single, African-American mother, Mike had learned early to solve problems before they came back to 'bite him in the ass.' He grabbed the wooden cutting board on which his second sandwich rested and smacked the pirate, crushing the man's nose with one strike. Mike then retracted the board and quickly struck again at the pirate's wind-pipe, forcing a guttural cough from the man as he collapsed.

Satisfied that he'd ended the incident, Mike paused to listen for other trouble. Hearing no immediate threats, he leaned over to pick up the pirate's knife, thinking he'd better check on his two less physically capable friends right away. The pirate could have already attacked one of them before coming down to the galley, he thought.

Rising back to nearly his full height, slumping slightly, so his head didn't hit the galley ceiling, Mike heard a metallic click that he didn't recognize. Before he had a moment to consider it further, a gunshot from the fourth pirate hit him in his left shoulder. The impact of the bullet spun Mike around, so he was now facing the pirate who'd just shot him. Neither of them moved as the gun's loud report still wrung in their ears.

Mike glanced down at the wound on his shoulder and then peered through narrowed eyes at the pirate. As the man raised his weapon again, Mike used the cutting board, which was still in this right hand, to swipe upward, across his body. The force of the blow dislodged the gun from the pirate's hand and broke the cutting board in half.

Not waiting to give the pirate another chance, Mike hurled his large body up the steps toward the back deck. "Damien! Watch out—." His warning caught in his throat as he found Damien's body slumped in the chair at the helm, a gaping hole where his neck used to be, and his chest covered in blood.

Grabbing his bleeding shoulder, Mike stepped around the edge of the wheelhouse and moved as quickly as the narrow walkway would allow toward the bow. The shock of seeing his friend dead was briefly tempered by the adrenaline surging through his body. Perhaps if he could get to Stephen in time, they could escape together.

He could hear someone coming behind him, but before he could turn around, Mike had arrived at the portion of the walkway that opened onto the *Innovator's* bow, revealing Stephen's lifeless body lying against a hatch. "Oh, my god."

Briefly stymied by the realization that his friends were no longer with him, Mike hesitated. At that moment, a pirate appeared around the edge of the wheelhouse. The man expertly tossed a large knife in the air, caught it by the blade, and then threw it directly at Mike's chest.

Mike frantically deflected the knife with his right forearm, the blade slicing deeply into his muscle before dropping to the deck and sliding over the side.

Now nursing two wounds, Mike determined that in the increasing darkness, his best course of action was to flee. He grabbed the rail with his bloodied right hand and launched himself over the side.

Plunging deep into the warm Pacific water, Mike surfaced away from the *Innovator* and began stroking toward the shore, leaving blood in his wake. He could see lights shimmering at multiple spots along the edge of the large cove from what he hoped were houses or hotels. Someone there would be able to help him.

It was a long swim for Mike, at least the length of a football field. He was not a natural swimmer, and with both arms impeded by injuries, his progress was slow. Approximately halfway to shore, he heard what he thought was the sound of a small outboard motor. He paused to listen over his labored breathing; it sounded as though the small boat was headed away from him. Maybe his plan was going to work.

Struggling with declining mobility in his limbs and significant blood loss, Mike continued to make progress toward land. He could see the silhouetted shapes of people walking along the shore, but he was too tired to produce a coherent cry for help. Pausing again to catch his breath, new hope swelled in Mike as his feet drifted down to touch the sandy bottom below. He'd made it!

His feet on solid underwater ground, he could now use both his legs and arms to make progress toward shore. Exhausted from the effort and delirious from the blood loss, Mike failed to process the tugging he sensed down by his right leg. When it persisted, he started to wonder if he'd become tangled in something.

Reaching down to remove whatever was holding him back, Mike was briefly shocked back into lucidity when he realized that his right leg was gone below his mid-thigh. His hand brushed against the end of what must have been his femur, surrounded by strands of tissue dangling in the water.

"What the f—?" exclaimed Mike, just before he was pulled underwater. He could feel the rough skin of the shark's nose on the underside of his right arm as it clenched its jaws around his torso.

Seconds after the attack began, it was over.

Twelve minutes later, the *Innovator* was once again underway, this time alongside the *Langosta Espinosa*. Neither the simultaneous departure of the two vessels nor Mike's struggle for survival registered among the partying crowd in nearby boats or along the shore. As the boats disappeared over the horizon, the bodies of Damien and Stephen joined Mike one last time as the pirates tossed them over the side, wrapped in an old fishnet and anchored down by the dive weights that Jared Wood would never have the chance to use.

2

Chris Black stood tall on the back deck of the fishing vessel *Elizabeth Margot*. He saw the small drone flying overhead before he heard it; the noonday sun reflecting off the drone's camera lens, giving away its position. Shielding his eyes with his hand, still gloved in neoprene from the SCUBA dive he'd just completed, Chris tracked the craft's approach against a backdrop of the mountainous region of Big Sur, along California's central coast.

"What's up?" asked Paulina, Chris's dive buddy, as she removed her tank and placed it on the deck.

"Drone," replied Chris, his eyes tracking it as it came directly toward the boat.

"Shouldn't be any drone activity out here."

Flights of unmanned aerial vehicles were closely regulated along California's coastline, particularly in sensitive areas like the kelp forest in which they were working. He could see the Point Sur Lighthouse high on a rocky outcrop just north of their position.

Just as the whir of the drone's propellers became apparent, Chris heard a small outboard engine cut out as three masked attackers climbed over the gunwale onto the fishing vessel's back deck. Though panic never crossed his mind, Chris would later admit that the sight of the attackers in the midst of a research cruise was so bizarre as to give him pause. But that pause lasted only seconds.

The three invaders split up immediately. One ran toward the stern, and though the figure was wearing a full ski mask, Chris was fairly certain she was female. One ran toward the bow, or at least that's what Chris assumed to be the guy's plan. The third attacker, the largest of the three, extracted a club from a sheath on his calf and started running toward Chris and Paulina.

At thirty-nine years old and six-foot-two inches tall, Chris was still fit and not at all afraid to fight if he had to. The lines on his face and the grey streaks in his otherwise dark hair suggested a lifetime spent in the outdoors; a lifetime that to-date had put him in contact with more than his fair share of society's criminal element. He watched the larger attacker come across the deck and processed what was going on. The man's black ski mask obscured his face, but his large, tattooed forearms were visible, and he was wearing a sweatshirt emblazoned with the words 'Deep Sea Corals Forever!'

"Eco-terrorists?" Chris asked aloud; he was that bewildered. He'd heard of such raids on boats around the world, but he'd never experienced one directly. He was now beginning to understand why the drone was there. These guys were trying to make some kind of point and were recording the entire event to showcase later to their membership.

Paulina, standing between Chris and the attacker yelled, "Hey!" A push from the large attacker lifted the five-foot-six Paulina off her feet, sending her flying into a pile of nylon line and inflatable floats.

With the move against Paulina, the entire event took on a new flavor for Chris. Chris and Mac, his friend and colleague, had argued about many things over the years as they'd encountered thugs and scum in many forms at various locales. But one of the things they agreed on was that you don't hurt members of their team.

Armed with nothing but his wits and dressed from head to toe in neoprene, Chris assessed his options. He did not know precisely how this was going to be resolved, but he was certain of one thing: this guy was going down.

Behind Chris stood a large shipping container that had been placed on the fishing vessel's back deck to serve as a mobile dive locker during SCUBA operations. As the assistant director of the Center for Marine Exploration (CMEx) in Central California, Chris spent a great deal of time in and on the water. With the university's primary research vessel, *MacGreggor*, headed south to Ecuador for a research cruise in the Galapagos Islands, Chris and his team had chartered a converted fishing vessel to serve as a platform for a research diving trip down the coast.

The family that owned and operated the *Elizabeth Margot* had fished off Monterey for generations. When increasingly stringent state and federal regulations had made commercial fishing less profitable, the family had converted the boat to support scientific operations. This was the third time Chris had chartered the vessel. He had come to like working with the family very much.

The attacker turned toward Chris, pulling a club from behind his back. Chris lunged forward, keeping his eyes on the club. When the inevitable swing came, clearly broadcast by the attacker, Chris was able to dodge it and grab the guy's sweatshirt with both hands. He then intentionally fell backward, pulling along the much larger man with all his strength.

The combined forces of gravity, the attacker's momentum, and Chris's strong pull resulted in exactly what Chris had hoped for—the attacker's face-first collision with the side of the shipping container. The forceful thud of the crash dented the side of the container and knocked the attacker unconscious. Chris sought, and to his relief, found a pulse on the man's carotid artery.

Seeing that Paulina was conscious, he asked as he pulled off his wetsuit gloves, "Are you okay?"

She nodded her head and grunted, "Go!"

Chris scanned the water to the left of the vessel, looking for bubbles at the surface. His four-member undergraduate dive team was still underwater and would be for several more minutes if the dive went according to plan. They were down in a kelp forest using a large virtual reality camera system to collect imagery on fish behavior. He wanted to resolve this situation before they returned to the boat. While he was completely comfortable, given their experience, with the team diving on their own as they were now, Chris didn't want them injured by some ill-conceived attack at the surface.

Chris picked up the attacker's club and spied around the right corner of the shipping container. Seeing no one, he moved quickly along the full length of the container. Peering slowly around the back corner, Chris could see the woman doing something to the A-frame crane mounted on the stern to deploy oceanographic instrumentation and small inflatable boats. He could hear the drone's propellers whirring overhead.

"Hey!" shouted Chris. "Whatever you're planning here is basically over. Your friend back there assaulted one of our staff, so you're all in big trouble. Just show me your hands."

The woman remained with her back to Chris and said nothing. He was briefly concerned that she might have some kind of explosive device. He hoped that the attackers weren't that extreme.

Chris approached the woman and nudged her shoulder with the end of the club.

"I repeat, turn around and show me your hands."

"Hey, asshole, I can't," replied the woman, and Chris could hear jingling metal. Glancing around the woman's side, he realized that she'd handcuffed herself to the crane.

"Okay, well, at least you aren't going anywhere," Chris said. Looking up at the drone, he added, "And I guess maybe you should have put your message on the *back* of your sweatshirt. As it is, you're just getting footage of some idiot in a dark sweatshirt handcuffed to an A-frame crane."

"Fuck you! We're going to stop you from destroying the seafloor no matter what the cost."

"Listen, lady, I've spent much of the past fifteen years sitting in ugly hotel ballrooms at too many management council meetings trying to provide scientific data on the impact, or lack thereof, of bottom trawling on deepwater corals and other habitats. And I can't think of a single meeting, not a single one, in which anyone from your organization was present to try and help move management forward."

"Yeah, you're part of the problem!"

Chris shook his head as if trying to ward off the insanity. "You idiots are handcuffing yourselves to research vessels and clubbing scientists, and I'm part of the problem?"

"Corals are dying, man! They can live for over a thousand years. But along comes a trawl, and they're knocked down forever. They die. The fishes that use them for habitat die. *Everything* dies."

Chris rolled his eyes. "This is not a trawler; this is a research vessel." Chris had serious doubts that any of the years of research he'd conducted precisely on the issues the woman was talking about would help the conversation. Coming back around the container, he found Paulina still lying tangled in lines and floats, but apparently uninjured.

"Don't look at me!" she demanded, in what had become her signature line in the past few weeks since she had fallen while exiting the surf after a SCUBA dive. "I'm a disaster over here."

"Are you sure you're okay?" asked Chris as he delicately untangled the lines.

"Yes. But what just happened? Where did those people come from?"

"I don't know. Maybe they were tracking this boat."

"Can you see any divers at the surface?" Paulina asked. When not conducting science, she served as the university's assistant Diving Safety Officer.

The burly boat captain came out of the galley dragging the third attacker by one arm. "This one didn't have anything to say. He screamed something incoherent and raced onto the bridge. I just punched him, and he went down pretty hard."

Chris smiled inwardly at the shock the attacker must have felt upon encountering the captain in the wheelhouse. Maybe the guy had conjured images of an old salt smoking a gnarled pipe as he slumped over the wheel. But what he'd found was a former amateur wrestler who'd become a fisherman like the rest of his family, only after it was clear that professional wrestling was neither professional nor wrestling.

Chris pointed to the attacker lying next to the shipping container. "Same thing with this guy." Then he motioned with his thumb toward the stern. "The woman back there says she's here to stop our trawling efforts."

"Our trawling efforts?" exclaimed the captain, two veins prominently bulging on his deeply tanned forehead. "Jesus, we just can't win. We're out here trying to support scientific research. There's no trawl gear onboard the boat. We've clearly got a dive flag flying overhead and divers in the water."

"I know," said Chris. "I don't think these activists recognize that level of nuance." Looking up into the sky, he added, "Where's the drone anyway?"

"Gone," noted the captain.

The vessel's first mate, a gangly, balding man whom Chris liked immensely, disappeared for a minute behind the container before returning with a smile. "If they were trying to disrupt our efforts, they didn't plan it very well. I can cut those cuffs off easily, but we can also use the crane with her cuffed to it. That should make for some great video if the drone comes back."

Looking at his watch, Chris explained to the captain, "We've got divers in the water for another twenty minutes. We'll need a couple of hours at the surface to download imagery from the VR camera and replace batteries for the next dive, if there is a next dive. What are we going to do with this trio?"

"Oh, we're not disrupting research for these clowns," replied the captain. "I put a call in to the Coast Guard. We'll just stow them down in the fish hold until the Coasties arrive."

"Perfect. The smell alone should teach them the error of their ways."

3

"You two are getting up off the couch and downstairs in the next two minutes," said Jessica Thornburg, "or, well, I don't know what will happen. But it won't be good."

Following the *Elizabeth Margot's* return to port in Monterey, Chris had gone straight to his old friend Tony's house and immediately occupied a comfortable spot on the Thornburg's large living room couch.

Like Chris, Tony had grown up in nearby Carmel-by-the-Sea. After high school graduation, while Chris moved to New England for college and graduate school, Tony moved to Berkeley for a degree in philosophy and stayed on at the university's law school.

Graduating near the top of his class, Tony had briefly worked for the California Attorney General's Office in San Francisco before accepting a position with the U.S. Attorney's office. It was only recently that his job allowed him to work from home, and he was taking full advantage of it.

"You made the view far too compelling, Jess," replied Chris waving his hand toward the ceiling-to-floor window facing west. "I mean, this is absolutely spectacular."

Unlike Chris, Tony had already found his partner for life before going to college. Jessica Thornburg, who was now an architect and developer of green buildings across northern California, had met Tony in high school. The two had been together ever since.

They were in the living room of one of the Phase 2 townhouse units of *PERCHA*, a designed community on the coast just south of Carmel that was Jessica's latest undertaking. She'd conceived the plans for every detail and seen it realized. Phase 1, *ROOST* on Bainbridge Island off the coast of Seattle, was complete, with *PERCHA* serving as a southern variation on the theme that paid homage to California's Spanish history. The living room of the 'inverted' townhouse was on the third and uppermost story, with living quarters immediately below it and commercial spaces on the ground floor. This gave the primary living area the best views in the house.

"Plus," Tony continued, "Chris almost got taken out by an unruly group of eco-terrorists today, so he needs to rest."

"*What?*"

"Well, 'taken out' may be a bit exaggerated," Chris said.

"Tell me what happened." Jess sighed heavily as she joined the guys on the couch, draping her legs over Tony's. She had been privy to the exploits of Chris's team for years. Chris knew that while she often put up an exasperated affect, Jess keenly followed events.

Chris gave Jess a condensed version of the day's events. "I blame Tony, of course," he concluded to put a lighter, non-sensical spin on things. "And speaking of blame, I really like the way the stairwell is so well illuminated by natural light."

The brilliant orange rays of the setting sun lit up the stairs.

"You're both still dead meat if you don't get off the couch," said Jessica, "but keep the observations coming."

Chris obliged by bouncing up off the couch. "I honestly love this place, Jess," he observed as he stepped closer to the large window. "It almost makes me want to sell the place in town and move down here.

All these new units are beautiful, the foliage is coming in nicely, and the connection to the water is almost tangible."

"Keep going," encouraged Jessica, her eyes tracking Chris as he walked around the perimeter of the large living area.

He reached down to pick up one of their dog Tucker's gnarled playthings. "Waterfront property in California is obviously unattainable at this point for a simple working stiff like me. But maybe you guys can give me a deal? My only concern is the name."

"Oh, god," said Tony under his breath. He'd relaxed into a horizontal position on the couch once Chris got up. Chris and Jess knew each other nearly as well as he and Tony after so many years in each other's company. They rarely missed an opportunity to playfully push each other's buttons.

"What do you mean the name? *PERCHA*? *ROOST*? What's wrong with it?"

"*PERCHA*'s not bad. The connection to the flying goat of *ROOST* is pretty cool. But I've taken to calling the place *KNICKERS*. I think it has a certain je ne sais quoi. Try it for a bit. I think you'll find it's catchy."

Tony lowered his head and pinched the bridge of his nose. Jessica had worked hard to cultivate the concept for ROOST and PERCHA, and she didn't like people questioning it. Earlier, Tony had mentioned some of the pushback local politicians had given Jess about the name of the housing project. He'd explained that his brilliant wife's design sensibilities were frequently just too far beyond the locals' more parochial viewpoints. They almost always came around to appreciate Jess' designs; it just took time.

Knowing this, Chris had settled on the non-sensical Knickers as a way to tweak Jess just a bit while also conveying to her that he was aware of the name controversy and its ridiculous nature and that he supported her.

She stared at Chris for several seconds. "You can call it whatever you want once you've moved down here," said Jessica with a calm that disturbed Chris.

"I can?"

"Yep."

"And why would I? Move down here, I mean."

Jessica smiled broadly. "Because after our dinner tonight, after you've met Molly, you'll definitely want to."

Chris turned toward Tony with a look of panic on his face. "Who's Molly?"

"Didn't I mention her? I must have. She was a fellow law student with me at Berkeley. Now she works up in Seattle for a firm that regularly contracts with the United Nations. She's down here for a week only, but she just bought one of the units up the hill."

Chris turned toward Jess. "Sounds awesome, but you know I'm not ready to meet anyone, however incredible she might be."

"I know," said Jess, smiling. "I know. But I have to say, though you can certainly dish it out, you don't take it nearly as well."

Chris exhaled deeply, well aware that she was stabbing at the casual way he had ended many romantic relationships in his time. But the sting of the recent end to his relationship with Abigail Wilson still lingered. He had to admit that Abby's sudden departure from his life had hit him harder than he cared to admit. Being the one left was infinitely harder than leaving, even if he knew and perhaps even understood that her decision had more to do with a recent incident in Carmel Bay than him personally. He was sure he'd have to answer Jessica's scrutinizing questions about that sooner rather than later.

"Look, you've got nothing to worry about. Right, Tony?"

"Right. Nothing to worry about. I'm not worried," replied Tony.

"You're not worried?" asked Chris.

"Well, maybe I'm a little worried," said Tony. "I think Jess may have told Moll that you looked her up online and were a bit, what was that word you used?"

"Smitten," said Jessica.

"Smitten," said Chris, with no affect.

"Smitten," said Tony.

Jessica patted Chris on the shoulder as she walked past him into the kitchen. "Look on the bright side, Chris. It's one dinner. You'll have fun. And maybe you'll have legal representation next time you get kicked out of a country."

"Ouch," said Tony.

"Knickers," said Chris. "I'm going to make t-shirts."

Thirty minutes later, the three friends walked into a Mediterranean restaurant that was just minutes away from PERCHA. While waiting for a table to open up, they approached the bar where a tall woman, with the darkest shoulder-length hair Chris had ever seen, turned towards them. Her green eyes looked from Tony to Jessica and then settled on Chris. Chris's internal dialogue immediately sounded alarm bells, and his mind quickly envisioned spending an evening talking about the law with the stern-looking woman standing in front of him. But then she smiled, and the severity that he'd seen a minute before was replaced with genuine kindness.

The foursome started at the bar, then migrated to a table. The conversation never wavered over the next hour, touching primarily on Chris's recent adventures in South Africa. Molly grabbed Chris's forearm in surprise as he told her about his involvement in the rescue of some hostages. "You chased after a machete-wielding bad guy, in a Boston Whaler, in large surf? Are you kidding me?"

"That's our Chris," said Jessica.

"And then," Tony added, "he was ushered out of the country by someone from our embassy."

"It's been suggested," said Chris, smiling at Molly, "that you could have helped me out in that situation."

"Oh, I don't know," said Molly. "It would have been preferable to find someone with particular knowledge of South African law. My expertise is focused on the open ocean, in international waters."

"How's that different," asked Jessica. "It all seems like international work to me."

"You're right, it's all international. But the law on the high seas is a different animal altogether than the laws of formalized countries. An international agreement called the United Nation's Convention on the Law of the Sea, or UNCLOS, specifies that a coastal nation's boundaries extend out two-hundred nautical miles from its coastline. Everything, more or less, beyond that two-hundred-mile limit is international waters."

"And out there, no national laws apply," added Tony. "Right."

Chris had been talking continuously through much of the meal, so he hadn't eaten very much. He picked at some cold eggplant with a piece of naan bread while he listened to the conversation.

"So, if no national laws apply," continued Jessica, "then why doesn't chaos reign out there?"

"In some ways it does. But there's still some order."

"Where does that order come from?" asked Tony.

"The best way to think about high seas is like a frontier," explained Molly. "What's the first thing that comes to your mind when I say frontier?"

"Cowboys," said Jessica. "And outlaws."

"Exactly. The type of people drawn to frontiers fit into several classical stereotypes. Some are visionary entrepreneurs; some are simply looking to feed their families. Some are people persecuted elsewhere looking for freedom; some are looking to do the persecuting. It is a place of few laws and broad jurisdictions, and it's populated by some of the most ruthless people on earth."

Chris was enjoying this conversation immensely. While he'd spent his life in and around the ocean, the vast majority of that life had occurred within several hours of the mainland. He'd had very little experience thus far with the open seas.

"Are you talking about pirates?" Jessica's voice betrayed both concern and excitement.

"What's a pirate's favorite letter?" asked Tony.

"Argh!" said Jessica and Molly nearly simultaneously.

"No, that would be the sea!" finished Chris.

"Dad jokes," replied Molly laughing. She continued, "Yes, pirates are still out there. They aren't spending so much time on sailing ships, and there aren't as many peg legs and talking parrots as there may once have been, but they are still very much with us."

"Really?" said Jessica. Looking at Chris, she continued, "I thought sharks were the worst thing you could run into out there. At least that's what you always say, Chris."

"Well, I'd agree, the odds of running into pirates anywhere in U.S. waters are pretty low at this point. But it's a lucrative business in some areas of the world," explained Molly. "Somalia, for instance. More than half of the world's shipping comes right past Somalia on its way through the Suez Canal. They actually made a movie about it starring Tom Hanks."

"Yup, *Captain Phillips*. I've seen it," Chris acknowledged. "Are pirates ever motivated by ideology?" Concerns about the eco-terrorists that had boarded the boat earlier in the day were still looming in the back of his mind. "You know, like terrorists. Something to prove or gain beyond just the accumulation of wealth?"

"Not so much, in my experience. There are some that claim to be, but the bottom line really is money. Think about it, piracy isn't happening where societies are functioning well, and people have economic opportunities. Piracy is the consequence of massive income inequalities. These people are desperate, and that makes them dangerous."

"So much for that plan to sail around the world," said Tony.

"Sailing around the world is dangerous on many levels," said Molly. "I think pirates would be low on my list of concerns. Again, depending on where you are, the odds of encountering a pirate are extremely low. But if you do run into them, you'll probably wish you hadn't."

4

Tonya Gordon slowly awoke from her concussion-induced stupor. Staring out with one eye from her fetal position on the floor, she could tell she was still in the main salon, or bedroom, on Tom's boat. Her other eye was swollen shut from a vicious beating she'd received, but she couldn't remember how long ago that was. Tonya's grey-blonde hair was plastered to her sweat-drenched forehead, and her entire body ached.

Despite the pain, Tonya forced her arms into action. She adjusted her position so she could look around the room. For the moment, she appeared to be alone. The door and all the windows were closed, which was why it was so hot and stuffy. She and Tom had come up with a strategy to keep as much air flowing through the boat as possible during the daylight hours, as the tropical sun beat down upon the outer hull and deck. Tom. Oh my god, Tom!

Tonya collapsed back down to the floor and returned to the fetal position. The momentary respite provided by her confusion at waking up passed, and the horror of her experience washed back over her in waves. Her torso literally shook under the weight of the trauma she now remembered so vividly.

Only twelve hours earlier, she had been embarking on the adventure of a lifetime. She'd met Tom Simpson through an online dating service the previous year and had been truly surprised when a romance blossomed. A marriage and family counselor by profession, Tonya had refused her friends' suggestions to join the online dating scene for more than a year, confident that a lasting relationship needed to blossom in more traditional ways. But one night, alone on the couch with a glass of wine and her giant cat, Mo, spread across her lap, she'd decided to try it.

Tonya had swiped left on virtually every profile she'd seen for the first week. Too many New England Patriots fans with beer cans visible in their profile pictures, even for her, a native from Scituate, Massachusetts. She never understood why people felt it was so important to have alcohol prominently featured in their pictures on a dating site. And then she'd come upon a fifty-five-year-old pediatrician with the pseudonym 'Christopher Robin.'

He had less hair than most men she found attractive, and he carried a few more pounds than her image of the ideal partner, but something about his eyes and the things he emphasized on his profile captured her interest. As a counselor, Tonya prided herself on her ability to evaluate people's character, and 'Christopher Robin' struck her as authentic. His brief description of his relationship with his son struck a chord, reminding her very much of her own relationship with her twenty-year-old daughter, Beth.

Their first date had been a total disaster. Dr. Tom Simpson had somehow determined that going clamming on the tidal flats near Plymouth might be a fun way to break up the tension of a first encounter. After Tonya lost both her shoes and her smartphone in the deep, sulfur-smelling mud, she'd been very near calling it quits. But then they'd shared a laugh over the whole thing at a nearby coffee shop as the other patrons looked on disapprovingly at the strange, muddy couple sitting in the corner smelling strongly of the bay. From that moment on, Tonya was hooked.

Tom, and his nineteen-year-old son, Ben, had fit into Tonya and Beth's lives like it had been planned that way. Ben had a physical confidence that his father lacked, but his obvious kindness was very much in concert with Tom's.

Beth, who was also an only child, found in Ben the type of friend she'd longed for. In all the years of Tonya's practice, with untold numbers of failed relationships coming through her door, finding one that worked so well, in so many ways, on an online dating site, was extraordinary in her experience.

Tonya's joy at finding Tom and Ben had come at the end of a dark period in her life. The previous two years had been an emotionally grueling ordeal. First, her husband of twenty years announced that he'd fallen in love with someone else. He'd met a woman while working on a new house down in Plymouth, another contractor.

They had 'worked on' the marriage for several months, but it was clear to Tonya early on that the marriage was destined to suffer when compared to her husband's new love. She remembered what new love felt like and remembered that nothing stood in its way. A marriage, particularly one that had been on autopilot for years, was distinguished by the daily grind of life, errands to run, bills to pay, and dinners with the TV on. In contrast, a new relationship represented all possibilities during its early stages. There were no hurdles too high for new love, particularly while flatulence and back hair shaving had yet to make an appearance.

Tonya had briefly thought the crushing pain of her failed marriage was the bottom; the nadir as her brilliant daughter would say. But then Beth came home from college in New Hampshire after she'd been sexually assaulted in her dorm room. That was the nadir of the nadir. And yet, while her divorce had been a period of what Tonya considered to be indulgent self-pity, Beth's plight had stirred in Tonya a fortitude she hadn't realized she possessed. There was no option for self-pity where Beth was concerned; only resolve.

Beth had shown her own considerable strength, and the two of them together had been 'coming out the other side,' a phrase Tonya had used frequently in her practice. And then Tom and Ben had come into their lives, and both she and Beth had started to heal. Tom had been everything her ex-husband was not: sensitive, thoughtful, unconcerned with college sports. He had listened to Tonya talk for hours upon hours, simply nodding his head with an empathy that Tonya could not fathom at first. It simply didn't seem possible that someone would come along and simply 'get' her. But eventually, she had come to trust Tom's faith in her, and the prospect of a new future seemed very promising.

It was the promise of a full life with Tom and Ben that had lead Tonya and Beth to embrace Tom's plan to sail from Ecuador out to the Galapagos Islands, and back. Neither Tonya nor Beth had ever done anything like it. They'd been to Europe like everyone else, but adventure travel had not been on their proverbial horizon.

Pushing herself to a sitting position again, Tonya leaned heavily against the starboard bulkhead. She'd already thrown up once. Now nausea returned as her mind replayed the horror that they'd found themselves in so quickly after leaving port in Guayaquil on the Ecuadorian mainland.

The wind had been non-existent that morning, so they'd been slowly motoring westward as the sun rose behind them, playing card games on the stern as Tom manned the wheel. Tonya remembered seeing the other boat, a cabin cruiser, approaching fast on the port side. Her natural instinct was concerned, but Tom had said something about the 'brotherhood of the sea' and explained how people helped each other out when on the water. She'd relaxed a bit at that and had gone below with Beth to put on clothes over their bathing suits.

From the galley, she could hear the thump of someone jumping on board but initially didn't think anything of it. But when she came up the stairs, she was face to face with three muscular and brawny men, two of whom were holding knives to Tom and Ben's throats. Primal fear flooded every fiber of her being instantly. Their eyes, that's what scared her the most. She'd met many violent men in her practice—wife beaters and child abusers—and they came in all shapes and sizes. Their eyes, though, they betrayed a violent burn she'd come to recognize. But the eyes of the men before her now, they didn't convey violence. They conveyed nothing. Their eyes were devoid of emotion. Empty. Desolate.

"What do you want?" she'd asked, hoping against hope to avoid violence. "We have money."

The largest of the three men had bandages with what looked like fresh blood on his nose as well as the arm he used to hold a knife to Tom's throat. He'd said something quickly in Spanish to the man next to him. At that moment, Tonya had been startled from behind as a fourth man emerged from the galley behind her, pushing Beth along in front of him.

"Mom . . ." said Beth, clearly frightened.

"It's going to be okay, honey," replied Tonya with little conviction. "Let's just find out what these men want."

The man standing behind Beth pushed her to the deck. When she stumbled, Ben lunged to try and help, and that's when the man holding him sliced Ben's neck open just below the Adam's apple. Blood poured from the wound. Beth screamed as the man had effortlessly tossed Ben's body over the side.

Tom struggled to free himself from the man holding him, uttering a guttural cry that Tonya knew she would never forget. As upset as Tom was, Tonya could see that he proved no match for the man holding him. Tom's horrified eyes locked on hers seconds before a knifepoint erupted from his chest. Blood sprayed everywhere, coating the white fiberglass deck. Some sprinkled on Tonya's face.

Tonya had watched Tom's eyes as the life drained from him in front of her. She'd been mute then, but now she screamed at the abject horror of that memory.

While the two murderers had wiped the blood off their knives, one of the other two pirates, as she now thought of them, had looked at Beth with a stare Tonya knew only too well. "No! You leave her alone," she'd screamed. "Take me."

That had earned her a punch in the face and a second in the gut. Lying prone on the deck gasping for air as her eye swelled shut, Tonya had heard Beth say with a resignation that belied her years, "Don't worry mom, there isn't anything they can do that hasn't already been done."

Tonya's turn had come soon enough. She now sat awkwardly against the salon wall, her entire body hurting, but resolved to remain strong for Beth. No matter what happened next.

5

"We found something in the kelp; something big," said Kong, one of Chris's student research assistants.

Chris walked into the Image Analysis Lab at the CMEx in Monterey, wishing that he'd stopped to take a nap. With water temperatures in the low fifties, long, deep dives like those he and his undergraduate dive team had been doing for the past seven days aboard the *Elizabeth Margot* induced a special kind of fatigue.

His core temperature took hours to return to normal, and nearly every part of his body was either raw from too much contact with his neoprene wetsuit, sore from the accumulated strain of four to five dives a day, or both.

"Please don't tell me you've found barrels, Kong," replied Chris as the five students and Mac looked on, only partially joking about the prospect of finding more toxic waste underwater.

As Chris had described to donors many times in the past, the Image Analysis Lab was an ironic juxtaposition to all the work his team conducted out in the field. Where SCUBA diving and ROV cruises took place in the great outdoors, closely aligning with the general public's conception of marine biology, the processing and analysis of the video and still photographic imagery they collected in the field was conducted in a windowless room with the only illumination coming from multiple computer screens.

To give it some character and flair, the darkened lab was adorned with memorabilia from past trips, past projects, and past students. A boomerang was displayed over the door from a trip to Australia. Hanging off the edge of the boomerang was a strand of monofilament fishing line strung through a number of ancient shells collected along the Mediterranean coast of Israel. An entire shelf on the western wall contained a curious line of shrunken Styrofoam cups with various messages written on them. It was a well-established tradition for marine scientists around the world to memorialize submersible dives by shrinking cups on each dive. Participants on a dive used colored pens to decorate cups, which were then mounted to the outer hull of the sub in a mesh bag. As the sub dived deeper, the cups, which were 95% air at the surface, were condensed into miniature, misshapen and contorted versions of themselves by the extreme pressure of the ocean depths. And in the corner, hanging from the ceiling, was a cardboard figure of a recently graduated doctoral student that had been used to decorate the room for her dissertation defense.

Chris looked at all the students. They were a tight-knit team, often operating with a kind of group consciousness. It was clear to Chris that they were all anxious for him to see something.

"Not exactly barrels," Mac Johnson offered. "I think you should sit down and put on the VR headset."

Robert 'Mac' Johnson was a physical and temperamental counterpoint to his close friend Chris. He wore his hair a bit longer, in a small pirate-like ponytail, which usually poked out from under one of Mac's many baseball caps. Where Chris was taller and longer-limbed, Mac was a compact five-foot-nine inches and a dense one-hundred and ninety pounds. His ponytail and perpetual smirk gave him the appearance of youth, though he was the same age as Chris. And where Chris was quick to start up a discussion with a stranger, Mac was far less conversational, often even when among friends.

It was common for Mac to play the role of naysayer to Chris's can-do optimist. Where Chris's upbringing had been a picture of stability, Mac's experience growing up had been different. His parents had divorced when he was eight years old, leaving Mac the "man of the house" at an early age. Absent a paternal authority figure, Mac had found his way to stability, and this had, in his own words, left him grumpy most of the time.

Mac and Chris had grown up surfing, swimming, and climbing together as well as pursuing a few less-than-productive activities. After high school, Chris took off for college and graduate school on the East Coast. Meanwhile, Mac joined the Navy, where he earned a coveted spot with the SEALs before an injury brought a premature end to his military career.

Now, Chris and Mac worked together at the CMEx, with Mac serving as the chief engineer on most of the research activities that Chris lead.

The goal of the SCUBA dives over the past week was to test the relative merits of stereo video and virtual reality video to understand fish-habitat interactions along the underexplored Big Sur coastline. With stereo video, two cameras collected video of the same area from slightly different vantage points to produce stereo images. With virtual reality video, multiple cameras collected imagery in all directions.

While the team had done enough work with the stereo video system to understand what it offered, the use of VR was new to the team, and they were still trying to figure out the utility of the system for collecting data. However, the potential for outreach and education was unambiguous. The six cameras enclosed in a special housing, each with its own glass dome port in front of it, offered scientists the opportunity to virtually immerse non-divers and future divers in the subtidal ecosystems of coastal California and beyond. And that, Chris knew, was a powerful way to cultivate a new generation of citizens interested in the con'servation of the marine environment.

Chris put one of the lab's new VR headsets on, securing it with the head strap and picking up the two dedicated joysticks. "Okay, Kong, walk me through what you found."

Having spent the past seven days in the water together, iteratively freezing and laughing their way through many challenging dives, the team now functioned as a unit.

Much to the dismay of Mac, to whom they'd reported their dive activities before and after each dive, the team had assigned nicknames to each member based on auto- suggestions made by one of their smartphones each time they texted Mac.

In this way, Kameron had become 'Kong.' And for some reason, while the other nicknames only seemed to last the morning, Kong had become his name well beyond all diving activities.

"We have all forty minutes of the imagery loaded up onto the headset," Kong responded. "I haven't had a chance to edit it yet."

"Right," said Chris, "and we don't get to the kelp for what, ten minutes?"

"That's about right."

Wearing the VR headset, Chris was able to look around in all directions to re-experience the morning's dive from the comfort of a chair in the lab. They'd been experimenting with the use of virtual reality for several months, and Chris was still marveling at the possibilities. He was redoing the morning's dive, albeit from the relative comfort and warmth of the lab.

"So, what am I looking for here?" Chris was tired and ready to move on to the next event of the day, a party at his mom's house in Carmel.

Kong and Mac looked at each other with palpable excitement. "Just fast forward to around minute eighteen," Mac responded.

"Okay." Chris used one of the joysticks to advance the video. "That was about when I came out of the kelp forest and swam along the reef's edge if I recall correctly. And where should I be looking?"

"Um, behind you," said Kong, with a tone that caught Chris's attention.

Chris paused the video and lifted the headset to look at Kong and Mac in the eyes. "You've got to be kidding me," he said, thinking he knew where this was going.

"Just put the headset back on," encouraged Mac, "and enjoy."

Chris did as he was told and resumed the video. By swiveling the chair around to look behind him, he could see himself swimming along approximately six feet back from the camera. As he swam, the camera housing was extended out in front of him on a custom-made "mono" pole. By virtue of the way the imagery from the six cameras was 'stitched' together, the pole was not visible, just the diver. At various points, he could also see other members of the team swimming along to his right and left.

It didn't take long for the enormous shadow to appear behind him on the video. It first swam past at the edge of visibility, a shadow that an untrained eye might dismiss as an optical illusion. But then it returned, passing close enough to the camera system to be clearly identified as a giant, male white shark. It swam past, apparently taking only a passing interest in the Chris on the video before disappearing into the murk. But that passing interest had brought the shark's mouth to within inches of Chris's head.

"Holy crap," said Chris instinctively recoiling from the shark on the video. "That was a close one." He watched the footage three more times while Mac and Kong sat quietly. Two other members of the crew— Megapixel, or Megan as per auto-correct, and Tammy, a.k.a. Tommy, who'd come to enjoy his genderbending nickname—joined them while the others were immersed in a different project.

"He really does come close, doesn't he? And yet . . ."

"And yet, none of you saw him," finished Mac.

"Not only that," replied Chris. "This didn't feel like a particularly 'sharky' day, right Kong?"

"Right," replied Kong. "At least not compared to many of the other days we've been out there. I didn't get any sharky feelings."

"I've heard you say a million times that they see us far more often than we see them," Megapixel added.

"Yep, I do say that. Though probably not a million times," said Chris. "But it is still unnerving to see such a large beast checking us out without any of us catching even a glimpse." He had reminded students that the creatures of the deep are far more aware of humans than they might imagine. That was never clearer than when he discussed the actions of large predators, who had a wide array of sensory organs for the identification of potential prey.

"Is seeing this going to change your behavior?" asked Mac.

Chris looked at Kong, Megapixel, and Tammy. As if rehearsed, all four of them responded simultaneously, "No."

"Right. So, consider yourselves lucky, and make sure to get that video posted on the website ASAP, Kong!"

"Good idea," said Chris. To Mac, he added, "And we have to get ready to head over to Margaret's."

Shrugging his shoulders, Mac asked, "What do you mean by 'we'?"

"Peter is going to be there, and I think he wants to talk with us about the Galapagos."

"Oh, man. I thought we'd dodged that bullet."

"Only you would think of a trip to the Galapagos as a pain." Chris shook his head.

"Yeah, yeah," said Mac. "I've barely unpacked from South Africa."

"So put the three pairs of underwear you own back in that sad-looking thing you call a suitcase, and stop talking about it."

"It's actually only two pairs now . . ." Mac held up two fingers for emphasis.

"Whatever. I'm sorry I brought it up."

6

Parties at Chris's mom's house were usually a thing to behold.
Walking in the front door, Chris was confronted first by the myriad sounds and smells of a party in full bloom. Conversations on so many topics among so many people that the individual words were lost and only a constant hum hit his ears. The scent of musty tweed combined with perfume and the legacy of nicotine addiction assaulted his nose. The mayor, a local author, one of Chris's elementary school teachers, all nodded as he meandered through the crowd. Working his way toward the kitchen, Chris could see people across the room look down toward their feet and smile. Moments later, the crowd immediately in front of him parted to reveal his dog, Thigmotaxis, pushing her way through. "Thig" was named for an ecological concept that described an animal's attraction to its habitat. She had spent more time with Margaret than with Chris over the past several months due to Chris's travel schedule.

Kneeling slightly and tapping his thigh, Chris welcomed Thig up into his arms. "Gooooood, girl. Gooood, girl. I've missed you, furball."

Having reconnected with her human, Thig jumped down and led Chris into the kitchen. Chris extracted a beer from among the many bottles of wine. Behind him, a familiar voice proclaimed, "The prodigal son returns."

"I just came to borrow money. Won't be here long." Smiling, Chris turned to greet Margaret's friend Steven.

"Sounds about right. And I see you've found my beer," said Steven as he reached in to hug Chris. He was still wearing his surgical scrubs from the hospital and a pair of well-loved running shoes. "How was your trip down off Big Sur?"

Dr. Steven Larsen stood two inches shorter than Chris, his brown hair close-cropped on the side and thinning on top. He and Margaret had been dating for over a year.

"Oh, you haven't heard?" replied Chris. "It was . . . not dull."

"In other words, a standard Chris Black affair, eh?"

"More or less," said Chris. "But that's all about to change. In fact, I pronounce this a new period of crushing normalcy. No violence, no bad guys, not even eco-terrorism; just the humdrum of the daily grind."

"Crushing normalcy," observed Margaret as she came into the kitchen. To Steven, she said, while nodding toward Chris, "I guess that's the only kind of normalcy we can expect with this one."

She hugged Chris and then looked down at Thig, wagging her index finger. "What are you doing in the kitchen, young lady? Have you already forgotten our mutually agreed upon rules?"

Thig spun around in circles to express her enthusiasm for Margaret and, Chris was sure to demonstrate her disregard for the house rules. The sound of her claws scraping across the kitchen tile brought a smile to his face.

Chris set his beer down on the granite counter-top and kneeled next to his dog. "I don't get the impression that Thig suffers under totalitarian rule when she's over here."

"You've got that right," Steven added as he pulled out a chair from the kitchen table and sat down. "And it's pretty clear that she's more welcome in the house than either of us."

Chris could see a thin scar running from Steven's forehead down the right side of his face, the legacy of the attack he and Margaret had been through in Cape Town.

Kneeling to hug Thig, Margaret said, "You and I understand each other more than either of these two philistines ever will."

Chris looked up at Steven. "I wish I could claim that philistine was the worst thing I've been called recently."

"Same here," answered Steven. In a quieter tone, he added as he opened a beer for himself, "Or even the worst thing I've been called today, in this house."

"Okay," said Margaret, standing up and expertly repositioning the bobby bins that held her mostly grey hair back. "That's enough of both of you. Chris, you can find your fearless leader holding court with some of the ladies on the back patio. I know he's interested in talking with you, so perhaps you should go interrupt."

"Copy that. On my way."

Finding his way slowly through the crowded hallways, Chris emerged on to the back patio to find Dr. Peter Lloyd, Director of the University's CMEx, huddled around the firepit talking with some of Margaret's friends.

Peter and Chris had hit it off years before when Chris was in graduate school. Unlike many of the other people that populated academia, Chris had found Peter's approach to the world to be refreshing. Wearing his grey hair pulled back in a small ponytail, and existing almost entirely in Hawaiian shirts and shorts, regardless of the weather, Peter exuded a kind of confidence rarely achieved by the more formal academics—a confidence borne of experience.

Peter had a track record of success around the world, both with respect to scientific research and the application of that research to policy and management. Chris knew that Peter rubbed people the wrong way from time to time, often people in positions of power. But they ultimately couldn't fault Peter's reasoning or his extraordinary grasp of the facts.

However, more important to Chris was the fact that he connected with Peter on things unrelated to science, including what Margaret characterized as a 'warped sense of humor.'

When Chris approached the patio, Peter announced to his audience, "I guess we'll have to continue this later, dear friends. Chris here knows all my best stories and might contradict something at a key moment." Peter had never married, which, Chris had observed, seemed to add to his allure among his mother's female friends.

"Came back to spoil the party, Chris?" one of them asked with a facetious smile as she gave him a brief hug and then followed the others inside the house before he could respond.

"I would never contradict," Chris said to Peter. "Clarify, perhaps, but never contradict."

Peter waved his hand. "Yeah, yeah. Neither of us has an audience now, so we can cut the bullshit. Where's Johnson?"

"Supposedly on his way," replied Chris. "He was excited to receive the invitation."

"I'm sure," replied Peter, motioning away from the artificial fire pit. "Let's sit down over there. I'm getting too hot next to this contraption."

As if on cue, Mac came walking through the back gate. He sat down next to Chris on a bench across from Peter. "It is my honor to serve."

"I'll bet," replied Peter, leaning forward and resting his arms on his thighs. "Look, I need you two to head down to San Cristobal at the end of the week."

"The end of *this* week?" asked Chris, sitting up. San Cristobal was an island in the Galapagos.

"That's correct." Peter folded his arms as if bracing himself against an onslaught of criticism.

"That's, um, a bit of a shocker," said Chris. "We weren't expecting to go until the end of the month."

"I'll miss yoga," added Mac.

"Plans have changed," said Peter, smirking at Mac's comment. "The *MacGreggor* was supposed to spend three weeks working along the mainland to the north and south of Guayaquil, but our collaborators down there were not able to raise the money to support their end of the bargain. Consequently, I'd like to send the boat out to the Galapagos sooner rather than later."

The RV *MacGreggor* was the multi-million-dollar research vessel that Chris and his CMEx colleagues used to conduct scientific research off-shore. It was equipped for everything from shallow SCUBA dives in the kelp forests to deep dives into the off-shore canyons along California's coast using a remotely operated vehicle (ROV).

Now serving as the Assistant Director for the CMEx, Chris had encountered firsthand the many challenges of keeping a large research vessel fully-funded and operational. A ship sitting at the dock, as Peter often remarked, was nothing more than a pit from which money never returned.

"So, you still want us to implement our same plan, just earlier?" asked Mac. Chris was not scheduled to teach any courses for the current semester, because he'd expected to be in South Africa, conducting research for several months. His earlier return due to his run-in with a group of individuals intent on illegally obtaining a Krugerrand gold treasure had freed him up for other university activities.

"Essentially, yes," said Peter. "You can head out to Darwin and Wolf Islands first, then work your way back through the main islands to San Cristobal. I trust the ROV is ready to go?" The operation and maintenance of the remotely operated vehicle, a robot named *Seaview*, was a core part of Mac's job description.

"It was when we loaded it on the boat before she departed," replied Mac. "As long as nobody touches it until we get down there, it should be fine."

Peter nodded. "Good. The instructors for this trip, Abigail Wilson and Dr. Oliver Chumley-Smith, flew down and met the boat in Guayaquil last Friday. The students got on board today. They have all been instructed to avoid the ROV until you are on site."

Chris inhaled deeply, but then caught himself when he realized Mac was looking at him.

"Abby's out there?" asked Mac. Abby and Chris had been in the midst of a new relationship when the team discovered toxic waste dumped in the Carmel submarine canyon. The violent events that followed, and Chris's reaction to those events, had led Abby to step away from the relationship.

"I have no doubt," said Peter, "that Ms. Wilson and Dr. Black here can work together for the betterment of the students' experience."

Chris stared at the bushes lining the inside of his mom's fence and wondered if Peter's surmise was accurate. How would being on the boat with Abby work?

"Who's Smidgen-Smythe? The math guy?" Mac asked.

"It's Chumley-Smith," replied Peter. "And yes, he's a mathematical modeler. He comes to us from the University of Bristol via a Fulbright Scholarship. Chris was on the committee that approved his request to spend a year at the CMEx."

"I was. His application was solid; British prep schools before attending Oxford. Solid credentials in mathematical modeling. But he's not an obvious fit for a field research cruise to the Galapagos," said Chris. "How many students signed up?"

"The final number is eighteen; ten from the US, four from Canada, and four from Ecuador. It's the international angle that allowed us to pay for this trip. Training students from different countries together is the latest trend. We would never have sent the *MacG* that far without the support from the State Department."

"It's going to be cozy," observed Mac. "Obviously we have enough bunks on board, but that is a lot of people for a long trip offshore. I wish we could take some of the undergraduates from up here to help us manage the situation."

"They're all too deep in their own work to leave for this long. We'll deal with it," said Chris. "Anything else, boss?"

They discussed details related to on-going SCUBA diving operations through the CMEx for the rest of the week, and for when both Mac and Chris would be gone in the Galapagos. All research diving operations through their university, as well as all other universities in the United States, occurred under the umbrella of a national diving academy. To participate in that academy, a university was required to have a Diving Safety Officer (or DSO) on staff, a Dive Control Board populated by approved faculty, staff and students to help advise the dive program, and a Dive Control Manual that explained all the protocols and safety measures required for any diving under the auspices of the university. With Mac, the current DSO, away in the southern hemisphere, responsibilities would temporarily fall to the assistant DSO.

"She'll do great," said Chris of the new assistant DSO. "Paulina's been there and done that with research diving. And she's much scarier than Mac here when she's mad, so I expect everyone will fall in line pretty quickly."

"You've got that right," said Mac. "She'll do great."

While the three had been talking on the back patio, the sun had set, and the fog had moved in. "That's good for now, team," Peter said. "But I wonder if I can talk to Chris for a minute before you leave."

"That's my signal," said Mac. He placed his hand on Chris's shoulder and pushed himself to a standing position. "I'll see you both tomorrow."

They watched Mac exit through the same gate through which he'd entered. Peter leaned a little closer to Chris and said, "I'm sorry if I sounded overly cavalier earlier about you and Abby. I need to warn you. My understanding is that Abby is actually seeing Oliver Chumley-Smith socially. That can't make this any easier for you."

Chris felt the bottom of his stomach drop out. Peter's statement confirmed something he'd heard the students discussing in the lab the previous week. The months since Abby and he'd parted ways had been so full that he'd been successful in keeping that part of his life at a metaphorical arm's distance. He knew there would be a reckoning at some point where he'd have to face the situation with Abby head on, but he wasn't going to push it.

He looked at Peter and measured his response, "I won't pretend it's under control, but I'm handling it. Thanks for addressing this, though."

"But what do we think of Dr. Chumley-Smith?" asked Peter, pressing the issue.

"*We* don't think about Dr. Chumley-Smith at all, and *we* think about his dating Abby even less," said Chris, sitting up and squaring his shoulders. "But if *we* did, I'm sure *we'd* want Abby to be happy."

Chris had thought about this new coupling frequently since he'd heard Kong and Megapixel talking about it. He found that during daylight hours, it bothered him very little, as long as he was not around either of them. However, late at night, Abby's new relationship could take on outsized importance in his mind. Chris knew the forthcoming trip was going to be difficult in this regard, and he was grateful that Mac would be along.

"But I maintain that he's an odd fit for this cruise," continued Chris. "My undergraduates have more field experience than he does."

"You know I could make life somewhat miserable for him," Peter offered conspiratorially. "Absolutely miserable, in fact. Just say the word."

Chris smiled. He knew this wasn't normal territory for Peter, and he appreciated Peter's efforts to bring it up, but also to keep it light. "I appreciate that boss. I really do. But don't worry about it. We're going to have our hands full just keeping the ROV working and in the water. And if I'm right about his lack of field experience, I think Dr. Chumley-Smith is going to achieve misery all on his own."

7

The pirates had bothered neither Tonya nor Beth Gordon for more than twenty-four hours.

Late in the evening the day before, the two women had been moved to the *Innovator* and into the small cabin at the bow. There they'd found personal items spread throughout—paperback books, well-read film magazines, and men's underwear—all suggesting that an American male had occupied the space at some point. The novels on the bookshelf ranged from adventures, to westerns, to soft-core pornography. For a moment, Tonya had been slightly offended at the latter reading material, but then had to laugh out loud at the absurdity of her outrage, given that the images of naked women were so utterly harmless compared to their recent experiences.

Below the bookshelf was a small cupboard that held a variety of games, including *Cards Against Humanity, Exploding Kittens,* and *One Night, the Ultimate Werewolf,* all further evidence that the former occupants were American and likely young.

Looking at the remnants of someone else's life as she curled up on the bed, Beth's eyes swelled up with tears. "We aren't the first people they've done this to." Beth was wearing a USC sweatshirt she had found in the cabin. She'd been wondering who might own it, hoping against hope that he—because it clearly was a man's sweatshirt—would still be alive and might have gotten away somehow. But deep down, she knew that chances of that were slim.

"I know, honey," whispered Tonya as she gently removed several strands of hair from her daughter's bruised face. Both women had considerable black and blue marks from multiple assaults by the pirates, but neither appeared to have any broken bones. Tonya's eye was still badly swollen, but she could now see from it.

It was dark out, with a thin sliver of moonlight shining down through the pair of small portholes at the front of the cabin.

"Okay," Tonya continued, "tell me again what you've overheard, and we can compare notes." Though the situation was horrific, she found herself thankful that both she and Beth had a reasonable command of spoken Spanish. This allowed them to glean information from the pirates, who frequently spoke in the women's presence as if they didn't exist.

"I've heard a lot of arguing," whispered Beth in return.

"Arguing about what?"

"I think they're scared. This boat we're on, and Tom's boat I guess, they aren't worth much money. Or at least not enough. And they fear their boss is going to be mad," explained Beth. "The smaller guy with the skull tattoos on both forearms keeps repeating 'debemos encontrar mas.' Sounds like they feel like they have to hunt other boats. The other guy just keeps saying 'fuck.'"

"That must be what I heard them fighting about last night," said Tonya. The walls between staterooms were transparent to the yelling that had ensued recently. "It's like they've been sent out to bring back treasure, and the two boats are all they've found so far."

"I guess we weren't rich enough targets. I wish they'd figured that out before they attacked us." Beth was still choking up a little. "I've also

45

heard the smaller guy mention 'silencio' multiple times," she added. "I don't know why they'd keep talking about silence."

"Maybe they're just asking each other to shut up and be quiet?"

The two women stopped talking as the weight of the horror they'd endured the past week sat between them.

"My grasp of Spanish isn't that great," Tonya broke the silence first, "but I don't think we're dealing with the sharpest tools in the shed here. I think it's possible they assumed that anyone riding around in a boat this size must be rich. But why on earth they'd assume anyone would carry their wealth around with them on a boat is beyond me."

"Maybe they are hoping for ransom. But in our case, who would pay? There's no one left who cares!" Beth put her head in her hands, defeated.

"Don't think that way, Beth." Tonya reached out and wrapped her arms around her daughter. "We need to stay positive. Have you heard them talk about where they are going?"

"No, I haven't heard anything about where they're taking us. The big one keeps complaining about his broken nose. I think he's having difficulty breathing. Maybe they're going somewhere where he can get medical attention."

Tonya planted a kiss on her daughter's head and then stood up to look out the small porthole. "And have you seen our, I mean Tom's boat?" She turned around to face her daughter. "What happened to it? Are there more pirates somewhere?"

Beth shook her head, and Tonya once again directed her attention to the porthole. "I can see land!" she exclaimed.

Beth got up with some difficulty and stood next to her mother. "That looks like an island."

"You're right. It looks so dry, like a volcano," replied Tonya.

The small island rose rapidly on all the sides the women could see. Waves crashed around its rocky base. Up the steep cliffs and into the sky above, hundreds of birds were visible, even at night, flying in and out of large crevices on the rock face. The ledges that were large enough supported small shrubs.

Tonya tried to recall the charts Tom had shown her. "I think we might be in the Galapagos. There are dozens of small islands like this one. Why would they bring us here?"

"So, nobody lives on these islands?"

"No, people live out here," continued Tonya as she stared out at the island. "Tom told me that two of the islands have entire towns."

"Mom, what if the 'silence' they are talking about is a euphemism for death? What if they are talking about killing us?" Beth looked at Tonya with an expression she hadn't seen in years. It was the look of a daughter seeking comfort, a daughter begging her mother to explain away this horrifying situation, a daughter desperate for hope.

Hope Tonya didn't have.

What Tonya hadn't mentioned to Beth was the bit of conversation she'd overheard earlier in the day while Beth was asleep. The pirates had argued. It wasn't their job to take hostages, one of them had said, and that they were going to get in trouble with their captain. The other one had responded with a laugh and suggested an easy way to handle the problem. They'd simply use the women for a few more hours and then dispose of them.

Suddenly the door slammed open, and the big pirate stormed in, grabbed Beth by her upper arm, and yanked her off the bed. In seconds, she was gone.

8

"Okay, the ROV is non-functional," Mac said to himself. Toggling his radio, he continued, "Alex, the ROV has lost power. Let's bring her up right away." Alex Smith was a former student and current CMEx technician who'd literally begged to come on the trip. Given how hard Alex worked, it had been an easy decision for Mac to make.

He and Chris were in *MacGreggor*'s ROV lab, or mission control, a darkened, fourteen by eight-foot windowless room in the interior of the state-of-the-art ship. Like the video analysis lab back in Monterey, solar glare at sea made watching video difficult, so no windows were provided. When the ROV was in the water, the only illumination in the room came from the six large flat panel screens arrayed on one wall from the ceiling to the top of the control console. Each displayed the output from one of the *Seaview's* cameras or sonar.

Chris leaned back in his chair and stretched. He could feel the rattle in the deck as the hydraulic winch on the *MacGreggor*'s back deck labored to recover the ROV. "Is there anything we can do to help?" He didn't expect a positive response, but he wanted to ask anyway. He knew that once Mac was in 'ROV-mode,' it was best to give him space.

"Negative," said Mac. "Once we get her back on deck, Alex and I will look her over."

They'd been down on the bottom for thirty minutes. After motoring overnight from the main Galapagos Islands, the *MacGreggor* had reached Wolf Island just after dawn. Wolf and Darwin Islands were one-hundred and fifty-five miles to the northwest of the rest of the Galapagos. As a result of that distance, the water could be as much as fifteen degrees Fahrenheit warmer because the two islands were bathed by a separate set of underwater currents. The warmer water temperature attracted more tropical fishes than were present in the main islands. Despite having made two prior trips to the Galapagos, this was Chris's first trip out to Wolf and Darwin. Like many of the small islands elsewhere in the Galapagos, they were both characterized by very steep, volcanic rock walls. But underwater, Chris was excited to see something else altogether.

Wolf Island did not disappoint during the first half-hour with the ROV. Chris had seen five fish species he'd not recorded in the main islands during previous trips, and the biomass of sharks was literally the highest in the world. They'd counted forty-five scalloped hammerhead sharks in the first twenty minutes, each swimming along the reef at ninety-feet below the surface in the very strong current that the islands were known for. Mixed in among the hammerheads were a number of large Galapagos sharks, which could be distinguished by a very pronounced triangular dorsal fin.

The extreme topography above the surface was evident below as well. Mac piloted the ROV expertly along the edge of a steep rock wall. The sharks swimming slowly in the current made it all look easy, but Chris suspected that the ripping currents had likely contributed to the ROV's problems. The thrusters had to work much harder under significant currents, which drew down considerable power. And each of the cameras and thrusters was connected to the ROV's main circuit board by rubber, waterproof connectors. Those connectors came under great strain when the ROV was in currents.

Frustrated with the ROV, but long adjusted to the challenge of using electronics in seawater, Chris stood up and stretched further. Leaving the ROV lab, he slowly walked down the corridor to the much larger lab where all the students on board had congregated to watch the ROV video live on a big screen TV.

They were clustered in groups of twos and threes at small tables spread around the room. Chris noted that all the tables had open boxes of crackers sitting on them, each surrounded by a lot of crumbs. There was nothing better for an uncomfortable stomach at sea than a whole bunch of crackers, he knew.

Chris reached for the nearest box and pulled out a handful. He asked, "So what do we think so far?"

"Very cool!" said several students simultaneously.

"Those sharks were amazing!" said a young woman from Ecuador. "I wondered if they were going to attack the ROV."

"Ha!" replied Chris. "We have had curious sharks approach the ROV before, but really they don't want anything to do with it. To them, it's just a big, bright and loud thing they can't eat."

"Dr. Black, have you ever dived with sharks before?"

Out of the corner of his eye, Chris spotted Abby feeding a cracker to Oliver. "Yes, indeed, I have. Remind me later to bring out the VR goggles and show you guys a dive we did last week in California."

"That sounds great!" said one of the students from the U.S. He was wearing a Boston University Marine Program sweatshirt. "Should we remind you after dinner?"

Chris arched his eyebrows. "Remind me of your name."

"It's Roberto."

"Got it," said Chris. "I'll know everyone's names soon enough. Roberto, I'll tell you what. I'll let you use the VR headset first in exchange for a good story about my friend Dr. Les Kaufman."

Chris had known Les for years, dating back to his time in grad school, but hadn't been in touch much since. He assumed that any student going through the BU marine program would have at least one good Les story.

"I can do that!" said Roberto.

One of the Canadian students raised her hand, "Dr. Black?"

"Yes?" He could see Oliver passing Abby his drink. She took a sip and handed it back. An unwelcome reminder that their relationship had entered a phase of tight familiarity.

The woman appeared to hesitate, and then she said, "I am supposed to tell you to leave some of the chocolate for us students and that you should record any deep-water corals you see on this trip."

All eighteen of the students looked at Chris in unison, as did Abby. He squinted his eyes. "Where do you go to school?"

"I'm studying at Dalhousie University in Nova Scotia."

Chris kept squinting. "Really?"

Eventually, she added, "But last semester, I studied abroad at the University of Cape Town."

"Well, two things. Three things, really. First, it is indeed a small world. You'll have to send my dear friend Karen a message." He had worked with Karen during his recent adventures in South Africa.

"Second, we now should plan on both a Les Kaufman story and a Karen Li story tonight. I'll counter every story you offer with one of my own."

"You said three things," Roberto said.

Chris walked over to the freezer, opened it, and pulled out an ice cream sandwich for himself. Abby was laughing quietly at something Oliver said.

"Yes, I did, didn't I? And third, I can't make any promises about the chocolate!"

Roberto, followed by two of the other students, jumped up out of his chair and staged a mock race to the freezer. They each grabbed ice cream sandwiches. Chris laughed, and several more students rose to join the growing crowd at the freezer. Abby and Oliver continued to talk quietly by themselves. Chris couldn't help but notice.

Raising his arms in the air and stepping back from the crowd at the freezer, Chris added, "Looks like we're going to need some time to work on the ROV. Everyone take ten. But please stay clear of the area where Mac and Alex are working." He suspected that Mac was likely going to need hours rather than minutes.

Needing no further encouragement, the students all filed out of the lab in unison and into the fresh air of the back deck. The rolling four-to-six-foot swell had been rocking the boat since they'd arrived at Wolf. The majority of people on board were still in the process of getting their sea legs.

Chris saw Abby file out with the students, but Oliver Chumley-Smith came over to him looking wobbly and a little grey. He smelled strongly of suntan lotion. "I didn't expect the ROV to break down this quickly."

Chumley-Smith had the physique of someone who spent all day at a computer. He was as tall as Chris but rail-thin and paler than any adult Chris had ever met. Chris had no reason to doubt the man's intelligence, but in the few short interactions he'd had with him, it was pretty clear that Chumley-Smith lacked the dry wit that Chris so loved in the British people. In fact, it was not clear to Chris that the man had any sense of humor at all.

"I'd keep that thought to yourself if I were you."

"It's just that these students have paid a great deal of money for this trip, and we have a lot that we want them to accomplish," said Oliver.

"I understand," Chris said as he began to walk toward the door. "That is why Mac and I flew all the way down here on a few days' notice. But the students are also here to learn about the conduct of field research. And nothing will prepare them better for the challenges of field research than to actually experience those challenges. And one of them is equipment issues."

He stopped and turned back to Oliver. "That goes for you too, by the way. I recommend you treat this cruise as a learning opportunity."

"I am. I just didn't expect things to break so quickly," persisted Oliver.

"Shit happens, dude," Chris replied, barely hiding his irritation. "Get used to it." With that, he stepped out into the brilliant sunlight. There, he took a deep breath, berating himself for losing his cool. He knew he might have to have a conversation with Chumley-Smith at some point, but it would not be during this cruise. He wasn't ready to face the man. Unless the complaining continued. Then he'd have to deal with it for the sake of the trip.

Thirty-six hours after leaving Monterey, Chris and Mac had arrived at the airport in San Cristobal, one of the main islands in the Galapagos. The trip to Quito, Ecuador, had been uneventful, with the minor exception that none of their flights had had power outlets or entertainment options in the seats. Mac had considered this an affront to twenty-first-century principles and told whoever would listen about his grievances.

"Look, Mac," Chris had said when his patience with Mac's disinterest in the trip had run out, "we're flying to one of *the* places in the world to conduct marine science. And we're getting out of Carmel right before the golfing madness starts."

Mac had just waved him off.

"Four-hundred thousand additional people on the peninsula!" Chris had continued. "The traffic on Highway One is going to be all-time.

Given how much I know you love traffic, you should be thanking me for this trip." The U.S. Open of Golf was returning to Pebble Beach two days after they departed, and the traffic predictions were indeed dire.

Mac had never conceded Chris's point, but he had quieted down for a while. So, Chris had privately declared a victory.

They'd spent the night at a hotel close to the airport in Quito and arrived in San Cristobal early the next morning.

The RV *MacGreggor* had been a welcome sight sitting at anchor in Wreck Bay. During his two previous trips to the Galapagos, Chris's experience with the local dive boats had been mixed. The *MacGreggor*, by comparison, was equipped for everything that Chris and Mac would need to conduct their research.

Chris knew he'd have to get a handle on being on the same boat as Abby and her new boy toy. Staring out at Wolf Island, watching thousands of brown-footed boobies and frigate birds come and go from the sheer cliffs, Chris calmed down. He could almost imagine himself in Darwin's position, looking out from the deck of the Beagle at this same island, and very likely the same species of birds.

Lost in thought, Chris could feel Abby's presence by his side before she said anything.

"You should give him a chance," said Abby.

"I hope you're talking about Mac," said Chris without turning.

"You know who I'm talking about."

Chris turned to face Abby. "Why is he on this cruise? I read his resume. It's impressive. But there is nothing in his experience that would suggest this is a good idea."

"It's true that he doesn't have much—"

"Any," interrupted Chris.

"Okay, *any* field experience. But he's a very smart guy, with a lot to offer. And I think he thought it would be fun," answered Abby.

Chris leaned forward on the rail and stared at the birds divebombing overhead.

"You don't have to make this so hard," said Abby, filling the pause in the conversation. "Oliver is a good man, and he cares about the students."

"Isn't it a little early in the trip to be trotting out the 'good man' narrative?" asked Chris. "Besides, if Mac hears him questioning the ROV or the ROV team's work, it won't matter how good a man he is."

A flood of complicated emotions poured over Chris as he stood there at the railing in such close proximity to the woman he had cared about so much in the very recent past.

"Look, Abby. We don't have to have this conversation now, or ever, really. I understood your decision back in Carmel, and I'm not questioning it now," replied Chris. "But that doesn't mean I have to get on board with your new love interest."

"I appreciate that. I really do," said Abby. "But please consider it from my perspective. I was utterly exhausted worrying about you. I never knew if you'd be killed or if you'd kill someone else."

"It wasn't always like that," replied Chris. "Was it?"

"It kind of was," said Abby. "And it didn't exactly end when we broke up. For instance, we haven't had a chance to talk about what happened in Cape Town."

Chris recalled vividly Abby's concern about the danger and violence that Chris and his team seemed to encounter so frequently. "I guess it went about as you would expect," he said. "Bad guys attacked us, and we stopped them."

"And people got hurt."

"Yes. In fact, people died," said Chris, a hint of challenge in his voice. "People I cared about. But we did everything we could to prevent it."

"Mac told me, and I'm sorry," replied Abby. "But to finish my earlier thought, you have to understand that spending time with Oliver is not like that. Oliver would never hurt a fly. And we don't have to worry about anyone trying to hurt us."

Abby's assessment bothered Chris, but he understood it. "I'm glad that you feel safe and aren't stressed about the dangers out there. I really am. But those dangers are still out there. I don't cause them. I just react to them."

"Well, I hope this trip will be different." Abby turned abruptly and walked away.

"Don't we all," Chris called after her as he watched her step back into the lab. She moved with the efficiency and grace of the distance swimmer that she was. Even with the boat shifting under the rolling swells, she rarely put a foot out of place. Chris noticed that she'd cut her hair recently, which meant that with her hair pulled up in a short ponytail, the curves of her neck were exposed.

Shaking his head quickly, Chris directed his attention elsewhere. From where he stood, there were several other dive boats visible in the vicinity. The captain had communicated with the National Park to coordinate when the *MacGreggor* would be on station at various islands and dive sites to minimize overlap with other dive operations.

On the far horizon, Chris could see what looked like an all-black vessel moving north toward Darwin Island. Surprised, as black boats were unusual, he was about to chase down a pair of binoculars to investigate further when Mac called him down to the back deck.

9

Tonya Gordon sat uncomfortably on the edge of her bed, looking out the small cabin's porthole. Day in and day out, man after man had violated her again and again. Though it seemed like the frequency of the assaults had abated over the past eighteen hours, the accumulated soreness from the pirates' repeated visits to her cabin since she'd been captured made it difficult to sit comfortably in any position. Large blue-black bruises had expanded to fill the inside of both her thighs. Contusions on her lower back made lying down difficult. And now, with her lower lip split in two locations, the simple act of talking was becoming difficult.

She had not seen Beth since the previous evening, and Tonya feared the worst. With nothing to do other than contemplate the hopelessness of her situation, she'd spent much of the time curled up in a ball on the unsheeted mattress. In the early afternoon, she was awakened by something bumping against the boat. She'd sat up in front of the porthole to find out anything she could about where they were and what was going on around her.

The boat had pulled up next to a much larger vessel, which is what had awakened her. All she could see through the porthole was the matte black paint of the larger ship. The size of the other boat had at first caused Tonya briefly to hope, thinking that it was a military vessel or possibly the Coast Guard. From the thumping on the deck above her stateroom, it seemed to Tonya that many people were coming and going from the other vessel. She could hear shouting, but also a great deal of laughter. With the laughter, her hopes of rescue dissipated.

Suddenly she heard two men talking excitedly in Spanish in the hallway right outside her door. The door burst open, and Tonya steeled herself for the worst. But instead of an onslaught from the pirates, they pushed another woman into the stateroom and closed the door.

The woman lay prone on the floor, breathing heavily. She wore a man's buttoned-down oxford shirt and jeans. The rolled-up sleeves exposed tattoos on both arms, but Tonya could not tell exactly what the tattoos depicted. She could see from the top of the woman's head that her blonde hair was bleached.

The shock of this new person being cast into the room left Tonya speechless as she processed what had just happened. Eventually, the woman rose unsteadily to her hands and knees and looked up at Tonya.

Tonya moved to help, but the woman screamed, "Don't touch me!"

That brought about another period of protracted silence. The silence lasted so long that in her exhaustion, Tonya's mind began to drift to other things, as though the woman were not there. She was deep into a vaguely coherent memory of a New Hampshire skiing trip with Beth when the woman spoke.

"Do you speak English?"

"I do," said Tonya.

The woman sat down on the edge of the bed. Tonya winced and gingerly touched her lip where one of the pirates had slapped her the night before, "I'm . . . I'm an American."

"American? Is this your boat?" asked the woman, her grey eyes looking directly at Tonya.

"No, I was on a different boat when we were attacked," replied Tonya with difficulty. "We were sailing with my friend and his son on their boat. These men killed both of them. They took my daughter and me."

"I'm so sorry," said the woman, as she gingerly moved to a standing position and looked out the porthole.

"Where . . . how did you get here?" asked Tonya, her mind racing.

The woman spoke without turning her head from the window. "I'm a doctor from Mexico City. I was sailing with three friends off Panama. We were attacked in the middle of the night."

"Panama? How long have you been held by these people?"

"I think, perhaps, a month. I'm not really sure."

"Oh, my gosh. What happened to your friends?" Tonya asked, although she knew the answer.

"They killed them. Right in front of me. We didn't have enough money on board to appease them." She didn't look at Tonya, but Tonya was sure she was fighting back tears. "And they took me prisoner."

Tonya reached out for the woman's hand. "My name is Tonya."

The woman remained quiet, then turned to Tonya. "Maria. I am Maria." She took a deep breath. "How old is your daughter?"

"Beth is twenty."

"Looking at you," said Maria, "she must be very beautiful."

Tonya suddenly couldn't hold back any longer, and the floodgates opened to an onslaught of uncontrollable tears. Maria returned to Tonya's side, draping her arm around Tonya's heaving shoulders.

Eventually, Tonya found words to respond. "She is beautiful. Thank you. But it's a beauty all her own. She's so talented, so capable. She doesn't deserve this. What they've done. It's unforgivable." She thought about what Beth had endured the previous year in college and realized she'd experienced it many times more just in the past few days.

Quietly, Maria agreed as she continued to hold Tonya. "No. Nobody deserves this."

"Do you have any children?" asked Tonya, as the interval between sobs increased.

"I do," replied Maria. "I have a son. He is twenty-six. Lives with his father more these days."

"He wasn't with you when this happened?"

Maria peered up at the ceiling. "No, thank heavens. He lives in the States."

"Oh. Where does he live?" Tonya said, no longer sobbing.

"Pennsylvania. I went to school there long ago. Samuel, that's his name, he does too. Law school, just like me."

Furrowing her brow, Tonya asked, "You went to law school too?"

"What?" replied Maria. "Oh, no. Sorry. I meant like his father."

"Oh."

Suddenly changing tacks, Maria said, "Look, Tonya. If you have any money, you may be able to purchase better treatment for both you and Beth. Did you have any money? Maybe on the other boat?"

Tonya remembered her conversation with Tom when they were making the final preparations for the trip. He'd been so excited about the prospect of sailing to places he'd never been before.

In his excitement, Tom had talked endlessly about the 'brotherhood of the sea.' He'd read many accounts of people taking care of each other on the open ocean.

"Imagine it," Tom had said while putting away his maps one night back in Scituate. "You're thousands of miles from home, and your generator dies. Or maybe your rudder is destroyed by a log floating just below the surface. And now you're adrift at sea."

"Aren't you trying to convince me to come with you?" Tonya had asked. "I'm not sure being adrift at sea is what I'm looking for."

"But that's just it!" Tom had walked over to stoke the dying embers in the fireplace. "You might be adrift, but if you put out a radio call, people will come. Sailors, fishermen, military, everyone basically drops what they're doing to help other people in need. Just reading about it makes me feel so much better about humanity. I can't wait to get out there!"

"So," Tonya had asked. "Given all this goodwill we're going to experience, why are we hiding money in the galley again?" They had hidden away fifteen-thousand dollars in a bench earlier that afternoon. It was nestled deep under several bags of rice and other staples.

Tonya shivered as she remembered Tom's reply. "Just in case. I'm sure we won't need it, but I've read online that you really want to have cash on hand to, you know, smooth things over once and awhile."

Back then, she'd imagined bribing fishermen for faster care of their needs. Paying ransom to pirates had never even entered her mind. Thinking now that her money might buy better treatment for Beth, Tonya felt cautious hope. "Why do you think so?"

"Several weeks ago, just after I was taken," Maria explained, "I met another woman who'd been kidnapped just like us. She was able to buy her freedom."

Exhausted and confused, Tonya sat back on the bed. "I don't understand. Why would these men . . . these pirates . . . why wouldn't they just take the money? Nothing I've seen suggests there is any honor in any of these men."

"I don't know, but isn't it worth a try?" asked Maria. "I overheard them planning to go after a larger boat somewhere. Perhaps if we can give them some money, they'll let us go while they go after this other boat."

They are going after a larger boat, Tonya thought, which must mean a lot more people.

"God help them," she said aloud.

10

Dawn was still an hour away when Chris came out onto the back deck to check in with Mac. He wore a fleece and his favorite CMEx hoodie to stay warm. The ROV was illuminated by four deck lights, and Chris could see several important pieces of the Seaview were still sitting on the deck unattached. Alex Smith was sleeping awkwardly in a canvas deck chair nearby.

"Hey. How're we doing?" asked Chris as he handed Mac a hot chocolate.

"Thanks. The ROV is non-functional." Mac was visibly exhausted; there were grease stains all over his bare arms and across his face. "Like we discussed, I'm pretty sure the currents yesterday stressed the connection to the umbilical, but I can't seem to isolate the problem."

Chris knew from innumerable days at sea with ROVs that the hardest problems to solve were the intermittent ones with no clear cause. And there were so many things that could go wrong it made life difficult for engineers like Mac. "Understood. If you tell me we can have it in the water by the end of the day, we'll plan accordingly. But if that looks unlikely, I think we'll switch over to SCUBA ops for the rest of today and perhaps tomorrow."

Mac sipped some hot chocolate then rubbed his eyes.

"I think you'd better go with dive ops. I don't like it, but it's the reality we're faced with."

"Copy that," said Chris. "I'll go back up and let Captain Dennis know that's the plan. What's your assessment of him, by the way?" The *MacGreggor*'s regular captain had had a family emergency before the trip, so a contract captain was hired to drive the boat.

"I like him," said Mac. "As you know, the toughest part of the job is driving the boat when the ROV's in the water. He's got a ton of experience with other ships and ROVs. I thought he did fine yesterday. Is there a problem?"

"Not at all," replied Chris. "I like him too. I was just up there talking to him for about forty-five minutes. He was telling stories about transporting sailboats across the Pacific. Gnarly stuff. He's been there and done that."

"Yeah. I've heard a few of those. Did he tell you the one about the night shift?"

"That's what I'm talking about," answered Chris. "Freaked me out. We'll have to get into that later. Switching topics, how much sleep did master Alex over there get last night?"

"More than I did, but not enough," replied Mac. "But I wouldn't worry about him. He's young and full of enthusiasm. He'll be fine if you need him."

"Okay, then. Dive operations it is," said Chris. "We can have Alex run them from the deck, and Ricardo and Abby can help me underwater."

Ricardo Estrella was a naturalist provided to the *MacGreggor* for the duration of their stay in the Galapagos as a condition of their permit with the National Park.

All naturalists employed by the Park were natives to the islands. It was an added benefit, from Chris's perspective, that Ricardo was an expert on whale sharks.

"Why don't you go grab some shut eye, Mac? It's hard to solve problems if you can't see or think straight."

"I think I might do that." Mac leaned down to start cleaning up the mess around the ROV. "Don't let me sleep past noon." The fact that Mac so readily agreed to get some rest suggested to Chris exactly how tired his friend must be.

Chris walked over to the wall-mounted phone and called the bridge. "Captain Dennis, we are going to switch over to SCUBA operations. I think we should move the *MacG* over to Darwin."

"Copy that."

"I'll get them together for a dive briefing in about an hour," Chris added, "and then we'll start to gear up. There are eight students getting in the water with me, Abby, and Ricardo. I'll need Alex to lead dive ops once we are at anchor, but for now, let's let him sleep, and Oliver will keep the other students busy on the upper deck studying all these birds."

"Understood," replied Dennis. "I'll alert Alex to that fact when we get on-site and send him your way once we are anchored. We should be there in two hours." He hung up.

Chris could feel the *MacGreggor*'s large diesel engines power up beneath them.

"Go to sleep, man," he said as he caught Mac yawning. "We can deal with the ROV later."

"On my way. Tell that wanker Hortley-Chumfrey that I can feel his disapproval and the feeling's mutual."

Chris didn't even try to suppress his smile. "Right, I'll tell him. Good night."

As the MacGreggor made the short trip from Wolf Island to Darwin Island, Ricardo gave an animated presentation to the students in the main lab about his favorite animal, the whale shark. He explained that whale sharks, *Rhincodon typus*, are the largest species of fish on Earth, reaching lengths of sixty-five feet. And like several of the largest marine mammals, they subsist entirely on microscopic plankton for food.

"Wait a minute," one of the students from the U.S. had interjected. "That's it? Little plants? How does anyone actually know that?"

"Well," replied Ricardo. "I've been studying whale sharks since I was fourteen, and I've seen them eat, I've seen them mate, and I've seen them die. That's how science works. We observe."

"I don't buy it," the student continued.

"That's the great thing about science," said Ricardo, demonstrating what Chris thought was incredible patience. "You don't have to buy it. You can go observe it for yourself."

After all the students filed out of the lab to begin getting ready, Chris asked Abby, "How did non-science majors get on this cruise? They all seem like nice kids, but some of those questions . . ."

"I understand your concern," answered Abby, sitting down across from Chris at one of the small tables. "But it's increasingly common on trips like this to have a wide variety of participants. I think the goal is to be as inclusive as possible."

Chumley-Smith, who was standing nearby, added, "Yes, we want to be inclusive. And I think you might want to think about their experience differently."

"How so?" asked Chris.

"The science students will no doubt learn a great deal on the cruise," Chumley-Smith observed. "But think about how impactful this all will be for the non-scientists who've never done anything like this before. It might literally change their lives."

"That's a fair point, Oliver. And I'm all in on inclusivity, Abby. You've seen what Mac and I have done to bring marine science to the masses. In fact, I'm going to lug along the VR camera on this next dive for precisely that purpose. I'm just concerned that if students haven't met some minimal level of preparation for a cruise like this, they'll be really limited in what they can take away from the experience."

"I don't disagree with you, Chris," said Abby, reaching out and placing her hand on his forearm. "I really don't. But there is also a great deal of pressure, both from the university and from donors, to include a wider array of people on activities like this."

"Even without sufficient training?" asked Chris, still looking at the spot on his arm where Abby had touched him. "Peter was aware of this?"

"Oh, yes," Oliver interjected. "Peter, Abby, and I had a number of conversations about this particular issue. I think he felt similarly to you, but he also understood the benefits to the CMEx of expanding the potential list of participants."

"Okay, but—"

"But bringing a diversity of students along on the cruise alone is not sufficient," Oliver continued. "We need to make sure that they have equivalent experiences to the other students."

Chris whirled toward the Brit. "First off, don't interrupt."

"Chris!" said Abby.

"Second, there was always going to be diving on this trip, and since your selection criteria for participants obviously failed to select for students trained for diving, fewer than half are going to be able to join us in the water, including you."

Only eight of the eighteen students aboard the *MacGreggor* were checked out as research divers, so the rest of the group would have to appreciate the island from the surface and from the video footage they would take with the ROV once it was operational again.

"Yes," replied Oliver, getting as far away from Chris as he could while remaining seated at the table. "That is precisely why it is so important to get the ROV back in service. Watching the live ROV video feed provides an equivalent experience to all the students."

Chris knew he should concede this point but sure wasn't going to give Abby's boyfriend the satisfaction. Looking at his watch, he pushed back his chair and stood up. "I will take the VR camera with me on the dive in the hopes of bringing back some whale shark video that the non-divers can experience in one of our headsets.

"Let's talk about this more later, Abby." Ignoring Oliver gave him unwarranted satisfaction. "I think we can come up with some other ideas to keep the whole group engaged in the coming days. We've got to go get suited up for the dive."

As he left the lab, Chris turned back to see Abby resting her hand on Oliver's forearm.

11

Everyone in the group wore full neoprene wetsuits. Though the islands were right at the Equator, the oceanography around the Galapagos made the water much cooler than other tropical dive locations.

Chris knew from his research during his first trip down that, depending on the time of year, the islands were bathed in one of eight separate currents. Several of those currents brought cold, nutrient-rich water up from the coast of South America. The water temperature at the main islands in the summer hovered around sixty-eight to seventy-two degrees Fahrenheit. Out at Darwin and Wolf Islands, the water warmed to the high seventies. That was considerably warmer than Chris and the team usually faced back in Monterey, but he still wore his full wetsuit. He knew that ultimately, any temperature below ninety-eight point six was going to wick warmth away from the human body. And the more dives one did in a day, the more heat was lost. So even if he had to feel a bit warm on the first dive of the day, by the last dive he was always glad to be wearing his full suit.

Chris received a little push back from the students when he handed out the colored Lycra hoods to be worn over their neoprene hoods for identification. With so many unfamiliar divers in the water, and given the potential for other dive boats to show up on-site during the dive, the colored hoods helped keep track of everyone while underwater. Undergraduates received magenta hoods, grad students yellow, and Ricardo and Chris were resplendent in rainbow.

The goal for the afternoon dive, likely the only dive they would complete on this first day of operations, was to introduce the students to whale sharks at a site called 'Darwin's Arch,' where the animals were frequently observed. However, as both Chris and Ricardo knew all too well, the ocean had a tendency to disrupt even the most well- constructed plans, so they weren't counting on anything.

Hoping to collect some imagery for the students not making the dive, Chris brought along the virtual reality camera system mounted on a telescoping carbon fiber pole. He figured that if he could record a white shark without trying back home, perhaps he'd have the same luck with a whale shark.

Thirty-five minutes into what was expected to be a forty-five-minute dive, the group had seen a lot of fish, but no whale sharks. They'd started the dive on the shallow edge of a rocky reef, which dropped off steeply into the abyss. From that location, they could see the multitude of fishes swimming along and above the reef. In the swift-flowing current just off the reef, large schools of hammerhead and Galapagos sharks swam past just as they had in the ROV video the day before, giving many students their first direct experience with sharks of any kind underwater.

They'd watched the procession of sharks, which were occasionally joined by green sea turtles and gold-spotted eagle rays, for twenty minutes before Ricardo had motioned the group to follow him into the blue water. The divers used their buoyancy compensator vests to maintain neutral buoyancy, meaning they neither sunk nor rose to the surface as they swam away from the reef.

Out in the 'water column,' the group quickly lost sight of the reef. With the bottom deep and out of sight below them and the surface well above them, they were left suspended in a deep mosaic of shifting blue colors. Large schools of small fish would emerge out of the blue to the left and quickly pass out of sight, followed just as quickly by larger predators seeking sustenance. At one point, a large school of scalloped hammerhead sharks, *Sphyrna lewini*, moved close to the group. The sharks were following bait fish and ended up circling the divers for several minutes.

Chris estimated that there were at least seventy-five individual sharks, each ranging in length from eight to ten feet. Watching the students, it was pretty clear to him that they had no idea how dangerous the situation was. Two of the students swam quickly toward the sharks, both with small cameras thrust out in front of them. If just one of those sharks decided to take an interest in any of the divers, which could very easily happen given the students' movements, many of the other sharks would respond as well. Seventy-five sharks feeding simultaneously on eight student divers was not the type of inclusivity, Chris knew, that the university was looking for.

Despite clearly being enthralled by the hammerheads, Chris suspected that expectations were running high for an appearance by a whale shark. And since the ROV had broken down, Chris was hopeful that the students would see something large soon. He thought that he'd seen one or more of the animals out at the very edge of visibility, which he estimated was likely fifty feet, when the group moved away from the reef. But the whale sharks were elusive, and he couldn't be sure that it was what he'd seen in the ever-shifting light.

Looking at his wrist-mounted dive computer, Chris could see that they were going to have to begin their ascent to the surface within eight minutes in order to avoid any problems with decompression. He also knew that two of the eight students were breathing air faster than usual in all the excitement, adding another reason to surface soon.

Just as Chris was about to signal to Ricardo that they should wrap it up, something very large above him blotted out the sun. He turned to see the silhouette of a huge whale shark slowly passing by. The animal, which Chris estimated to be at least forty-five feet in length, was swimming only ten feet above him.

He could hear Ricardo hooting loudly through his regulator, and he could see the students all pointing their cameras at the enormous shark.

Chris used a magnetic wand to start the VR camera recording. The shark was so large that it effectively served as a habitat for many other fishes. He could see large black jacks taking turns swimming in and out of the shark's open mouth to pick off small fishes hiding there.

Next to the shark's dorsal fin, and along both of its pectoral fins, multiple individual fish from several species swam close, seeking protection from predators. And along the tail fin, Chris counted no fewer than twenty-five separate fish.

The shark appeared to be barely moving, but had the divers not moved along with it, it would have been gone in moments.

As exciting as it was to meet one of their main objectives for the day, Chris motioned for everyone to begin their ascents to the surface. By pressing three fingers under the palm of his other hand, Chris signaled to the group that they would conduct a three-minute safety stop when they were fifteen feet shy of the surface. These three minutes would allow the divers to 'off gas' some of the nitrogen that had accumulated in their bloodstreams as they dove.

Hovering close by the students during the safety stop, the excitement in the group was palpable; their body language radiated enthusiasm. Ricardo swam by and gave Chris a look that suggested he too could see how pleased the students were. Chris, too, was eager to see how the VR footage he'd just shot turned out.

At the surface, they all signaled their status to the boat and then commenced with a recap as they slowly swam back toward the *MacGreggor*, which was several hundred feet away.

"That was amazing!" exclaimed Abby. Chris admitted to himself that it was nice to have Abby out there with them. Without Oliver.

"Dr. Black, have you ever been that close to a whale shark before?" asked one of the Ecuadorian students.

"Did you see that thing? It was incredible!" asked Roberto.

"Right over our heads. I've never seen anything like it," said another student whose name Chris couldn't recall.

Eduardo, another of the Ecuadorian students commented, "It was like three feet away from me! Biggest thing I've ever seen."

"Dr. Black, what did you think?"

Chris didn't respond immediately because his attention had been drawn away. A sailboat had tied itself up to the side of the *MacGreggor,* and Chris couldn't see anyone on deck. Lying on his back, supported by his buoyancy compensator vest, Chris kicked along at the surface toward the stern of the *MacGreggor* with a trepidation that he couldn't immediately explain. He signaled to Abby to stay put with the students. And then he began his approach alone.

12

Something about the boat tied up to the research vessel made Chris very nervous. There were no plans for a rendezvous with anyone that he was aware of, and it struck him as odd that anyone would seek to tie up to a research vessel they couldn't possibly know. His sense of foreboding had started very early that morning, as Captain Dennis had recounted a tale that uncharacteristically unnerved him.

Years before, Dennis had joined three other sailors to transit a sixty-foot sloop from San Diego, California to Sydney, Australia. It was just one of many such trips Dennis had made by that point in his life, but it still stood out in his mind even decades later. One of the other sailors had been a former British special forces operative. Dennis had described him as a tough guy in all respects. "You didn't fuck around with this guy, if you know what I'm saying."

One night when the boat was halfway between Hawaii and Australia, deep in the central Pacific, about as far from land as a person could get on the planet, Dennis took his turn at the wheel from midnight to three in the morning.

As he sat there alone in the dark, slowly steering the boat through tranquil waters under the stars, he became aware of a deeply menacing presence in the water around the boat.

"Do you mean a shark?" Chris had asked. "We've all had that feeling of 'sharkiness' on or in the water."

"No," Dennis had answered, "this was very different. It was much more intense. With a shark, sure it's a little concerning, but you know it's just doing its shark thing. It doesn't actually mean to threaten you. This was, for lack of a better description, pure evil."

Chris had actually gulped upon hearing this consummate professional recount such a story.

"There was something out there, and it wanted to get me. And I was close to getting out of there, but then my shift ended and I came down into the galley to warm up and get something to eat. I don't remember the guy's name who replaced me, but it was the guy from the British Special Forces. And that's when things got really interesting."

"Interesting how?" Chris had asked.

"After that experience, I couldn't go to sleep, so I sat down in the galley and tried to read a magazine. About an hour into his shift, the Brit comes down to get some coffee. At first, he just nodded at me. But then after he'd poured himself a cup of coffee, he turned to me and said, 'Did you feel that out there, mate? There's something nasty out there.'"

Dennis had pulled back the sleeve on his sweatshirt and shown Chris the goosebumps he was getting just by recounting the story.

"He didn't ask me to join him, but I did. I went out there and we sat together until dawn. By then, the feeling had dissipated. I never felt anything like that again, but I will never forget it."

Chris shivered just thinking about the captain's story.

As he approached the ladder he called out, "Hey, Alex! A little help back here." Chris exhaled deeply, the accumulated anxiety washing away when Alex's smiling face appeared at the rail. "Didn't realize we were expecting guests," said Chris, nodding his head toward the sailboat which he could now see was named *D-fens* out of San Diego. "What's going on?"

"Oh, you should come up on deck to see," replied Alex as he reached out to take Chris's fins.

Climbing to the top of the ladder quickly, Chris peered over the gunwale to see the captain and several students talking to none other than their old colleague Hendrix, a former military colleague of Mac's, who now ran a very lucrative security business.

Seeing Chris at the rail, Hendrix called out, "Ahoy, Dr. Black! Cheated death once again, I see."

"Well, the day is young." Chris laughed, feeling far more relieved than the situation required.

"What's up with the rainbow hood?" asked Hendrix. "Not that it doesn't look good on you, of course."

"It reminds me of unicorns and fluffy bunnies," said Chris.

Hendrix, Chris had never learned his first name, stood on the back deck sandwiched between two very strong looking women. He himself was shorter than Chris but gained a few inches based on toughness alone. Chris had seen Hendrix with his head shaved clean and at other times with thick black hair and a matching beard. The man adjusted to whatever the current mission was. One thing Hendrix couldn't hide was the fact that his neck was permanently scarred from what appeared to be a failed hanging. Hendrix usually wore sunglasses with reflective lenses, so one rarely got a direct look at his eyes. But during the few moments that Chris had seen Hendrix without his glasses the previous year, he'd looked right into the eyes of a warrior.

Sure, there was kindness and mirth visible from time to time, but when Hendrix wasn't directly engaging him, Chris could see the man constantly taking the measure of everyone and everything within his cone of vision.

If Hendrix and his crew hadn't helped to find Chris when he'd been taken hostage during the Carmel Canyon Incident or had they not arrived on the scene in South Africa at precisely the right moment, Chris knew he'd have been dead on both occasions. Mac's description of his friend was dead on. "Hendrix is the Keyser Söze of the security world; he's a figment of your imagination right up until he's not. And then, you can't get rid of him." The guy simply had the ability to show up, literally anywhere in the world, and then disappear as quickly as he appeared.

"I don't recall that we even told you we were coming down here, let alone when and to which islands. How did you find us?" asked Chris.

Hendrix ignored the question, as he frequently did, and said, "Where's Johnson?"

"I'm here," said Mac, climbing down the ladder from the deck above.

"Ah. Well, Dr. Black, let me introduce you to my two colleagues, Dana and Sam. Dana and Sam, the esteemed Dr. Chris Black. And this guy over here is Mac Johnson."

Sam was a tall African-American woman with a big smile, a firm handshake, and a black t-shirt that read "Trust No One." She also had eyes similar to Hendrix; Chris could tell she was sizing up threats all around her. He liked her immediately.

"Trust no one. I like it," said Chris.

Sam seemed to ignore him and directed her response to Hendrix instead. "You're right, he does look a little bit like Mulder. Especially if you turn your head sideways and squint."

"Okay, now you're just flirting," said Hendrix. Chris laughed.

Dana did not appear to be as friendly as her colleague. She was several inches shorter than Sam but looked every bit as strong. Her brown hair was cut shoulder length. Chris shook hands with her as well, feeling pain in his fingers from the strength of the grip.

"You may have outdone yourself this time, Hendrix," he said.

"Okay, now you're flirting. It's time to cut this off before it gets out of control," said Hendrix. "You guys should motor over to our yacht for dinner tonight. We'll be anchored right around the corner."

"What's for dinner?"

"It's not the meal," said Hendrix. "It's the conversation."

As Chris pondered Hendrix's suggestion, he noticed the black vessel that he'd seen earlier, hovering out on the horizon between Darwin and Wolf Islands.

13

"Okay, now turn slowly to your right about ninety degrees and then look upwards," said Chris to Terra, a student from South Florida, who was wearing a VR headset.

After all the dive gear from the morning's activities had been cleaned and hung up to dry on racks lining the back deck, the students had prepped and consumed lunch and then cleaned up the galley. Prior to their arrival on the *MacG*, Abby had assigned each of the eighteen students to a three-person color group. A meal plan for the entire cruise was then mapped onto a calendar posted on the main refrigerator, with each group rotating through preparation or clean-up for each of the day's meals.

While all that had happened, Chris had quickly produced a preliminary version of the video from the morning's dive with the whale shark. Since the *MacG* did not have eighteen VR headsets on board, he'd rallied all the students back into the main lab late in the afternoon, where one of the headsets was synched with the large monitor on the wall. This allowed everyone in the room to simultaneously see the same thing as the person wearing the headset.

"This is very cool," noted Terra, as the massive whale shark swam across the screen. She had not been able to join the morning's dive, but was getting to experience one of the highlights, nonetheless.

Standing in the middle of the room, Terra instinctively held her arms out in front of her as she turned around in circles. The VR goggles completely constrained her view, literally immersing her in the video. The students, all seated around Terra, watched the action on the big screen, but watched her as well as she spun.

"It is, right?" noted Chris as he sat with the rest of the students watching the large screen on the wall. "I was obviously on the dive this morning, and I still can't stop watching."

"I want one of these headsets."

"We should probably get you trained to SCUBA dive first, no?" Chris suggested. "Now please, for the sake of your colleagues, make all your movements a little slower."

One of the primary challenges of linking a VR headset to any other type of screen was the fact that the headset wearer invariably looked all over the place very quickly. That made for some uncomfortable stomachs among the people watching on the screen.

Smiling, Terra spun quickly in a circle, causing the image on the screen to move dizzyingly fast. "Like this?"

Several of the students groaned, and everyone looked down or away from the screen.

"Hey, Terra. Let's let someone else have a look, eh?" Roberto said.

Terra shifted the headset up onto her forehead, immediately grabbing the back of the nearest chair to steady herself. "Whoa. It's not easy coming back to reality."

Eduardo was the next to use the headset. After everyone had already seen the whale shark several times through, the focus of the group changed to finding each of the divers on the video as well.

"That's me!" said Eduardo, pointing up and to the right.

"That can't be you," joked Roberto. "That guy's buoyancy control is too good."

"Ouch," said Terra.

Chris chuckled. "You better be careful, Roberto, or we might have to apply that same scrutiny to you."

Chris stood up to get the students' attention. "Okay, here's the plan for the rest of the day. Since we skipped forward to watch the whale shark first, Ricardo is now going to take you all through the entire video, and I think he has some questions for you to answer after. Everyone should get a chance to watch on one of the headsets.

"By the way, please remember to wipe down the headset with those wet wipes before you pass it along to the next person. All we need on this cruise is a pinkeye epidemic."

"Gross!" exclaimed several students simultaneously.

"Remember, there's nothing gross in science," noted Chris.

Mac stuck his head in through the lab door. "Except spider bites. Remember that kid in eighth grade who got bit by a brown recluse spider on his leg?"

One of the Ecuadorian students asked, "What's a brown recluse?"

"Just do a Google image search for 'brown recluse spider bite,'" suggested Mac. "You'll see what I mean."

To Chris, he added, "We've got to get moving. And I need to talk with you."

"Right, I'll catch up. Mac and I are going to eat dinner over on our visitors' boat, but later I'd like to meet up with everyone back here to talk about the behavior of all those fishes swimming around the shark. Can you guys handle that?"

"Definitely," said Roberto.

"Totally," added Terra.

"What time do you want us here?" asked Eduardo.

"Let's say nine, to be safe," said Chris.

"Dr. Black?"

"Roberto, since we're all thousands of miles from home, and we spent the morning together surrounded by sharks, I think you can call me Chris."

"I'll try," said Roberto. "Are we going to get a chance to use this VR system again?"

"You can count on it. We're just getting started. We'll get you divers underwater collecting the imagery, and the surface team will help collect data from the videos. Actually, now that I think about it, do any of you have skills with photography or image processing software?"

Several hands shot up.

"Of course, you do! I forget I'm talking to a bunch of millennials. You guys know more about this stuff than me. Alright, I've got to talk to the captain about tomorrow's plan. I'll see you guys later tonight."

Eduardo blurted out, "Nasty!"

Chris turned to see Eduardo and two other students grimacing as they hovered close to a computer monitor. Several other students jumped up to check out what Chris assumed were images of festering wounds. He was certain that Peter Lloyd would appreciate the *MacGreggor's* expensive WIFI being used so productively.

14

Leaving the main lab through the interior door, Chris turned right to head toward the bridge. Proceeding up the hallway, as he neared the galley on his left, he could hear Mac talking in a voice that was uncharacteristically agitated.

Coming through the galley door, he found Abby and Oliver sitting at a table in the corner, with Mac standing very close by

"What's up?" asked Chris.

Turning toward Chris, Mac's eye initially flared with an intensity usually reserved for more tense experiences. But within a second, he had dialed the intensity down.

"I just received an urgent sat phone call from Peter." Pointing at Chumley-Smith, Mac added, "Our Fulbright Scholar here apparently found it necessary to call back to California to complain about my handling of the ROV."

Looking first at Abby, then directly at Chumley-Smith, Chris said, "Go on."

"Not only did he call to complain about the vehicle breaking down. He also apparently told Peter that I was sleeping all day rather than working to solve the problem. And he's demanding that we go back into port."

"I was perfectly within my rights to contact Dr. Lloyd," suggested Oliver. "And if you can't solve the problem out here it is entirely logical that we return to port to find someone who can."

"I built the *Seaview*," said Mac. "I know her systems from back to front."

"And yet," noted Oliver, "she is not functioning. I'd say it was high time that we come up with another strategy, don't you?"

Putting his hand on Mac's shoulder, Chris said, "I'd already notified Peter via email last night, and again this morning, about the situation with the ROV and all the work that you and Alex were doing to fix it. I wouldn't worry about Peter. Where do we stand with the ROV right now?"

A visibly calmer Mac explained, "We've checked everything on the vehicle at least three times, and everything looks good. It is, as we discussed earlier, very likely that the strong currents during yesterday's dive stressed the connection between the umbilical and the vehicle."

"That's the first I've heard of it," stated Oliver flatly.

"That's the first you've heard of it because—"

Chris interjected, "Mac, can we re-terminate the umbilical out here?" The umbilical was essentially a combined power cord and audio-visual cable. To fix it, the damaged end would have to be cut off, and then each of the wires inside the umbilical would need to be soldered to new connectors. And then it would need to be waterproofed.

"Already done," replied Mac. "Alex and I just finished. But we will have to wait twenty-four hours before we put it back in the water."

"Twenty-four more hours?" asked Oliver. "Another day lost. That is just splendid."

"This isn't computer modeling," said Mac, his voice rising again.

Chris placed his hand on Mac's shoulder again. "Thanks, Mac. Why don't you go get the inflatable ready to go? I'll be out there in a minute."

Chris and Mac had been through so much over the years that Mac easily picked up on Chris's verbal and physical cues. He took a long look at Chumley-Smith, nodded toward Abby, then left the galley, closing the door behind him.

"Mac, please, wait a minute," pleaded Abby.

"Hang on, Abby," said Chris as he waited for Mac to leave.

Grabbing a chair from a nearby table, Chris turned the chair around so he could rest his forearms on the seatback as he spoke. He positioned himself very close to Chumley-Smith.

"Mac is my oldest friend and I know he's your friend too, Abby," said Chris. "But in this situation, he's a staff member and we don't talk about staff members' performance in front of them."

"It really wasn't about him," said Abby.

"I'm sure we could argue about that, but let's move on."

"Fine," Abby conceded. "The fact is, we came all the way down here to the Galapagos, and the ROV barely made it a day. That just isn't satisfactory. You have to see that."

Chris rubbed his face with both palms. "Of course, I see that. I've done everything I can to keep the students engaged since. And Mac just explained what he's done to get the ROV back in action." He was surprised that Abby was continuing to press the point. She'd been at sea back in California enough to know that these things happen.

"Look," Chris continued. "This is on me. We should've had this conversation before we left port, but I let my personal concerns about the two of you cloud my judgment."

"Chris . . ." whispered Abby.

"I don't see how my relationship with Abigail has anything to do with the functioning of the ROV or the success of this cruise," said Oliver, resting his hand on Abby's. "If you are preoccupied with our relationship, I recommend that you figure out a way to move beyond it."

Chris took a deep breath. "As I said, this is on me. And you have my blessing to email or call anyone you'd like to complain to about my leadership. But don't misunderstand me on this point, I am in charge here. You report to me, and you will not antagonize Mac, or any of the personnel on this ship, any further. Do you understand that?"

"I resent that," said Oliver.

"Fine. Resent away," Chris said, stood up and carefully put back the chair. "You're a smart guy, Oliver. Two weeks from now, when we're all back in Monterey, I want you to remember this moment as an important one. You can opt to piss off those around you, or you can try and join the team. Your choice."

And then Chris walked out.

15

"Wait a second!" interjected Hendrix as he cracked open an *Endemica* beer and handed it to Chris. "Are you telling me that Abigail is over there on that boat? And that she's doing the hokey pokey with some other dude?"

The sun had set as the five of them sat in near total darkness on the stern of the *D-fens*. With no man-made structures in sight, the pitch black was punctuated by extraordinary starlight, though an approaching storm front was blocking out the stars as it advanced.

They were anchored so close to the island that, other than the conversation, the only background noise came from the thousands of birds nesting in the cliffs.

Chris and Mac had motored over to Hendrix's yacht on one of the *MacGreggor*'s inflatable dive boats two hours before, neither in the mood to socialize. As they feasted on assorted vegetables prepared by Sam and Dana, they'd learned that both of the two women were former special forces who now worked for one of Hendrix's competitors. The trip, contrary to the image that Hendrix had jokingly asserted, was actually a recruiting effort on his part. He'd hatched the plan to meet up with Chris and Mac in the Galapagos, and when he learned that Sam and Dana were already in South America, he'd organized the trip.

Chris, preoccupied as he was with other concerns, stared out at the approaching storm. Rain was exactly what this disaster of a cruise needed to bring on true misery. He had an overwhelming desire to get out of there, to head somewhere where irritating British computer modelers and old love interests couldn't get to him. Even Hendrix's seemingly boundless enthusiasm was not enough to shake him out of his funk. And though he couldn't see Mac very well in the light provided by Hendrix's small camping lantern, Chris was pretty sure Mac was feeling the same thing.

But as romantic as the notion of escape felt, he knew that they couldn't abandon the students.

"That's about the size of it," answered Mac, who sounded grumpy and near sleep. He was lying on three cushions and considering spending the night right there on the back deck.

"And how's our boy handling it?" asked Hendrix.

"You know I'm sitting right here?" asked Chris. He looked over at Sam's silhouette. "This is exactly the kind of stimulating conversation I was hoping for."

"You two are a couple of huge downers tonight," observed Hendrix, taking a long swig on his beer. "I convinced Sam and Dana here to travel hundreds of miles by sail, out into the middle of the Pacific Ocean, in order to meet the great Dr. Chris Black and the incredible Mac Johnson. I regaled them with stories of buried treasure and big white sharks. And this is what we get? Two duds?"

"You'll have to excuse us, ladies," explained Mac. "Chris is having image problems, and I'm suffering from a severe lack of sleep. You aren't exactly catching us at our best."

"Ha! That much is true," said Hendrix.

"Image problems?" asked Sam. "That sounds interesting."

"It isn't," grumbled Chris.

Mac repositioned himself on the cushions with newfound animation, "Young Chris here—"

"Mac."

"Just let me get it out and then you can clarify where needed," said Mac. "As I was saying, young Chris here saved the girl, more than once, really. But the girl basically thinks that it was Chris's fault that she needed saving in the first place. So, our boy gets no credit for the saving. Do you get the picture?"

Dana said nothing. She'd been the quietest of the group all night. "Ah, yes," Sam offered, "the under-appreciated hero. Not a failed hero, or even an anti-hero. Just a simple hero who lacks the recognition he deserves."

"That's it, exactly," said Mac.

"A true tragedy," said Hendrix. "We must explore this further. Dana, what do you think?"

"Oh, my god," said Chris.

"I think we should leave this poor guy alone."

"Thank you, Dana!" said Chris, glancing at the luminous hands on his dive watch. "Look, as much as I relish the opportunity to have my personal failings critiqued by the group, that storm is coming on quickly, and I told the students that I'd meet them back at the lab at nine o'clock."

Sam glanced toward the bow before getting up abruptly and rushing off silently. Chris noted that Dana watched Sam go with some concern. He asked quietly, "What?"

Before Sam could answer him, a knife came flying up from the galley, embedding itself deep into Hendrix's chest just below his right collarbone. He fell backward with an audible grunt.

"Mac!" yelled Chris, "Galley!"

Gunfire erupted from the door to the galley ripping through the deck where Mac had been reclining only seconds before. One round hit Hendrix in the opposite side from the knife.

Hearing the click of an expended magazine, Chris leaped into the dark hole leading to the galley, his eyes still reeling from the bright flash of the weapon. He collided immediately with the guy who'd fired the gun.

Struggling in the pitch black, unsure of exactly what he was dealing with, Chris grabbed the man by the shoulders and quickly head-butted him in the face. He could hear and feel the man's nose break.

Not waiting for the man to recover, Chris jabbed his right fist at what he hoped was the man's throat. The punch landed solidly, crushing the man's windpipe.

His eyes now adjusted to the dark. Chris grabbed a handgun from the now unconscious man's belt and paused to listen. Hearing nothing, he crept back up the short flight of stairs to the back deck. Dana was on the deck administering aid to Hendrix, who was laid out on the decimated cushions Mac had been using. Chris started to look around for Mac when he heard from behind him, "Here."

Chris turned to see Mac walking back from the bow.

"Sam's dead. But she took two guys with her. I finished off a third."

Chris recognized in Mac's tone the total focus that he always brought to bear in these situations; the legacy of his military training.

"I put the guy in the galley down," Chris said. "He may still be alive."

Mac turned to Dana. "What's Hendrix's status?"

"He'll live, but he's going to need more care than I can give him on this yacht." Chris didn't know Dana at all, but he could sense in her the same training that Mac and Hendrix so frequently demonstrated.

"We have a pretty good sick bay on the *MacGreggor*," Chris interjected. "Let's get him over there ASAP."

Dana nodded.

Mac agreed. "Get the motor started. I'll pull up the anchor."

Chris was moving toward the wheel and console when he caught movement out of the corner of his eye. A fifth man was coming out of the galley, pointing an automatic weapon right at him.

Before Chris had a chance to react, the man was thrown backward from the force of the knife that hit him squarely in the chest. Chris turned to see Dana applying direct pressure to the wound on Hendrix's chest. It was clear that she'd pulled the knife out of Hendrix and used it to stop the fifth man.

"Thanks."

"No problem," said Dana. "Let's get this thing moving. I don't want to lose Hendrix too."

Chris fired up the motor and turned on the deck lights. He could hear the anchor lock into place on the bow. He slowly brought the bow around and began motoring to the other side of the island to rendezvous with the *MacGreggor*. He could see a second inflatable now trailing behind their yacht bobbing along in the wake next to the one he and Mac had used to come over from the *MacGreggor*.

Mac came up out of the galley carrying a first aid kit, which he set down next to Hendrix. "They destroyed both the radio and the satellite phone. There's zero cell coverage out here, so we've got no comms."

"Doesn't seem like a random attack," said Chris, thinking aloud.

"No, it doesn't," said Mac. "Not professional either, and yet coordinated."

"And where'd the inflatable come from?" Dana asked. "The island?"

"I don't think so." Mac was helping Dana secure a bandage on the still unconscious Hendrix. "We've only been out here a day, but that sheer cliff face seems to go all the way around the island."

"Yeah, there's no place to go on the island," Chris explained. "No structures, no landing spots. At least no official landing spots."

Chris thought for a minute and then said to himself, "The black boat."

"What?" asked Mac.

"In the past two days I've seen a large black vessel on the horizon a few times."

"There's been a lot of boat traffic out here. Why did you notice the black one?"

"Because unlike all the other traffic," Chris replied, "this one stayed just far enough out to maintain visual contact without being seen much itself. Just like that white shark in the VR back home. A predator. It was acting like a predator."

"Okay. We'll find it," said Mac.

With Hendrix's wounds now dressed, Mac stood up and approached Chris.

"Thanks for the timely warning. That was a close one."

Chris was deep in thought. It was difficult to believe that they'd met Sam only hours before and now she was gone. He wondered how Dana was dealing with it.

"My pleasure," said Chris, after a moment.

"I saw the second guy down in the galley," answered Mac

"As soon as we get to the *MacG*, I'll help Dana get Hendrix to sick bay." Chris looked at his friend with an urgency reserved for too many dangerous situations they'd shared recently. "You get to the bridge and reach out to the Ecuadorian coast guard."

"Roger that," said Mac.

Minutes later, the yacht rounded the southern tip of the island. Even in the dark, Chris could instantly see that they had a much bigger problem.

The *MacGreggor* was gone.

16

"Mac, she's not there."

"What?" said Mac as he came up out of the galley. "Who's not there?"

"The *MacG*. She's gone."

Mac whirled around to face Dana. "Do you have any long-range night vision goggles on board?"

"Affirmative, they're down in my cabin," said Dana. "All the way forward on the port side. There's a waterproof bag above my bunk."

Chris was cycling through a number of scenarios in his head simultaneously. The attack on the *D-fens*, though shocking, was not outside of his life experience to-date. He and his colleagues had been attacked before, and they'd thwarted those attacks. But the disappearance of the *MacGreggor* was pushing the limit on what he was capable of processing. It was like coming home from work to find your house missing from its lot. It just didn't happen.

"Chris?" Mac had somehow appeared back at Chris's side without his noticing.

"Sorry. Got lost there for a moment."

"You've got better eyes than I do," said Mac. "Let me take the wheel. You see if you can find the ship."

Chris took the night vision goggles and started to scan the area. He started from his right, panning slowly along the horizon in a counter-clockwise fashion until he encountered the island.

The cloud cover was now almost total, but the goggles easily penetrated the dark.

"Nothing," he observed. "No, wait a second. There's something over there to port about 200 yards. It's one of our inflatables. It looks like there's someone in it."

Mac brought the *D-fens* around and motored toward where Chris was pointing. Chris did not take his eyes off the inflatable for fear of losing sight of it in the dark.

"Do you have it yet?" asked Chris.

"Not yet," replied Mac. "How far off the rocks?"

"Not far. Maybe fifty feet. I can see two people," said Chris. "It looks like Alex and maybe Ricardo."

"Are either of them conscious?" asked Mac.

"Not clear," said Chris. "They aren't moving."

Mac surveyed the back deck. "What's Hendrix's condition? Can you leave him for a second Dana?"

"Yes. I think the bleeding is under control."

"Okay," said Mac. "Here is what we're going to do. I'm going to put the bow right next to the inflatable. Chris—if one of them is conscious and capable, throw them the line and have them tie it off. If that's not possible, I'll need you to get into the inflatable yourself and do it."

"Copy that," said Chris. Using the night vision goggles he quickly surveyed the island for any indication of other attackers. He saw nothing but knew that that didn't mean anything. The attackers had managed to board the *D-fens* without any of the highly-trained people on board noticing until it was too late. "But what if this is a trap? I don't see anyone, but we have no idea what we're facing."

"Good point. Dana can stand up on the bow and cover you while relaying the situation to me."

"Will do," replied Dana.

Mac expertly moved the bow of the *D-fens* to within a few feet of the inflatable. Neither Ricardo nor Alex responded to Chris's hail, so he swung out from the bowsprit and lowered himself gently into the bow of the inflatable, holding a line in his teeth. He secured the line to the inflatable and nodded to Dana, who, in turn, relayed the situation to Mac.

As Mac slowly backed the *D-fens* away from the island, which in turn moved the inflatable away from the rocks, Chris checked on Alex and Ricardo. Dana operated a searchlight from the bow to help Chris tend to the men. Both men were alive, but in the light, both appeared to have been beaten.

Of the two, Alex appeared the worse for wear. Chris noted that the knuckles of both Alex's hands were scraped and discolored, suggesting he'd put up a fight.

"Good man, Alex."

Mac cut the motor and came forward to help lift the men out of the inflatable. Using the sling from one of the rescue rings, Mac and Dana slowly lifted Alex up toward the bow while Chris supported his body from below.

Chris looked around him. The exercise was getting increasingly more challenging. Having moved away from the rocks, they'd solved one problem but created another. Now away from the island, both the *D-fens* and the inflatable were subject to the ever-growing swells, but responded very differently; at one moment the two could be nearly on top of each other, and in the next they'd be drawn apart, violently stretching the line connecting the two.

As he prepared to lower the sling back down to Chris, Mac lost his footing and nearly fell over the rail. Leaping to his side to assist, Dana was caught off guard by a large swell and knocked overboard. Drawing on quick reflexes, she was able to grab line between the boats to avoid being drawn under the sailboat's hull.

As the inflatable sunk into the trough of a swell, Chris was able to grab Dana's left arm and pull her into the small boat before it was pulled back toward the *D-fens*.

"Thanks, that was dicey." Dana had trouble catching her breath and was dripping wet from head to toe.

"We're not out of this yet," noted Chris, over the sound of crashing waves and increasing wind.

As the next swell lifted the inflatable toward the sailboat's bow, Chris leaped and grabbed the rail, pulling himself onto the bow with Mac's help. Together they were able to pull Ricardo's unconscious body up without incident.

While Mac attended to the two men, Chris untied the line from the bow and carefully walked toward the stern, allowing the inflatable to drift aft. At the stern, Dana was easily able to step from the inflatable onto the *D-fens*. She secured the smaller boat to a cleat on the stern and then helped Chris and Mac bring their two injured comrades out of the weather.

Twenty minutes later, Alex, Ricardo, and Hendrix were all secured safely in three of the four staterooms.

Chris was about to turn off the light in Alex's cabin when he spotted a slip of paper protruding from the breast pocket on his coveralls. He gently removed the paper, turned off the light, and walked back to the galley where Mac and Dana were talking.

"Anything?" asked Mac.

"They're all still out," said Chris. Unfolding the paper, he added, "But I found this in the pocket of Alex's coveralls. My Spanish is a little rusty."

Dana reached out for the paper and read, "We have taken your boat. Return to Puerto Ayora. You will be contacted within two days. You will then pay what we ask, or we will kill one passenger a day until there are none left."

No one said anything. Chris thought about the students and their boundless enthusiasm. He thought about the captain, and he thought about Abby.

"Why leave two guys rather than one?"

"And why leave them alive?" added Mac.

"I can't speak to why the two men were left alive," said Dana. "And you guys know the situation on the boat better than me. But with the two of you gone, as well as the two we just found, is there anyone left on the boat who can put up a fight?"

Chris and Mac looked at each other. "Only the captain, really," Chris replied.

"And they may have kept him to operate the boat," said Mac. "Driving a sophisticated vessel like the *MacG* is not easy."

Looking down at the table in front of him, Chris pulled a local chart out from under the first aid kit. "How long do you estimate it will take us to get back to Santa Cruz?" he asked.

"We'll be sailing into the growing seas, and I don't want to make it too rough for our wounded," said Mac. "Maybe sixteen hours. What are you thinking?"

Chris placed both hands on the wooden rail that ran along the edge of the table, squeezing the rail until his knuckles turned white.

"I'm thinking we get our wounded to the hospital, and then we set about tracking these fuckers down."

17

B ack aboard the *MacGreggor*, it had all been over in five minutes. While Chris and Mac were away, the group had been about to barbecue on the upper deck when the pirates struck. As the *Innovator* had approached, many of the students out on the deck, as well as Abby and Oliver, had assumed Chris and Mac were returning early from dining on Hendrix's boat. The delay in any response allowed the pirates to quickly take over the vessel.

Alex Smith was on the upper deck preparing for dinner and therefore had had the best vantage point for observing the early stages of the attack. He saw a large white yacht approaching. He knew it wasn't the *D-fens*, but given the afternoon's exciting arrival of Hendrix and crew, he hadn't ruled out some other type of strange visit to the *MacG*.

When Alex saw the first two pirates come over the gunwale wielding guns, he'd immediately sent Roberto, one of the students tasked with assisting with dinner preparation, to the bridge to alert the captain. He then grabbed the lug wrench he'd used to attach the propane tank to the barbecue and rapidly descended the nearest ladder to the back deck.

Abby and Oliver were talking with a small group of students on the opposite side of the back deck, partially obscured by the large ROV. For that reason, Abby had seen Alex racing down the ladder with a wrench before she saw what he was racing toward. As soon as she heard the ensuing struggle, she'd corralled the students.

"Terra, get everyone to the main lab and lock yourselves in. We'll be there as soon as we can. Hurry!"

As soon as the six students on the back deck were gone, Abby had then turned to Oliver. "We have to help Alex."

"How are we going to do that?" Oliver had asked but immediately followed Abby towards the scene of the struggle.

However, as they'd rounded the ROV, they'd found Alex lying unconscious on the deck next to one of the attackers, who'd been cradling a broken arm and bleeding from a deep gash on his forehead. The second attacker had immediately pointed his gun at Abby and Oliver and forced them to lie down on the deck.

Within half an hour, all eighteen students, along with Abby and Oliver, had been confined to the main lab, a guard placed inside the lab and outside, right next to each of the two doors. The students had removed personal floatation devices (or PFDs) and immersion survival suits from their respective cabinets and spread them out on the lab floor to provide cushioning. The bright orange immersion 'dry' suits were designed to prevent hypothermia when a person had to abandon a sinking vessel at sea. Made of thick neoprene, they were large enough to be put on over clothing and to cover the entire body except for the eyes and nose.

Though Abby was not aware, Captain Dennis had been confined to the bridge by two other pirates so that he could continue to operate the vessel. Ricardo had been in the lab when the pirates first attacked. Seeking to protect the students, he'd confronted the attackers directly and was badly beaten as a result.

Abby and Oliver were placed at a table nearest to where the guard was stationed inside the lab. While this prevented them from talking openly about their situation, it did allow them to overhear a conversation transpiring on the pirate's radio.

"Jefe, we have the boat."

"What of the other boat? Have you heard from Ernesto?" The reply was somewhat garbled.

"No, we haven't. But the other boat only had five passengers on it. They shouldn't have had any problems."

So, they are going after Chris and Mac too, thought Abby. She knew that they'd be doomed if they'd commandeer that boat too.

The radio had squawked again. "Very well. Secure the prisoners and leave two behind on the inflatable. Leave the instructions with one of them. Once you have done that, join the other group and proceed to the meeting point. Understood?"

"Yes, sir."

Before being forced off the back deck and into the main lab, Abby had seen two things that struck her as interesting. First, she could have sworn that she saw the attackers bring a woman aboard the *MacGreggor*. The woman had bleached blonde hair, and Abby assumed she was a hostage. And second, she'd seen a large, black vessel very close by. Something about the sheer size and blackness of the vessel had given Abby chills.

Abby's attention was drawn back to the present by the sound of the engines cutting abruptly. She could hear several loud voices of men rushing past the door to the lab.

The door opened forcibly and a man carrying a large assault weapon stepped into the lab. Abby noted that the look in the man's eyes showed both fury and fear in equal measure. The man surveyed the group then walked quickly over toward Oliver.

"Get up!" yelled the man in Spanish. Oliver stood up, his knees shaking.

"Who is on that other boat?" yelled the man. "Tell me!"

"I don't understand what you mean," said Oliver. "What other boat?"

"The sailboat that tied up to you earlier today. Who is on that boat?"

Abby noticed with worry that Oliver didn't answer, likely calculating the risk of mentioning Chris and Mac and deciding to keep the information to himself. Suddenly the pirate reversed his gun and hit Oliver squarely in the forehead with the butt of the handle. Oliver dropped to the floor.

"I want to know who was on that other boat! Soldiers? Policemen? Who?"

"Soldiers?" said Oliver, propping himself up on one elbow while using the other hand to rub his forehead. He looked at Abby. "I've never met those people before in my life."

The pirate again struck Oliver in the forehead, this time much more violently, causing Oliver to collapse to the floor unconscious.

"Stop!" pleaded Abby. "Our friends are on that boat. They are scientists, not soldiers."

"Come with me!"

The pirate grabbed Abby by her upper arm and forced her out of the room. They walked down the hallway and out onto the back deck. Abby could feel her fingers begin to tingle as the force of the pirate's grip cut off circulation to her lower arm.

The pirate abruptly turned toward the starboard rail and pushed Abby in that direction. She briefly thought she was going to be thrown overboard.

At the rail, the pirate grabbed the hair at the back of Abby's head and forced her to look downward. "You are telling me scientists did this? Bullshit. Tell me who is on that boat!"

It took Abby's eyes several seconds to adjust to the dark.

"Tell me!" screamed the pirate, yanking her hair and forcing her head downward.

Below her, bobbing in the water next to the *MacGreggor*, was one of the ship's inflatables. And in the inflatable were the bodies of four men Abby didn't recognize. She realized that these had to be the men these pirates had sent to kill Chris and Mac.

One of the pirates lowered himself down to the inflatable on a nylon line. Abby could see him look for signs of life among the bodies piled on the boat. He looked up at the man holding Abby and shook his head.

"Ernesto is not here." The man then reached down toward one of the bodies. Abby could see a huge knife that had been used to affix a piece of paper to the body. The man unfolded the paper and read the message.

"What does it say?" demanded Abby's captor.

The man briefly struggled to maintain his footing as the inflatable rocked in the increasing swells. He then held the paper up with both hands. One of the pirates on the back deck shined a light down on the piece of paper.

The large block letters were easily readable from above. "Vamos por ti." Abby translated in her head, "We're coming for you."

18

Motoring into the building seas, the *D-fens* rocked as the large swells passed under the boat. Every few minutes the crest of a larger swell would lift the bow to the sky before it plunged down into the trough, briefly submerging before emerging again.

Dana expertly steered the vessel through the frothing ocean. Alex and Ricardo were each secured in bunks down below. Neither had resumed consciousness. Hendrix was awake but very weak from the loss of blood. He was secured in his own stateroom.

Chris labored to walk back from the bow toward the galley where Mac was working on the pirate Chris had incapacitated.

"This is a little much for Hendrix, I'm afraid," said Chris. "But I don't see what our options are."

"Damned if we do and damned if we don't," replied Mac. "We can't go after anyone in this sailboat. Much too slow. We need to get Hendrix to a doctor, and without a radio we've got to get to shore to alert the authorities."

"Pirates," said Chris.

"What?" asked Mac as he secured the unconscious man's wrists with large, black tie wraps.

"That date that Tony set me up on? I think I told you she was a lawyer. Works for the United Nations."

"And . . ."

"We had a long conversation at dinner about international waters and the Law of the Sea. We ended up talking about pirates."

"That seems as good a label as any for the group that attacked us."

"Molly explained that there aren't really any ideological pirates," explained Chris. "They are all motivated by money."

"And so . . ."

"Well, if we know they want money, then I think we can hope that they'll keep their prisoners alive in the near term. That should buy us some time to find them."

Having looked at maps of the Galapagos an untold number of times in preparation for this trip, Chris was monitoring their progress in his head. On his mental map, he placed them about one-third of the way back to Santa Cruz Island.

A large wave violently rocked the boat. "We're basically out here in the middle of nowhere," he said. "There's no place to hide from the seas. What's this guy's condition?"

"You did a number on him, but he's coming around slowly," said Mac. "Let's sit him up."

Chris helped Mac move the pirate to a sitting position. Mac used his open palm to tap the man on both cheeks. "Despierta."

The large man awoke and immediately tried to get up. Chris and Mac each held a shoulder, keeping the man firmly in his seat.

"Don't do it," Mac said.

Another large wave rocked the boat, throwing both Chris and Mac off balance. The pirate used the opportunity to push up to a standing position. However, with his ankles bound and the boat rocking, he quickly fell to the floor when the next wave hit the bow.

"Okay," said Mac, struggling to maintain position himself. "We'll leave you there."

The man thrashed about on the floor, desperately trying to free himself. The boat dropped into the trough of a passing swell, and in an instant, the ties broke and the pirate's hands were free.

The pirate pulled himself up to a standing position and launched himself at Chris, uttering a deep, guttural cry. Standing awkwardly to absorb the swells beneath the boat, Chris was caught on the chest and knocked backward into a cabinet over the sink. The blow caused him to see stars in his peripheral vision, and he was briefly disoriented.

In that split second of disorientation, Chris reflected on the extraordinary strength of the man. He was lucky to have knocked the guy out so quickly earlier. As he watched the pirate move toward Mac, it occurred to Chris that Hendrix and his two traveling partners would not have gone to sea without a suite of defensive weapons.

Coming to his senses, Chris quickly surveyed the surrounding cabinets. Watching the pirate now wrestling with Mac out of the corner of his eye, he wrenched open the nearest drawer. Finding only nautical charts, and seeing that Mac was now in trouble, Chris grabbed the handle on the drawer below and yanked.

"Bingo." He extracted two sets of brass knuckles and fitted them on each hand.

The pirate was now pummeling Mac with a series of vicious blows. Despite the rocking boat that required that he constantly regain his balance, Chris swiftly moved toward the man, who by now throttled Mac with both hands, his back turned to Chris.

"Hey!" The pirate turned at the sound of Chris's approach. Chris wasted no time, jabbing the man in the face with his left hand, following closely with a right-hand punch to the gut.

The two-punch combination slowed the pirate considerably but did not knock him out. The man pulled a small knife out of his sock and sliced through the tie wrap that bound his ankles.

"Okay," said Chris as he moved back in. Chris swung fast with his right, connecting with the pirate's jaw, feeling a bone break. Pulling his right hand back and trying to adjust to the undulating deck beneath him, Chris then followed with an awkwardly placed punch to the center of the man's forehead.

This time the pirate dropped to the deck.

Keeping his footing, Chris stepped over the unconscious pirate to help Mac up.

"You okay?"

Mac had a partially swollen eye and split lower lip. "I think so. Would have been worse if you hadn't stepped in. That guy is a beast. How did you stop him, anyway?"

Chris flashed the brass knuckles. "Found some of Hendrix's implements in a drawer."

"Huh. Lucky for me."

Chris found more tie wraps and triple-wrapped the pirate's wrists and ankles.

"Why don't you get some rest," suggested Chris. "I'll go give Dana a break at the wheel."

Four hours later, the boat's electronic mapping software indicated that they were still one hour out from Puerto Ayora on Santa Cruz Island. The swells had diminished significantly as they approached the main islands of the Galapagos. The sun had not yet risen, but based on the cloud cover, Chris could tell it was going to be a stormy day.

Alex emerged slowly from the galley and took a seat next to Chris.

"I couldn't stop them."

"Hey, you risked your life trying to help. That was much more than we could ever ask of you. These guys are no joke."

"Pirates?"

"Yep. That's what we're calling them. They fought hard."

"Dana said you guys killed four and took out the big guy down in the galley," said Alex. "I should have done better."

"Hendrix is, hands down, the toughest guy I know," said Chris. "And he's lucky to be alive right now. I'd say you should consider your survival a win. I know I do."

Alex was quiet for a few moments. "What are we going to do about the *MacGreggor*?"

"We're going to get this boat back into port and alert the authorities— everyone; Ecuadorians and our own people. And then we wait for the communication from the pirates. Did you see anything that can help us?"

Alex shook his head. "Not much. I saw two guys coming over the gunwale and tried to fight them off. I think Ricardo did the same thing in the lab with the students. I guess there were more pirates than we thought because that was the last thing I remember."

"What about a very large black vessel?"

"No. I didn't see anything like that," said Alex. "There was a white cabin cruiser nearby. Its name was something like *Innocence*, or *Innovation*, or *Inner-something* or other." He let his head drop. "I'm sorry, Chris. I let you guys down."

"No, Alex. You didn't. If this is on anyone, it's on me. Mac and I should have been there."

19

Dana knocked once before opening the door to the hotel room. In the twenty-four hours since they'd made it back to Puerto Ayora on Santa Cruz Island, the room had been converted into an unofficial command center, and no one had slept. Though Chris and Mac were both anxious to get back out on the water to look for the *MacGreggor*, it had been clear to them that without some new intelligence on the pirates' whereabouts to help guide their search, any effort they made would likely be fruitless.

"Any luck?" asked Chris without looking up from the table, which was covered by nautical charts of the islands. Dana had left on a mission to collect information two hours before.

Dana deposited her bag on the bed. "Yes, some. By the way, I stopped at the hospital on the way over here. Hendrix is conscious and unhappy."

"What else is new," noted Chris. "Wounded or not, Hendrix is basically the same guy."

Once Hendrix, Alex, and Ricardo were at the local hospital. Chris, Mac, and Dana had spent approximately ten hours talking with the local authorities about the attack. About midway through, Chris calculated, a representative from the U.S. Embassy in Quito had arrived on the scene. The trio then had to reiterate the story from the beginning.

Compared to his recent discussions with authorities in South Africa, which had felt like interrogations and resulted in Chris's forced departure from the country, Chris was impressed by the constructive nature of the conversation with the Ecuadorians. It struck Chris as though they were somewhat embarrassed by the fact that this horrible event had occurred in their waters and wanted to do everything in their power to help resolve it.

An Ecuadorian naval vessel had been dispatched to Darwin Island to recover the bodies of the pirates that Chris and the team had left in the inflatable. Chris noted that neither the Ecuadorians nor the U.S. Embassy was particularly pleased with that portion of the story. Nobody directly questioned the obvious self-defense explanation, but as Chris had seen in South Africa, governments don't like to see body counts, whether good guys or bad guys.

"They were able to extract the bullet cleanly," continued Dana. "No major damage there. But the knife wound is more serious. Hendrix is going to be out of the game for a while."

Chris yawned loudly as he stood up to stretch. "Yeah. Years ago, I broke my shoulder bodysurfing. My surgeon referred to the shoulder area as a symphony of interacting bones and tissue. And that knife went pretty deep into Hendrix's symphony."

Dana dropped several glossy images on the table in front of Chris. "The WIFI out here is sub-optimal. Using Hendrix's connections, I was able to get these printed at the research station on the other side of town with some effort," she said. "It has the best connectivity on the island, I think."

Chris looked down at the satellite imagery they'd requested from Hendrix's security group. One of their best chances to figure out where the pirates went would be through satellite footage of the area. Each image covered the same area around Darwin and Wolf Islands from immediately before the attack to once every two hours for the next twelve hours. Chris organized them in the order they were taken and observed, "Clouds; nothing but clouds."

Standing next to Chris, Dana nodded. "These pirates couldn't have chosen a better time to strike. The cloud cover from this storm front extends thousands of miles in all directions."

"We're blind," said Chris. "But not out."

"What do you mean?" asked Dana. "New intel?"

"I got through to one of my colleagues back in the States. He's a computer modeler. Works on birds mostly, and sometimes traffic patterns. But he thinks he can come up with a model to predict where these pirates will go."

"What will he use as a parameter for the model?" asked Dana, who had explained to Chris earlier that she'd trained in computer modeling years before with the Navy.

"Well, he's going to have to improvise a bit. But the nature of the dive boat and tourism operations out here work in our favor."

"How?"

"By law, all commercial operations must be handled by residents of the Galapagos. That means there's a fixed number of vessels running at any one time. And they work together to avoid overlapping too much. For instance, I don't know if you noticed, but there were only two commercial operators out at Darwin."

"I noticed."

"Right. Sorry. No offense intended," said Chris, thinking it was unwise to antagonize someone like Dana. "Anyway, so the boats are dispersing across a multitude of specified dive sites to avoid impinging on each other's business. If we know where various boats are going, and we assume that the pirates are not going to want to risk being seen, we should be able to predict areas where isolation is most possible. Then we start with those areas."

"And if they leave the islands?"

"Then we have a new problem," said Chris.

"What new problem?" Mac asked as he came in the door. "By the way, I keep getting the strong sense I've been here before."

"Very funny." Chris stepped away from the table. He found an open space on the bed among the gear and documents and lied down.

"What?" Dana asked, obviously befuddled by the apparent joke.

Chris opened his arms wide and explained, "The hotel's name, *Déjà Vu*."

Dana looked at Mac, her head tilted and her eyes narrowed. He shrugged his shoulders. "Just trying to inject a little levity around here."

To the surprise of both Chris and Mac, Dana smiled. "That's not bad. We could use a little levity around here. It's been a long three days." From the first moment they'd met Dana, she had been much quieter than either Hendrix or Sam, the very picture of a professional soldier.

"What's your report?" Chris asked Mac.

While Dana was tracking down satellite imagery, and Chris was working on narrowing down potential locations for the pirates, Mac had gone off in search of a vessel that was faster and more capable than the *D-fens*.

"I think you're going to like what I found."

"Tell me," said Chris.

"A fifty-foot cabin cruiser, capable of making twenty-eight knots. And it gets better."

Chris sat upright in bed when he heard the vessel's ability to move quickly. More speed equaled more territory covered in a shorter period of time. "Better how?" he asked.

"The guy is ex-military, so it's stocked with weapons."

"Which military?" asked Dana, her arms folded across her stomach and with an edge in her voice.

"Does it really matter?" offered Mac.

"I suppose not, but I prefer more information than less," explained Dana.

"*Well*, it gets even better. SCUBA tanks and compressor."

Dana furrowed her brow. "How is that going to help us?"

"You never know," Chris and Mac said simultaneously.

Then Chris continued, smiling, "Nice work, Mac. Let's get provisioned up so that as soon as we hear back from Mitchell, we're ready to go."

"So, you were able to reach him, eh? Can he help us?" Mitchell was a friend of Chris's who worked for the U.S. federal government. He and Mac had met on a project years before. While motoring back to Santa Cruz, contacting Mitchell had seemed like one of their best options.

"I was just telling Dana that he thinks he can," Chris said. "Using known vessel patterns in the islands, he is going to give us an analysis of where the pirates would be most likely to go due to the least official boat traffic."

"That sounds as promising as anything else we've got. We should probably get some shuteye as well," suggested Mac. "By my calculations, none of us has slept in at least thirty-six hours. If we're going after pirates, we'll need to be firing on all cylinders."

Chris looked at his watch and then at his tired visage in one of the several mirrors in the room. "That's a good point. Now that you bring it up, I'm exhausted."

Dana agreed.

"Group nap?" suggested Mac with a wink.

"Uh, how about concurrent naps? Mac, you take the bed in here. I'll hit that couch. Dana can use the bed in the other room. Agreed?"

They all retreated to their designated sleeping areas. Chris could hear Mac snoring almost immediately. Dana had left the door to the other bedroom open, and it looked like she fell asleep very quickly as well.

Though Chris was exhausted, too, the disquieting reality that Abby and all the students were prisoners of ruthless pirates kept sleep at bay. There'd been no ransom demand yet. With every passing day without word from the pirates, his hope that the prisoners were being treated with respect dwindled. And he chastised himself for leaving the *MacGreggor* in the first place. If we'd been there, he thought, it would have gone differently.

Gradually, Chris could feel the weight of his eyelids increasing and in minutes he was asleep.

His slumber was interrupted in what to him felt like seconds by a loud knock on the door. Slowly rising, Chris was disoriented by the total darkness around him. The luminous dial on his dive watch indicated that nearly five hours had passed. That was also disorienting and very hard to believe.

The knocking continued.

The bed Mac was sleeping in was closer to the door. Before Chris had a chance to get up off the couch, Mac sprung from the bed in a frenzy of activity. He moved to the door, opening it as he shouted, "What?"

From his vantage point on the couch, Chris could not see who was standing at the door, but the voice was inimitable. "Good evening, Mr. Johnson. Might I come in for a moment."

20

"**F**rank Donagan," replied Chris, still shaking off sleep. "I don't know what to say."

"Good evening, Dr. Black." Frank Donagan was five-foot-eleven with close-cropped, completely gray hair and steely blue eyes. As far as Chris knew, the man was in his late fifties or early sixties. He wore a dark suit with a white oxford shirt, but no tie. Chris realized he'd never seen Donagan wearing anything else.

"It's been, what, about a month and a half since we last saw each other in South Africa?" Donagan said. "You were in trouble there. And now I find you in trouble in Ecuador. You really do get around."

Chris was pretty sure that Donagan had kept him out of a South African prison. But then again, it was also possible that Donagan had expedited Chris's departure from the country for other reasons. As far as Chris knew, Donagan worked for the U.S. State Department, but he suspected there were connections to certain clandestine agencies as well.

"As do you, it seems." Chris sat up on the couch and rubbed the sleep out of his eyes. "I thought no one would surprise me more than Hendrix by just showing up out of nowhere, but I think you win in that regard."

Dana came out of the bedroom and sat down on the couch next to Chris, looking much fresher than he felt. She conspicuously slipped an automatic handgun into the back of her belt. Mac remained standing, holding the door open.

"Ah, Hendrix. I just spoke to him at the hospital. He's quite irritated."

"Getting shot and stabbed will do that to you," Mac said, sweeping his arm into the room as an encouragement to Donagan.

"I'm sure," Donagan said. "And if anyone knows that, it's the three of you."

Donagan stepped forward with his hand out to Dana. "You must be Dana; I don't believe we've met before. Hendrix mentioned that you might be here."

Dana shook his hand without getting off the couch.

Chris was not in the mood for a battle of wits, or even a protracted conversation. "Why are you here, Frank?" Chris liked Donagan, but he had no time to spare for more repartee at the moment.

"I'm here primarily for two reasons. First, I'm supposed to update you on what has happened in the twenty-nine hours since you returned with news of the abduction."

"You have news? Spit it out." Chris leaned forward, the irritation in his voice palpable.

"I flew down with your Peter Lloyd. A fine fellow, I might add. He's at the police station, which is serving as a sort of command center. Upon receiving your call yesterday, Dr. Lloyd called the State Department, and they sent me."

"If you flew down with Peter, you obviously weren't in Africa anymore," stated Chris. "Where were you?"

"Around." It was quickly coming back to Chris how evasive Donagan was with details related to his own activities.

Donagan explained that Peter Lloyd had pushed every button he could as soon as Chris had contacted him and then headed to Ecuador himself. "There's a process for dealing with these types of situations.

The State Department contacted our embassy in Ecuador. The Embassy reached out to the Ecuadorian authorities. They, in turn, mobilized the Navy, which operates a vessel out here in the islands."

"Just one?" asked Mac.

"Yes, as it stands right now." Donagan motioned to a nearby chair. "May I sit down?"

"What is the protocol for dealing with hostages and ransom demands?" asked Chris.

"It's complicated."

"Complicated how?" Mac pulled a bottle of orange juice out of the room's mini fridge.

"I know you all remember President Reagan's famous 'We will never make concessions to terrorists' speech back in the '80s. The policy of non-negotiation has been in place ever since. It really dates back to the earliest years of the Republic and the Jefferson administration's dealings with the Barbary pirates off northern Africa. The pirates took hostages. We paid the ransom. The pirates took more hostages, and so on. Negotiation has not been a winning strategy for us."

"But . . ." said Mac.

"But there has been wiggle room in the years since Reagan's speech. We will negotiate when it is another state that has the hostages. We also tend to negotiate when the hostages are military service members. These kinds of negotiations usually happen behind the scenes, and the government does not discuss them. And there is also the possibility for negotiations if someone other than the U.S. is paying the ransom. Terror groups have made hundreds of millions of dollars in the last decade through ransom, so someone is paying."

Mac looked at Chris. "Do you think the university . . ."

". . . will pay? I have no idea," said Chris. "Has a demand come in yet?"

"No." Donagan pulled a folded piece of paper out of an interior pocket of his suit coat. "But this came in via email to the university two hours ago." He handed it to Chris. Mac and Dana both huddled next to Chris to see what was on it.

It was a grainy black and white picture that Chris supposed had already been copied multiple times. It showed the interior of the *MacGreggor's* main lab. Chris quickly counted and could see that all the students were visible in the image. They appeared to be unhurt. He could also see Abby, but the quality of the image was too coarse for him to read her expression.

"Where's Oliver Chumley-Smith?" asked Mac. "I don't see him."

"Good question," responded Chris. He was no fan of Chumley-Smith, but currently the man was one of their team, for better or worse, and he didn't like bad things happening to his team.

"We don't know what's happened to Dr. Chumley-Smith," said Donagan. "It's possible he was just out of the field of view of the camera. But the image suggests that the majority of the hostages were alive and apparently doing okay at the time the photo was taken."

"What time do we think it was taken?" asked Chris. "Or, what time did the email come in?"

"The image was received approximately ten hours ago," replied Donagan. "That's the only information we have about the timing."

"I'm going to talk with Peter. I would've appreciated knowing about that when it happened," Chris said.

"No kidding," Mac added.

"So, what does the command center think will happen next?" Chris asked.

"They are standing by for a formal ransom letter before doing anything else. There are hostage negotiators en route from the mainland right now. They have some experience dealing with this type of incident in South America."

"So, what you're really saying is that no action has been taken," Mac suggested.

"They've put out a call to all mariners to be on the lookout for the *MacGreggor*. But it's a large ocean."

No one said anything as Donagan's words sunk in. No one is looking, thought Chris.

"What is the second thing?" Chris asked after the moment passed.

"What do you mean?"

"You said you were here for two reasons. You've told us the first. What was the second reason?"

"Right," said Donagan as he looked around the room. To Chris, it appeared as though the man was measuring his words. "My recent experience with you gentlemen in Cape Town indicates that you're not likely to sit still while the formal protocols are followed."

"And?" asked Chris.

"And I am here to stop you from going rogue again."

21

Abby used a damp washcloth to dab the blood off the face of the unconscious Oliver Chumley-Smith. Her hands were shaking as she worked. She had been so close to Oliver when the pirate struck him that she'd had to wipe his blood off her own face as well. The wounds to the bridge of Oliver's nose and his cheek were very deep, but she'd been able to slow the bleeding.

Around her, students sat huddled together in small groups, some crying, some simply staring at the wall with vacant expressions on their faces. Abby noticed Roberto and Terra, both of whom had become de facto leaders of the students over the past three days, appeared to be deep in conversation. Every few seconds, Roberto would look back toward the guard to see if he was watching.

Abby secured Oliver on the floor among the immersion suits and PFDs before she got up to get some water. She measured her steps carefully as the swells rocked the *MacGreggor* and navigated her way through the huddled students, plotting a path that took her past Roberto and Terra.

"How are you guys doing?" she whispered. The guard was watching her, but he didn't appear to care if she was talking to the students.

"We've been trying to figure a way out of this," whispered Roberto, in return.

"We need a plan," Terra said, under her breath.

"*Please*, you two," implored Abby. "Just stay put and safe. These pirates will not hesitate to hurt you."

"Do you think that they killed Chris and Mac," asked Roberto, his wavering voice betraying his age.

Abby pretended to be unstable from the swells and leaned in close. "No, they're okay. Or at least they were after the initial attack. I know Chris well, and he won't rest until they've found us. So please, stay put and stay safe."

Though all smartphones had been confiscated immediately by the pirates, Abby had been allowed to keep her smartwatch. For that reason, she knew that they'd been motoring continuously for more than a day and a half without stopping. There'd been several fleeting moments in which the swells had briefly receded, but they were few. Many of the students had been sick multiple times. The lab now smelled from a combination of real vomit and very real fear.

The lab was situated on the main deck, amidships. The engine room was directly below, with the ROV lab just aft. Toward the bow was the galley, as well as a lounge. The staterooms were located on the deck above, as well as several on the deck below. During three trips to the bathroom in the past 24 hours, Abby had observed that there were always two pirates, either watching over the lab or staying very close. Sometimes both were in the lab while other times both were immediately outside the door. But most of the time, there was one pirate inside and one out.

The man currently inside the lab was considerably older in Abby's estimation than the other pirates, possibly in his early sixties. And she thought that he might have looked at her with a sympathetic eye when the other pirates were outside. Twice he had responded to her requests in Spanish for blankets and first aid for Oliver when the other pirates would not.

As she moved toward the sink to wash off the towel she was using for Oliver and to refill her water bottle, Abby briefly made eye contact with the man. Standing at the counter, watching the water flow into her bottle, Abby could feel him move closer to her.

"How is your friend doing?" he asked in English.

"Not well, I'm afraid," she replied. "He was beaten very badly."

"I am sorry about that," said the pirate. "The man who beat him is one of the 'verdaderos creyentes.' How do you say? True believers?"

"What do you mean?" Abby asked, hoping to get any information that she could.

"Los piratas," the man whispered. "Some are very, very bad men."

"Some?" Abby could feel her blood begin to boil. "You're all pirates. You took us hostage. I think you killed some of our crew. You're holding us at gunpoint right now as we speak. I'd say you are all very bad men."

Abby immediately regretted saying that, as the pirate's eyes flared in anger and he stepped back. She finished filling her water bottle and cleaned the towel, then moved slowly back to Oliver's side.

Thirty minutes later, Abby had just drifted off to sleep, when she was jarred awake by a particularly large wave shaking the hull. Looking around, she saw that the older pirate was moving toward her. He was close when the lab door opened, and one of the other pirates walked in. This man was much younger. Abby estimated his age to be in his late twenties. He had a rifle slung over one shoulder, and a large knife mounted in a sheath on his thigh.

"Hey!" yelled the young pirate. "Find out how many of them need the bathroom."

The older man approached Abby. "Can you help me with the students?"

She saw no benefit in being difficult, so she complied. "Everyone, if you need to use the restroom, now is the time. As with before, we will go two at a time. It may be several hours before we have another chance, so please take it."

As the students began their bathroom runs, Abby sat quietly next to Oliver. She was thinking about her parents when she realized the older pirate was standing right next to her.

"Lo siento," said the pirate, grabbing her upper left arm. "I really am sorry. Some are 'true' pirates, but some of us are not here by choice. My wife and family are in great danger back in Bogota. If I do not do as I am told, my wife, my daughters, and their daughters will all be killed. Or worse."

Abby shuttered at the recognition that there were worse things than death. A vision of the woman the pirates had brought aboard the *MacGreggor* briefly flashed in her mind. The young pirate scared her, but so did this old man, but for different reasons. She imagined the young pirate and his colleagues committing acts of violence in attempts to establish themselves in the pecking order. Men like this older pirate, however, would likely do anything to protect their families.

While she could empathize, she also realized that this made him and others like him even more dangerous. She couldn't trust any of these pirates, she knew that. And yet, hope springs eternal, she thought and asked, "How many are like you?"

"I know a few. We have to remain quiet or we'll be killed. So, I don't know all of them."

"How many pirates are there in your, um, group?"

"Many. Dozens, maybe. In charge of all of them is El Capitan."

"Have you ever met El Capitan?" asked Abby.

The pirate stole a glance over his shoulder to see if anyone was listening. "No, I am too low. I don't meet the big boss. I have heard stories, though. People fed to sharks, alive. People chopped up into pieces, alive."

"How many times have you taken hostages like this?" asked Abby. This was a question that had been on her mind since the beginning.

"I have not been with them very long. I don't know."

"Often?" asked Abby.

"No," replied the man. "I think this might be the first time."

Abby's mind raced as she tried to determine whether or not that was good news. Did inexperienced kidnappers make good mistakes or bad mistakes? Would they be more or less likely to hurt the students? She didn't have enough data to properly evaluate the situation.

Students had been coming and going to the bathroom while Abby had been talking to the pirate. She had not noticed that the angry young pirate had returned until he was standing inches from them. The young man's grin made Abby move back several steps.

The young pirate said nothing. He drew the large knife from its sheath and used it to point to the door. The older pirate didn't make eye contact with Abby as he walked out into the hallway beyond, which was illuminated by the afternoon sun. The young pirate then grabbed Abby by her upper right arm and forcibly pushed her out of the lab. The strength of the man's grip was considerable, particularly, Abby thought, given that he was missing two fingers on his right hand.

Coming out into the fresh air, Abby surveyed her surroundings. In addition to the older pirate and the young one holding her by the arm, there were five other pirates on the *MacGreggor's* back deck. They were standing in an open circle facing her. She could see islands on the horizon from which they'd come, so they weren't far from the Galapagos after all, she realized.

One of the five pirates stood several inches taller than the rest. Abby estimated his height at six-foot-three or six-foot-four, inadvertently comparing the man's height to Chris Black's. Though she could not see the man's eyes behind the black wrap-around sunglasses he was wearing despite the dark cloud cover and threatening rain. She sensed this man had more presence than the others. The other men appeared to stand in deference to him.

The waves were spraying water over both rails, and the sun was only just visible beyond the thick cloud cover.

The large man stepped out of the circle. Dense dreadlocks emerged from under a CMEx baseball cap. Abby recoiled. Despite being outside in the wind, she could smell a mix of alcohol and body odor reaching out from the man, and the fierceness in his eyes alone, made Abby shiver. She hated that he dared to wear one of their baseball caps. It felt—sacrilegious.

"Stand in the circle and take this man's hand," he said in English, motioning her toward the older pirate.

"What?"

"Stand in the circle and take this man's hand!" The dreadlocked pirate's voice was devoid of emotion.

Abby moved into the circle and accepted the older man's hand into hers. This time the old pirate's eyes met hers, and the fear she saw in them was contagious. Her heart raced.

Fixated on the old pirate's terrified eyes, she caught movement to her right in her peripheral vision. The next few seconds proceeded as if in slow motion. Abby first noticed a change in the weight of the older pirate's hand. When she glanced down to see why, it took her a few seconds to register what had just happened.

A lightning quick slash of the eight-fingered pirate's knife had, in one swift movement, severed the older man's forearm below the elbow. The lower arm was now hanging in Abby's grip.

Before she could scream, or release her grip on the severed arm, Abby inadvertently looked up into the older pirate's eyes again—just in time to see the knife now slashing through three-quarters of his neck before getting stuck. Blood spurted out of the now-exposed carotid artery. As the head slowly fell to the left, the man's horrified eyes kept looking right at Abby. His mouth hung open as if trying to form words.

That's when Abby realized that they were all going to die.

22

C hris sat in the dark and willed the hotel's imperfect wireless internet to work. Donagan had left a cloud of warnings hanging over the rudimentary command center before he'd left to 'attend to other business.' Mac and Dana had immediately departed on a supply run, while Chris had stayed to await the modeling results from his colleague to see where they think the pirates were hiding.

Just as he was considering throwing his laptop off the balcony and into the pool below, four bars showed up on the wireless power indicator. He quickly downloaded his emails and surveyed the contents.

Nothing from Mitchell. Chris took a deep breath and reminded himself that the modeling exercise they were conducting was not a trivial undertaking and that patience was going to be required on his part.

Working to demonstrate some patience, he scanned the dozens of messages that had shown up over the past several days while they were out of contact at Darwin and Wolf Islands.

"Not that one," he said to the dark. "Not that one either."

"No f'ing way," he observed in response to a poorly written message from an administrator back in California.

Then Chris spotted a message from his mom sent three days before.

Dear Chris. I hope your work in the Galapagos is going well. I was cleaning out my inbox and found the attached from your last mission to Poseidon. I found it both fun and sad, and thought you might like it for your records. Love, Mom.

At first, Chris was unclear what the attachment might be, but he recognized it immediately after opening. During his last mission to the Poseidon Undersea Laboratory in the Florida Keys, the team had been supposed to provide blog posts each day as part of a multi-pronged outreach effort to engage high school students around the country. Mac had refused. Alex had written two, two-sentence summaries that Chris thought hardly qualified as blog posts. So, he and Gretchen had taken over the duties for the entire ten-day mission, ultimately having a lot of fun with the job.

Margaret, Chris observed to himself, was right once again. Sitting alone in the dark, thousands of miles from home, he read the post from eight years before with no small measure of sadness. The post struck Chris as a written time capsule from a period before violence had come to impact all of their lives.

Day 3: A Predator-rich Environment!

Alfred Lord Tennyson famously wrote, "Tho' Nature, red in tooth and claw." He could just as easily have inserted "fin" for claw, but he probably had less experience with predators of the undersea variety. My friend Mac, on the other hand, has said much less poetically, "They all want to eat you." When he's in a really good mood, he adds, "And they're coming!"

Chris Black here. I'm reporting from Day 3 of our current mission to the Poseidon Undersea Research Lab in the U.S. Virgin Islands. And it's been a wild one, literally. For those of you just joining us, we're down here as part of a mission to study the movement behavior of coral reef fishes. By 'we,' I mean a four-person research team from Monterey's Center for Marine Exploration (CMEx), including myself (Dr. Chris Black), Mac Johnson, Gretchen Clark, and Alex Smith. Alex and Gretchen are dutifully narrating the mission with their own blogs, and Mac neither writes nor reads blogs, so I will say no more about them here.

To study fish movement, we have to first trap and anesthetize them. Then we surgically implant $1000 acoustic transmitters in their gut cavities. After surgery, we suture them up, revive them from the anesthetic, and release them back onto the reef where they are tracked by an array of acoustic receivers we've deployed out on the reef for miles around. Using scalpels and sutures makes me feel like the kind of doctor my parents always wanted, if only for a little while.

The great thing about this type of project here at Poseidon is that we can do this all at the seafloor, never leaving the water. Poseidon is a saturation dive facility. We spend eight hours diving each day for ten days, without returning to the surface. We come and go from Poseidon via a 'moon pool;' it's all very cool. If we did the same work from a research vessel at the surface, we'd have to catch the fish and bring them to the surface, exposing them to significant pressure and temperature changes. Putting aside the anesthetic and the surgery for a second, this approach is much better for the fish.

We've been working the past three days to trap one or more Blue Parrotfish (Scarus coeruleus), an herbivore that scrapes algae off the reef with fused front teeth. Interesting side note: when scraping off the algae, the parrotfish also consume coral, which they then poop out as they swim around. Something like 90% of the sand around coral reefs comes from parrotfish poop!

I'm sure many of you are wondering what it's like to dive for eight hours a day surrounded by Parrotfish poop. I'm the first to admit that it's pretty cool. But, as it turns out, baiting a trap to catch a fish that eats only algae is not as easy as it may sound. Indeed, it's quite frustrating to do that unsuccessfully for three consecutive days (frustration which you'd read about in graphic detail if Mac actually took the time to write a blog. Consider yourselves lucky that he doesn't.)

So, you can imagine our excitement when we caught five (that's right, five) beautiful Blue Parrotfish simultaneously this morning. While it may be nearly impossible to catch one Blue Parrot, once you've caught that one the rest are pretty easy, as they happily (my characterization) follow their friend (also my characterization) into the trap.

Now here's the rub: we caught those fish right before our mandatory break from diving just before noon. For those of you who are familiar with diving, you'll understand that like diving from the surface, you still have to do a "surface" interval, but here it's called a "storage" interval and you stay inside the lab. It's essentially a four-hour break to eat, sleep, and process data, usually in that order.

Gretchen and I were a buddy team for the morning dive and came back into the lab first. Mac and Alex followed shortly thereafter and reported our glorious haul of Blue Parrots, which they'd observed just before entering the moon pool.

We passed the four hours comfortable in the notion that we would soon be meeting our primary objective. And when the time came to resume diving, all four of us were geared up and ready to go the minute we were authorized to hit the water.

Now is the point in the story when I should introduce my nemesis. He is a six-foot-long Green Moray Eel (Gymnothorax funebris) that lives in a small cave located next to the lab. He earned his role as my nemesis by menacing us during fish surgeries on our last mission. Some of our surgeries are conducted on a platform immediately adjacent to Poseidon (while others are done out on the reef). I do the surgery while kneeling on the platform with the anesthetized fish sitting on a piece of mesh strung between two lengths of PVC pipe. My assistant, Gretchen, usually kneels on the other side of the PVC frame and hands me the various implements as I need them. It isn't glamorous, but remember, this is all happening underwater.

Even though most of you have never experienced this, I'm pretty sure you will understand the shock, horror, and ultimately, the frustration I've experienced on more than one occasion as a six-foot-long moray eel appeared between my legs from under the platform looking hopeful that he can eat my sleeping piscine patient.

My sense of scientific decorum prevents me from describing the way I have resolved these shocking intrusions into our work. However, up until today, I have considered this battle of wills with my nemesis to be a draw.

But it's a draw no more.

While my three colleagues and I rested during our storage interval, my nemesis saw his golden opportunity. He left his cave, swam several yards across the open sand, entered the trap, and ate all five Blue Parrotfish. All five. Ate them.

But the story does not end there. You see, much like your large uncle Bob who always threatens that you'll have to remove the front door of your house to get him out after a particularly indulgent Thanksgiving meal, my nemesis, full of five Blue Parrotfish, could not get out of the trap. He was stuck, and he was not happy about it.

Apparently, his thrashing about had been going on for a while, for it had attracted the attention of an eight-foot-long female Bull shark (Carcharhinus leucas). The shark circled the cage (as sharks do) in ever tightening circles, evidently expecting something to change. Bull sharks, by the way, are not to be trifled with.

Not to be outdone by the moray or the shark, a medium-sized Goliath Grouper (Epinephelus itajara) arrived on the scene. I say medium-sized because this fish was only about six-feet-long. There are much larger ones around. This fish is so large and powerful that one beat of its tail can knock a diver unconscious.

I hesitate to anthropomorphize more than I've already done, but the grouper showed much less patience than the shark, attacking the trap with vigor almost immediately. Next commenced what we call a positive feedback loop: the harder the grouper hit, the more exercised became the eel. The more the eel moved, the closer the shark circled, and the harder the grouper hit. Within minutes the trap was destroyed, the eel was eaten by the shark, and my five thousand dollars in acoustic transmitters were gone.

Nature red in tooth and claw, indeed.

Chris recalled that for several years after that mission, he'd used that story to highlight how many ways there were to get eaten underwater. It perfectly encapsulated the nearly omnipresent threat of predation, and it generally resonated with audiences. Now, thinking about Abby and the students captured by pirates, about the ecoterrorists, the treasure seekers in South Africa, and the toxic waste dumpers back in Carmel, he realized that the experience was an even more apt metaphor for life above the surface.

Danger was omnipresent. Yes, the trappings of society were there to protect citizens much of the time, at least within the United States. But that didn't mean that the danger wasn't there. And perhaps that was the difference he'd struggled to explain to Abby back in Carmel. He didn't seek out danger. It was always there. The key difference in the analogy was that the fish swimming around in the presence of the shark and the moray eel was always aware of that threat. But the trappings of society had led most humans to either forget or consciously ignore that danger was always lurking.

Abby opted to look for 'the best in people,' to give people, even those who were overtly offensive, 'the benefit of the doubt.' But for men like Chris, Mac and Hendrix, that option had long since been lost. They were forced, by circumstance, to realize the dangers lurking around every corner.

A new email pinged as Chris sat there in the shadows. It was from Mitchell. Chris sent the map enclosed in the message to the printer and stood up.

After the horrific events in Carmel and Cape Town, Chris had regained his composure. It hadn't been a religious experience or some stunning emotional insight that had granted him peace.

No. After weeks of sweating through his sheets at night in pure terror at the knowledge that his team might face danger once again, Chris woke up one night to a certainty he'd rarely felt before. A calm had settled over him as he'd realized with unprecedented clarity that he needn't fear ruthless men; instead, ruthless men should fear him.

He recalled a meme he'd seen floating around the internet years before: "Fate whispers to the warrior, 'You cannot withstand the storm.' The warrior whispers back, 'I am the storm.'"

Chris Black grabbed the map he'd sent to the printer and walked out the door in search of Mac.

23

"Okay, where are we going?" asked Mac, as Dana piloted the *Tiburon* away from its mooring in the embayment off Porta Ayora. The trio was standing on the bridge, protected from the sheets of rain pelting the fifty-foot cabin cruiser.

It was twenty-four hours after their conversation with Donagan. Dawn had yet to arrive, so Dana was piloting the boat in the dark using instrumentation.

The rain was coming down in torrents, and they fully expected the swell to increase once they cleared the embayment.

The previous day had been spent outfitting the *Tiburon* with the supplies they would need, avoiding direct contact with Donagan or any other authorities, and Chris and Mac had to acquire new clothes given that all they'd brought with them had left with the *MacGreggor*.

"Genovesa," replied Chris, zipping up the fleece he wore underneath his waterproof foul weather gear. "It's a small island about seventy-three miles to the northeast of here."

"Why there?" asked Mac.

He was wearing a similar outfit as Chris, but he'd added a black baseball cap emblazoned with "I Love Boobies." Below the ubiquitous catchphrase was a pair of feet from the well-known bird, the blue-footed booby.

"Mitchell's model predicts that the pirates are there at a fifty-seven percent probability," explained Chris. "It's a small, isolated island that doesn't get the same type of boat traffic like the other islands, particularly in weather like this. There's a large natural embayment, but landfall is not recommended, and there are no popular dive sites at the island."

"Fifty-seven percent? That's not a high probability," observed Mac. "In the SEALs, we probably wouldn't have mobilized for less than eighty percent."

Dana nodded her head. "That was my experience as well."

"I understand," said Chris, "but we've been sitting around for more than two days as the danger mounts for our friends on the *MacG*. I think we needed the time we took to get ready, but it's time to move."

"Copy that," said Mac. "I'm just trying to manage our expectations. This could be a long, rough night with zero success. That said, I'm obviously in." Then, turning to Dana, he asked, "What's our ETA?"

"Difficult to estimate with the swells we'll likely face. In calm water on a vessel like this? I'd say three and a half hours. In this weather, we should double that. We'll know more once we get out there and see what the swells are doing."

When they cleared the protection of the island, the conditions were considerably worse than when they'd arrived. But the *Tiburon* was a much larger and more powerful vessel than the *D-fens*, so the ride was a bit smoother.

The sun rose after an hour but offered little warmth or light, given the density of the clouds above. They made slow headway steaming directly into the oncoming swells. Chris watched as wave after wave broke over the bow and marveled at the stunning majesty of a storm at sea.

He smiled as he recalled Gretchen's favorite passage from Stephen Crane's 'Open Boat:'

When it occurs to a man that nature does not regard him as important . . . he at first wishes to throw bricks at the temple, and he hates deeply the fact that there are no bricks and no temples . . . Thereafter, he knows the pathos of his situation.

"It's rare to see you smile," said Dana, who sat at the helm with a cup of coffee in hand. Mac was below making breakfast.

"Penny for your thoughts."

"Oh, I . . . A quote about storms at sea. That's what I was thinking about. A colleague of mine, she really liked it. The waves reminded me of it."

"Of it? Or of her?"

"What?" Chris was taken by surprise and stumbled through his response. "I don't see the . . ."

He had grown to detest talking about Gretchen, or Claudia, or any of the horrific incidents they'd faced recently, with anyone other than the few close colleagues who'd been through the events with him. Somehow, Dana had cut through all of that with a simple question.

"She was one of the most positive people I've ever known, and she really enjoyed literature that challenges us to question our existence."

"Is she the woman on the *MacGreggor* right now?"

"Abby? No," said Chris. "Gretchen died over a year ago in a situation that developed back home in Carmel. We found toxic waste in an undersea canyon right offshore. What happened next didn't go very well."

Dana nodded in recognition. "Hendrix mentioned something like that. I'm sorry that you lost your friend."

Chris had the distinct impression that Dana understood what it meant to face violence and to lose people.

"Thanks. What is it they say? Time works its wonders. Somehow doesn't seem to work that way for me. The pain is never far from the surface."

"I think I understand." Dana nodded, never taking her eyes off the horizon. "We're trained to compartmentalize the losses of comrades in battle. It allows us to continue to function. But I've found compartmentalization is not the same thing as dealing with it."

"Yeah, my mother is a psychologist. She could talk about that all day long. And no doubt she would if she were here." Chris smiled, surprised he found himself longing for his mother's shop talk.

"I worry that there is something broken in our generation," Dana continued. "There are so many sad eyes on happy faces."

Chris turned to Dana with newfound respect. "I didn't think you could go up in my estimation after what I've seen you do these past few days, but did you just quote *To Kill A Mockingbird*?"

Dana surprised Chris again when she smiled.

"Atticus and Scout are perhaps my favorite characters in all of literature," he said. "If I ever have the good fortune to have a daughter, Atticus will be my model."

Mac came up onto the bridge from the internal stair and asked, "Who's a model?"

Chris looked at Dana, but said to Mac, "We were talking about you and your new hat."

Mac removed the hat and regarded it with pride. "It's simultaneously profound and ironic."

"Uh . . ."

"Relax," said Mac. "I overheard some of your conversation and wanted you literary types to know that I am not as simple as my good looks imply."

"Methinks he doth protest too much," Dana said.

"Even I know that's Shakespeare," Mac quipped.

24

Jared Wood's boat, *Innovator,* rounded a rocky headland and pulled into the calmer waters of a protected embayment. Through the rain, the crew could see the *MacGreggor* tied up adjacent to the much larger *Silence.*

Raul Sanchez piloted the *Innovator* to within thirty yards of the two ships before ordering the anchor dropped. He rubbed his broken nose delicately. The big black guy on the boat had nearly killed him with that cutting board. Though he didn't talk about it with his shipmates, Raul was amazed that he'd maintained consciousness after that blow. Raul shook his head; a silly college kid had nearly taken him down.

His thoughts turned to his brother Ernesto. He'd heard over the radio that Ernesto had gone missing during the seizure of the Yankee science vessel, and Raul didn't know how to feel about that. Ernesto had been a terrible older brother from the beginning. And more recently, he had compelled Raul to join this group of pirates despite the fact that he had no desire to do so.

Raul, like many young, male residents of Cartagena, had seen his share of killings. It was impossible to survive life on the streets without some experience with death. But up until the raid on the *Innovator*, Raul had only killed people that he felt deserved it; people with a good reason to die. Rivals in other gangs, for instance. But in his estimation, killing the three college students on this boat had been without any honor.

And then there was the way his comrades were treating the woman down in the hold, and her mother before she was moved to the *Silence*. Nothing in his life experience had prepared Raul for that. He knew his four colleagues were deeply distrustful of him because he refused to take advantage of the women. His objections to raping a teenaged girl rendered him suspicious in the eyes of the pirates.

Now they had a vessel full of hostages, students as well, he'd heard on the radio. And the captain apparently planned to leverage them for a ransom. Raul didn't know anything about collecting ransoms, but he was skeptical that these pirates would be capable of pulling off such an act. He'd seen enough movies, some even pretty good, like *Captain Phillips*, to understand that receiving the money, and then getting access to it, was very, very complicated.

Maybe the captain had a plan. Maybe. But Raul didn't see how it was going to work. And how long was it going to be possible to avoid the authorities? He'd heard that some of the passengers or maybe crew had gotten away, and a large scientific vessel such as the *MacGreggor* sure had money and power behind it. So, there must be people out looking for the vessel now. Even in this weather, eventually they were going to find it.

After the *Innovator* was successfully anchored, the five pirates motored to the *Silence* in a small inflatable. The relatively calm waters of the protected embayment made the ride easy, and so Raul had time to revel in the beauty of the sleek vessel.

His brother Ernesto had told him the *Silence* had been built in the nineteen-nineties for South American cruises. She was about three-hundred-feet long, ninety feet wide at the widest point, and had a draught of thirteen feet. Ten years after launching, the ship had run aground on a shallow reef off the coast of Colombia. The argument that ensued about who was to blame and who was going to pay for it took so long to resolve that the ship was washed off the reef by a storm, recovered by salvagers, and repurposed as a modern pirate vessel.

From afar, the *Silence* appeared to be uniformly black. Up close for the first time, Raul could see that the blackness resulted from many different coats of paint that had no doubt been applied over many years. Most of the ship's seven decks had been repurposed, with the lower two decks serving to hold the proceeds of piracy. Otherwise, there was nothing conspicuously pirate-related along the outer hull in the event that a curious passerby got close enough to see anything.

Raul was the last of the five *Innovator* crew to climb the ladder onto the second deck. He could hear excited voices talking above him. As he reached the deck, he found the reason for the excited voices.

A partially decapitated body had been laid out on its back. The corpse's right arm had been severed below the elbow.

Raul stepped over the body and into the main salon where a tall pirate, who he'd figured was the captain, was laying out a plan.

25

"Approaching Genovesa," announced Dana from the bridge. Chris and Mac were in the galley one deck below assessing the equipment they had available to them. Chris was focusing on the dive gear, while Mac inspected the weapons.

"Copy that," Chris replied via the intercom. "Any sign of vessel traffic on radar?"

"Visibility is still minimal out here," said Dana. "But there was a large ship on the horizon about forty-five minutes ago. Too large to be the *MacGreggor*."

Looking up at the electronic chart on the large screen in the galley, Chris could see the icon depicting their borrowed yacht approaching the strange shape of Genovesa Island from the south.

To Chris, the island looked like a tortoise head, with a small body of water mid-island serving as an eye, and the mouth-shaped embayment they were heading for gaping southward as though looking for food.

The swells under the boat, which had been plaguing their progress for hours, calmed quickly as they pulled into the lee provided by the island. Chris could still see rain pelting the galley windows, but at least they'd get a break from the swells.

Mac handed Chris a loaded forty-five-millimeter handgun and headed up the spiral staircase to the bridge. "We have to be ready for anything."

"Agreed." Chris was not a gun enthusiast and lacked Mac's military training. But he'd had to use guns before and was prepared to do so again if he had to.

As they arrived on the bridge, the yacht was enveloped in complete darkness. There were no structures on the island. The only illumination came from the bridge command screens and from what looked like two other small vessels anchored in the bay.

"Can we pull off a drive-by in these conditions to see who's here?" Mac asked.

"Risky," said Dana. "If our bad guys are here, they may think we're the authorities and try to rabbit. What do you think, Chris?"

Dana turned toward him with an open and honest smile that took Chris by surprise. Gone was her quiet mistrust, and she seemed genuinely interested in his opinion.

"I agree that it's a risk, but we have to try. And if the bad guys are here, perhaps they'll relax once they see that we aren't the cops. That could actually help us."

Dana brought the large yacht around to port and slowly motored toward the nearest vessel. "Target number one coming up."

Mac suggested, "Everyone look casual."

"I don't think they'll see much through all this tinted glass," replied Chris, spreading his arms out from side to side.

The first boat loomed out of the dark. It was a small, thirty-five-foot catamaran called *The Lonely Shark.*

"That's a mighty small vessel to be out in these conditions," observed Mac. "We should radio over to them to see if everything is okay."

Dana nodded as she reached for the radio mic mounted on the ceiling above her.

"*Lonely Shark, Lonely Shark*. This is the *Tiburon*. Do you read us? Over."

There was no response. Lights were visible below decks on the starboard pontoon.

"*Lonely Shark, Lonely Shark*. This is the *Tiburon*. Do you read us? Over."

"*Tiburon*, this is *Lonely Shark*," said a male voice with a German accent. "What can we do for you?"

Dana looked at Chris and Mac. They all knew that if there were pirates around, they'd likely be listening to radio chatter. She affected a southern accent and replied, "Just checking on y'all. This's some sporty weather we've got out here."

"Thanks, *Tiburon*. We aren't going anywhere. Think we'll ride this storm out right here."

"Copy that, *Lonely Shark*. We'll probably stick around here for a while as well. Let us know if we can be of any assistance. *Tiburon*, out."

"They didn't sound like they were under duress," observed Mac, his eyes still fixed on *The Lonely Shark*.

"True," said Chris, "but what would duress sound like? I think we may have encountered a drawback to our plan."

"Well, they didn't come out shooting," noted Mac. "So perhaps we try the next candidate but keep our eyes on *The Lonely Shark* as well."

"On to target number two?" Dana asked.

"Let's do it," said Chris.

As they approached the second boat, which appeared to be completely dark, Chris pulled out a pair of night vision goggles they'd borrowed from the *D-fens*.

"Can you make out a name," asked Mac.

"*Innovator*," said Chris. "It's from Newport."

Dana tried to raise the boat on the radio but received no response.

Chris continued to view the cabin cruiser through the night vision goggles. He couldn't see any movement. *Innovator? Innovator?* Where had he heard that name before?

Dana maneuvered past the *Innovator* and moved toward the other side of the small bay to anchor.

"Holy shit!" exclaimed Chris, once it dawned on him.

"What do you see?" asked Mac, stepping closer to Chris to see anything from his vantage point.

"Nothing," replied Chris. "Still blacked out. But that name, *Innovator*. Alex remembered seeing another boat but wasn't sure about the name. Thought it might be called *Innocence* or *Innovation*. If you ask me, that's darn close to *Innovator*."

"And you don't believe in coincidence."

"Nope."

"You think that could be one of the pirate ships?" Mac asked. "Sitting here alone, in the dark?"

"Don't you?"

"I . . . Wait, where are you going?" Mac asked as Chris bounded toward the stairway down.

"To make sure the batteries for the scooters are powered up. I'm going over there."

"Explain," said Mac.

"We go now, under the cover of darkness," said Chris, "with plenty of weather to provide us cover."

"An underwater assault on a pirate ship? At night?" asked Mac. "If the situation weren't so dire, I'd say this is a boyhood dream come true."

26

The top speed of the dive scooters was just over nine miles an hour, meaning that Chris and Mac could cover the distance to the *Innovator* in five minutes from where the *Tiburon* was moored on the other side of the protected embayment. Each scooter was essentially an underwater jet pack, consisting primarily of a large battery contained within a waterproof housing and a large propeller. At the back end of a scooter were two handles, one of which held the trigger to accelerate.

Both of the men had used similar scooters on many occasions over the course of their careers. Mac had passed the time as they'd prepped the devices talking about every cinematic use of scooters he could remember, spending most of his time talking about the 'epic' undersea battle at the end of *Thunderball*, his favorite of the original James Bond films.

"I'm telling you, it was epic," Mac had said.

"I'm not disagreeing," Chris had replied. "I'm just trying to stay focused on the task at hand."

"Right, right. The task at hand. Underwater assault on a pirate ship, in the dark. Also, epic. Do you remember that flick we saw in third grade, *Skyriders*? That was an assault on a mountain complex using hang gliders, but very much in a similar to vein to what we are going for here . . ."

Even under the cover of darkness, with the rain continuing to pour down, Dana had been concerned about the duo being spotted as they approached the vessel. The air bubbles exhausted from a traditional SCUBA regulator would, she'd pointed out, leave a literal trail for anyone watching from the vessel to see.

Speaking to Dana, but looking at Chris, Mac had pointed out, "Ah, but Mr. Johnson's mother didn't raise a fool." He'd then opened the cabinet to his left to reveal two black *Megalodon* closed-circuit rebreathers.

"I told you this boat came fully stocked."

Dana and Chris both knew that unlike traditional SCUBA units, which provide a fixed amount of compressed air to a diver from a high-pressure cylinder, with the diver's exhalations extruded through an exhaust valve on his/her regulator, a rebreather literally re-circulated the air through a closed-circuit system.

The air a diver inhaled contained roughly twenty-one percent oxygen and seventy-eight percent nitrogen. When that air was exhaled the percentage of oxygen decreased by as much as five percent, with the balance being replaced by carbon dioxide.

Because carbon dioxide could lead to unconsciousness, it had to be 'scrubbed' from a diver's air mixture. The major innovation provided by closed-circuit rebreathers was the introduction of a chemical 'scrubber' to the closed circuit. By removing the carbon dioxide from the air while also injecting additional oxygen, a diver could breathe from a device like the *Megalodon* for as much as six hours, depending on his or her depth.

Mac and Dana had both used various makes of rebreathers on military exercises over the years, while Chris had used them for other reasons altogether. As a scientist studying fish behavior, there were circumstances in which not extruding air bubbles allowed him to approach much closer without disrupting the natural behavior of the organisms he was there to study.

"Do you guys remember your physics? The Observer Effect basically says it all: the observed phenomenon is not the phenomenon," he'd explained to his students.

"Wait a minute. What?"

"As soon as you observe something, so the theory goes, you change what you're observing. In our case, the bubbles extruded by our regulators do have an impact on the fishes we are observing. Some fishes are attracted to the bubbles, while others flee. We know this."

"But aren't we supposed to be studying natural behavior?" a student had asked.

"Yep," Chris had replied. "None of our tools for sampling underwater are perfect.

All we can do is do our best to match the tool to the ecosystem and to the scientific question."

"I'm not sure I understand."

"It is all about tradeoffs. SCUBA produces bubbles but allows the scientist to immerse him or herself underwater where the organisms live. ROVs are too loud and usually too bright, but they allow us to explore much deeper than SCUBA diving.

"The key is to understand the limitations of the tool and to use the tool exactly the same way every time within a study. That way, even if we might not be observing exactly what happens in our absence, but studying things the same way repeatedly, we can learn important insights into subtidal ecology."

Clad head to toe in jet black SCUBA gear and the rebreathers, Chris and Mac had dropped into the water on the far side of the *Tiburon,* out of sight were any pirates to be watching, and immediately begun their rapid approach to *Innovator.* Each was armed with a pistol, a knife, and a telescoping ASP baton, as well as a radio for communicating with Dana. The simple plan was to board the vessel at the stern, subdue any pirates on board, and to subsequently interrogate them as to the whereabouts of the *MacGreggor* and the status of the hostages.

Chris surfaced first, gradually allowing his head to emerge from the water thirty feet behind the boat to check for guards. Mac surfaced immediately adjacent to the boat on the port side, ready to respond to any threat from the back deck.

Even in the near pitch-black conditions, Chris was able to see that no-one was on the back deck of the *Innovator*. In fact, he could see no evidence of occupation at all. He was concerned that the total lack of activity might suggest they were too late and that the pirates had left. He didn't want to contemplate what that might mean to the hostages. He also briefly considered the possibility that he was completely wrong on his recollection that *Innovator* was the name of the boat Alex had mentioned. In that case, Chris thought, this was going to be an awkward five minutes.

Keeping the scooter underwater, Chris triggered the accelerator and slowly moved toward Mac, making sure to minimize any visible wake created by his movements. Reaching Mac with no reaction from on-board, he quickly signaled to Mac that no one was visible up top. Mac had secured a suction cup to the hull just below the waterline to which they attached their scooters, fins, and masks.

They then slowly pulled themselves up onto the swim platform that ran the full width of the *Innovator's* stern. Chris led the way onto the back deck and nearly stumbled on a person lying prone on his back. The gun sticking out of the unconscious man's belt, and the empty bottle of rum still clasped in his hand suggested to Chris that they'd found the right boat and that the men on-board were not the rightful owners. He couldn't help but snicker at the fact that they'd encountered a pirate drunk on rum.

Chris looked at Mac, who mouthed, "Yo-ho, yo-ho." He hadn't missed the irony either.

While Chris watched the deck, Mac removed a roll of black Gorilla tape, and a pair of large tie wraps to secure the drunken pirate. Once that was accomplished, Mac moved up the ladder to the upper deck while Chris slowly entered the salon. He was grateful that the door made little noise as he carefully swung it open, for he found the galley to be illuminated by interior lights that the tinted windows had not allowed them to see in advance from outside.

Two men were sitting at the galley table with their upper bodies collapsed on the table in front of them. Chris delicately pulled the arms of the nearest pirate behind his back and secured them with tie wraps. The second man stirred as Chris was finishing, earning the man a tap on the head from the ASP that Chris had rapidly deployed.

As Chris secured the second man, he could hear footsteps on the deck above him. The radio remained silent, so he assumed that whatever Mac was involved in up there was proceeding to their advantage. He then heard what sounded like a subdued female voice from down the hall to his left.

Chris's first thought was of Abby, wondering if she'd been removed from the *MacGreggor*. His ASP still in his hand, he crept down the hall, listening carefully as he passed each door. Passing the second door on his right, he heard a muffled female voice and a man speaking in slurred Spanish.

On his nightstand next to his bed back in Carmel, Chris had a pile of partially read non-fiction books. He'd recently pointed out to his students that two of those books, in particular, were interesting to him. One of the books suggested that first impressions should always be acted upon, while the other argued with equal vehemence that one should never trust one's first impressions because humans were such poor observers that they regularly missed a great deal. After a very animated discussion, Chris and his students had reached a consensus, namely that both assertions were likely true. But as with so much in science, and in life, everything depended on context.

Standing in the hallway of a pirated ship, listening to what he expected was a drunken pirate about to attack a woman who is very likely a hostage, Chris went with his first impression.

Twisting the door handle slowly and finding it unlocked, Chris thrust the door open. Quickly surveilling the scene in front of him, Chris found a drunken man standing right in front of him, evidently struggling to unbuckle his belt.

On the bed in front of the man lay a young woman whom Chris did not recognize. She was wearing a battered USC t-shirt, and he could see multiple bruises on her arms as well as her neck and face. The woman's wearied glance moved from the pirate to Chris, at which point a quizzical look came over her face.

Through cracked lips, the woman uttered, "Who . . . who are you?"

Sensing a change in the situation, the pirate followed the woman's glance and began to turn his head toward Chris. Chris, however, was ready for that and struck out with the ASP. In the close quarters of the stateroom, he did not have the room to swing the baton, so he jabbed it straight at the man's temple. The blow struck true, and Chris followed with a sidekick to the man's torso, sending him flying toward the desk along the far wall.

Chris closed the door behind him and moved to tie up the pirate. He spoke calmly to the woman as he did so, "My name is Chris Black. I'm here to help. Can you tell me your name?"

The woman looked from Chris to the pirate and then back at Chris. "Beth. My name is Beth."

"Beth. Can you tell me how many people are on-board this boat?"

Responding with what Chris thought was determination increasing by the second, Beth replied, "I think there are five of them, but there may be more." That leaves at least one unaccounted for, Chris thought to himself.

"Is this your boat?" asked Chris.

"No, we were sailing out to the Galapagos when they attacked us using this boat. They killed our friends and then moved my mom and me here. But I don't think my mom's on board anymore."

"I'm sorry, Beth."

"They'll kill us too."

"My friend is upstairs right now, and we aren't going to let that happen," said Chris. "Will you be okay if I leave you in here while I go check on my friend?"

Fear came into Beth's eyes. "No, I haven't been out of this room in days. I want to come with you."

"Okay, let's go. You can follow me. Stay close."

As Beth climbed out of the bed, the pirate moaned and tried to move. She was on him in an instant, first kicking at the man and then clawing at his face.

Chris gently put his arms on her shoulders. "Beth, we have to go. He's not going anywhere." He hit the man again to make sure he stayed down.

Emerging from the stateroom, Chris led Beth down the hallway toward the bow.

At the end of the hallway was a circular stair that led to the deck above. Chris wound his way up, poking his head around the corner once he reached the top. The stair had led to the bridge, where Mac stood over an unconscious pirate while he aimed a gun a second man standing at the helm.

Without taking his eyes of the man, Mac said, "Chris, please tie up this piece of shit before I change my mind and shoot him."

27

"**D**r. Black, please," said Frank Donagan as he motioned to a nearby bench. He had met the two boats at the dock back in Puerto Ayora on Santa Cruz Island. Dana had called ahead to alert the U.S. consulate that they were bringing captured pirates and a liberated hostage back to shore, hoping that the consulate staff would help with local authorities.

Having just spent seven hours talking with Beth Gordon in between her naps as they motored back from Genovesa, and then another two hours explaining what had happened to the local police, Chris was in no mood to hear about rules and protocols. "Frank, I suggest you talk to the poor woman they just took away to the hospital before you start with your recitation on protocols." Beth had not wanted to separate from Chris and Mac, and he felt sick about it. But Dana had volunteered to stay with Beth wherever they took her, and Chris had assured her that they would visit her as soon as possible.

"Ah, recitation. Did you know the word is literally translated from the Latin as 'again to summon'?"

"I can think of a few other Latin phrases," said Mac as he climbed down onto the dock from the *Innovator*. Chris was too tired to wave him off.

"Gentlemen. Contrary to popular opinion, you are not actually in trouble with the authorities at this time. They were quite happy to have a hostage returned to them, and the fact that you didn't kill anyone also helps your case."

The satisfaction of catching the pirates and saving Beth from further assaults had been considerable for both Chris and Mac. But the realization that they were back to square one in their pursuit of the *MacGreggor* had dampened their moods.

"Where's Peter?" asked Chris, looking up at the dark sky. The rain had stopped, but the clouds looked threatening.

"He is at the hotel meeting with some of the families. A number of them arrived on the island while the two of you were out at Genovesa."

"I'm glad I'm not in his shoes," said Chris. "They must be having a rough time. And I'm sure they won't hold back."

"That's true," said Donagan. "A few are hysterical. Several are very angry. The rest are simply worried."

"Has anyone heard from the pirates yet?" Mac asked.

"Not yet. There are still six hours remaining before the original deadline for communication expires."

"What is it with these pirates?" asked Mac in response. "Isn't there a way these things usually go?"

Donagan nodded. "Yes, there is a formula for hostage situations down here, including a regular schedule of contacts with the authorities. These pirates are not following that formula."

"Is that genius or idiocy?" asked Chris. "Are they outthinking us, or do they simply not know what they're doing?"

Donagan shrugged but did not respond.

Chris rubbed his eyes and thought of what the students must be going through. The scene on the *Innovator* had not been a good one. After they'd secured the pirates and helped make Beth more comfortable, he and Mac had searched the boat for any clues to the pirates' plan or to the location of the *MacGreggor*. While they'd found no clues, there was a great deal of evidence suggesting that several people had been killed on the boat.

"Donagan," Chris said, "You are always critiquing my efforts after the fact. And that's fine. Maybe that's your job. But I'd like to hear what you think is going to happen next. You've got experience with this kind of thing. Tell us, how's this going to pan out?"

Donagan did not respond.

"Are they dead already?" Chris asked, nearly vomiting from the stress of putting words to what everyone feared but had not dared say out loud.

Donagan still did not respond.

"Okay, Mac. Let's go."

They picked up their SCUBA gear and began walking toward the Tiburon.

"Wait, please," Donagan said with an urgency Chris hadn't heard from him before.

Chris stopped, but did not turn around.

Donagan looked around to see who might be close enough to hear him and then said, "It might be resolved quickly and without loss of life. Or it could be a complete tragedy."

"I'm not trained in diplomacy or statecraft, but even I can see that," Mac spat. "What do *you* think is going to happen?"

"Yes, what does your gut say?" Chris added.

"I am not accustomed to making gut calls," Donagan said. "But if I were, I'd say I don't expect a positive outcome. There are too many unknown variables in play here. I've witnessed hostage negotiations before, but never like this." He shook his head. "I fear the worst for everyone aboard the *MacGreggor*."

Chris turned around. "Okay. So, then my next question is, if the situation is so dire, and no one appears to be doing anything, what would you have us do?"

Donagan did not respond.

"You saw what happened in South Africa first-hand." Chris took a few steps toward Donagan. "You know what we're capable of. Do you honestly expect us to sit around the hotel room and wait?"

Chris could see that Donagan was measuring his next words carefully.

"You're right. While I can't, as a professional, condone rogue efforts, I don't see any other good options. There's a certain randomness to this situation that defies prediction. Most hostage takers, in my experience, are predictable. It is essentially a business for them, albeit a business that is run differently than most. But the scene aboard that boat suggests violent intent. Angry, violent intent. I can't see how such people would have the patience to negotiate for anyone's release."

He took a deep breath, highlighting the gravity of his admission.

"No, I don't think this will go well. I fear that you guys may be the only hope those poor people have."

28

"That is how we deal with traitors," said the tall pirate, his face only inches from Abby's. "No one here is going to help you. The sooner you recognize that, the better it will be for you."

Abby could not speak. Nothing in her life had prepared her for this.

"But don't worry. I'll be back for you tonight." The pirate's voice dripped with sarcasm as he kicked the body of the pirate who'd offered to help Abby. "That will take your mind off your dead friend here. So, don't get too comfortable."

Laughing, the tall pirate pushed Abby toward one of the other pirates on the back deck and walked off toward the bridge. The man led her down the hallway and shoved her through the lab door, slamming it closed behind her.

"Oh, my god!" said Terra. "You're hurt!"

Looking down at herself, Abby could see the dead pirate's blood all over her. It saturated her blouse and shorts and covered her arms and legs.

"It's not my blood," Abby explained to the horrified group as she sat down at the nearest table. "Would somebody mind . . . helping me?"

Terra hopped up immediately and brought a damp towel to wipe off the blood. Together they were able to clean Abby's face and arms. Cleaning her clothes would have to come later.

Abby noticed that everyone was staring at her. She realized that this could be a defining moment. She could tell everyone about the violent death she thought awaited them, or she could try to give them hope.

She opted for hope but wasn't sure she could sell it. "They killed the guard who was helping us. But I don't think they'll hurt us. They are ransoming us for several million dollars."

"Will anyone pay?" asked Leah, one of the Canadian students.

"My parents will." Brian, from Texas, said with what seemed like forced confidence.

"How, exactly, would they do that?" Roberto asked.

"I'm certain the university has insurance for this type of thing." Abby doubted her own words as they left her mouth. "They won't want anyone of us to be hurt. I think the best thing we can do right now is to stay calm and to not risk antagonizing our captors."

"Maybe we should fight our way out," said Brian, sitting up straighter.

Abby held out the lower part of her blouse and looked at the deep red bloodstains. She wanted to scream but fought back the urge. "I don't think so. If you'd seen what I just saw, I'm pretty sure you'd agree. We have to remain calm."

"I think you're right," said a woman Abby hadn't noticed when she came in. It was the woman she'd seen earlier when the pirates had brought her onto the *MacGreggor*. She was kneeling next to Oliver. "They don't want to hurt us. They just want money."

The woman's surprise appearance and proximity to Oliver unnerved her. Looking at her more closely, Abby noticed the tattoos on the woman's forearms but couldn't tell what exactly they showed. "How did you get here? I thought I saw them bring you on board earlier?"

The woman stood up and approached Abby. Sitting down at the same table with Abby and Terra, she said, "My name's Maria. I'm a lawyer from Mexico City. I was on vacation in Panama when I was kidnapped. They are ransoming me too."

"How long have you been held?" asked Abby.

"I think I've been with them for three weeks, but I've lost track of time."

"Three *weeks*?" asked Anna from Ecuador.

Maria looked directly at Abby through striking grey eyes, "I was able to give them some money the first week after I was taken. That helped my situation. They've pretty much left me alone since then. It's buying time."

"Time for what?"

"For people to come looking for me."

Abby nodded. "How'd you give them money?"

"I had money in a special belt that they didn't find at first. And I gave them my bank card and PIN."

"You gave up your bank card and PIN?" asked Abby, looking around to see if any guards had appeared as well. "And you're *still* here?"

Of all the scenarios Abby had considered over the past three days as she'd struggled to keep her panic at bay, none of them involved giving up her personal financial information to these pirates, and none of them lasted three weeks. This woman's report was terrifying.

"Hey, I'm just trying to stay alive." Maria seemed offended.

"I'm sorry," said Abby. "Of course, you are. I just don't understand. If you gave them money and you're still here, what do they want? And what did your money buy you?"

"More money. That's what they want," replied Maria with a guffaw. She then leaned in so that only Abby and Terra were able to hear her speak, "And as I said, the money is buying me time." With a quick glance at the young girls among the students, Maria added, "It also stopped their visits to my cabin, if you understand what I mean."

The potential for sexual assault had been prominent on Abby's mind from the first moments of the attack. But as time wore on, and none of the females in the group had been attacked, Abby had begun to hope that perhaps the ransom was going to protect them; that if they were going to try and make money off the hostages, the pirates wouldn't abuse them. Considering the implications of Maria's comments, Abby shivered and hugged her arms to her chest.

"Why do you think they moved you onto this boat with us?"

"I'm not sure," replied Maria.

"Is this the first time you've been moved around since you were taken?" asked Terra.

Abby was proud of Terra's effort to keep it together, though she wondered if that effort was simply made easier by her youth. She may not have lived long enough to see the manifest horror of what people could do to one another.

"This is the third, no, I'm sorry, the fourth boat I've been on since I was taken."

"Have you encountered other hostages?" Terra continued her line of questioning.

"I have not *seen* anyone," answered Maria. "But that doesn't mean they weren't around. I've heard things to suggest that there are other captives."

Abby digested this news and tried to understand what it meant for her group.

"How long have they had you?" Maria asked as she turned back to Abby.

"We are on day three," replied Abby.

"Have they taken your wallets?"

Abby thought about this. "They may have. We've all been confined in here since they came on board, so I don't know if they've searched our personal stuff."

"I'm sure that they have," replied Maria. "Perhaps if we gave them information on how to use the cards, we can buy you women some time."

"Perhaps." Abby didn't want to imagine staying under these conditions for weeks, or longer. But she had to admit that she would gladly give up her life's savings to avoid being assaulted by these pirates.

She looked at Oliver, who was still drifting in and out of consciousness, wondering how long he would last without medical help soon. And she thought of Chris and hoped against hope that he and Mac would show up soon to help them.

29

Chris and Mac ran through the narrow streets of Puerto Ayora en route to the police station, dodging trucks and locals on scooters. Donagan had called the hotel to report that the captain of the boat they'd captured had agreed to talk, but only to them.

There were no rental cars in the Galapagos. So, the only alternative to a taxi, which could take some time to arrange, was to travel on foot. Fortunately, the rain had not yet resumed, so Chris actually appreciated the opportunity to run. Mac was less enthusiastic, but he kept up.

They rounded the last corner before proceeding up the hill to the station when they were brought to a halt by an incongruous sight. Coming down the hill toward them was a large, green mechanical caterpillar.

The huge white eyes rolled back and forth as it moved forward. Bright Christmas lights lined the edges of the lead car, which towed six other cars behind it filled with tourists. Eerie calliope music was projected from two large speakers that masqueraded as the caterpillar's ears.

"Are you seeing this?" asked Mac.

"I am," said Chris. "Did Stephen King ever write a book set on Santa Cruz? Because if he hasn't, I think there's a missed opportunity with that thing."

As the caterpillar rolled past, Chris noticed that none of the passengers were smiling. It was as if they'd all gotten more than they paid for with the freak show.

"Onward," said Chris, as he took one last look at the green machine before it turned the corner out of sight.

The duo reached the station and found Donagan standing inside among a mix of Ecuadorian policemen and likely U.S. consulate employees. All were talking among themselves right up until Chris and Mac walked through the dirty glass door.

Donagan walked over to greet them. "Come with me."

They were buzzed back through a locked door that Chris figured would neither hold anyone in nor anyone out if any real effort were made.

"Why does this guy want to talk to us?" Mac asked.

"Hold that thought," Donagan said under his breath. Mac looked at Chris and shrugged his shoulders.

As they moved down the narrow hallway, an officer stepped out of a door on the left to reveal three of the pirates they'd encountered at Genovesa. Chris and Mac stared at the pirates, recognizing them instantly. It took the three men several seconds longer to connect Chris and Mac to their current plight.

The first to act was the man Chris had interrupted in the room with Beth. The man's head was bandaged, and his arm was in a sling. As recognition dawned in his droopy brown eyes, the pirate tried to leap up from the bench where all three were sitting to attack Chris. He overlooked the fact that the chains on his ankles connected him to his two comrades, and he fell forward, landing awkwardly on his injured arm.

The pirate screamed through is pain, "Voy a matarte!"

The officer called for someone to help him pick up the pirate. In that moment, Chris took the opportunity to step into the room and kneel down next to the pirate. He whispered, "Not today, cabrón. And you better hope you never see me again."

The man squirmed on the floor in a fury, kicking his chained ankles and trying to lift himself up with his one functional arm.

Chris backed away and stepped out of the room as two additional officers came down the hall. They entered and closed the door.

"Has anyone interrogated those guys yet?" Chris asked.

"Not yet," Donagan replied. "We're hoping that your meeting with their colleague provides some useful information first."

Several more steps down the hallway, Donagan knocked twice on a room marked 'holding' and ushered them inside. The boat captain was sitting at one end of a long table, his wrists locked to a metal ring on the table by handcuffs. The room was barely large enough to hold the four of them and the table. The interior was painted a color that approached avocado green, giving the appearance that it hadn't been touched up in decades. The rusted metal fan hanging from the ceiling was not spinning fast enough to move any air.

Chris and Mac moved into the room and did their bests to position themselves to be ready should this guy harbor similar aspirations to his colleague down the hall.

Donagan spoke first. "This is Raul Sanchez. You gentlemen will recognize him from the vessel *Innovator*." Pointing at Chris and Mac, he continued, "Mr. Sanchez, these are my colleagues. You indicated that you wished to speak with them directly, so we have honored that request. May I stay?"

The man started at that request. "No, por favor."

"Fine," said Donagan. As he left, he handed Chris a smartphone and said, "Call me on this when you're done, and we'll let you out."

Chris thought this request to be strange until he looked down at the device in his palm and realized that the phone was already connected to another line. This was Donagan's way of being in the room, even if he wasn't in the room. It also indicated that Donagan was trusting Chris not to cut him off.

"Okay. We're here," said Chris. "What do you want to talk with us about?"

The pirate sat still and said nothing.

"I told you this was a huge waste of our time," said Mac. "We know the pirates have headed back to the mainland, and we should be going there as well. Not sitting here talking with this D-bag."

Playing the 'good cop' to Mac's 'bad,' Chris said, "I don't think he understands enough English, Mac. Why don't we go find him a police translator?"

Getting no response from Raul Sanchez, they turned to leave. Mac knocked hard on the door. "We're done in here!"

"They will kill you, you know?" Raul said. "You are dead men walking."

"Who's going to kill us?" asked Mac.

"My compadres."

"Those idiots down the hall?" asked Chris. "I think they'll be spending more time dodging much tougher guys in the shower for the next few years."

"No, not them," replied Sanchez. "They are drunkards. No, I am talking about my other shipmates. The guys who have taken your boat and your people."

"Well, we'll see about that, won't we?" said Chris.

"No one gets away from us."

Chris nodded at Mac, who instantly rounded the corner of the table and grabbed Sanchez' throat in a vice grip. "Tell us more about how we're dead men. We love tough talk."

Sanchez tried to shake himself loose of Mac's grip, but Mac held firm. "You have three seconds to tell us what you want to tell us. Three . . . two . . . one . . ."

Someone tried to open the holding room door, but Chris held the knob.

"Okay!" rasped Sanchez, his face a deep red.

Mac released the man's throat but stayed right in his face. Through gritted teeth, Mac asked, "*What* do you want to tell us?"

The knocking on the door increased in urgency. Both Chris and Mac looked at Sanchez.

"Your information is incorrect," he said, barely audibly.

"What did you say?" asked Chris.

"Your information is not correct. Your ship is not going back to the mainland. They are headed to Isabella Island, and when they get there, the plan is to sink the ship and to kill the passengers after the ransom has been received."

Chris felt his legs weaken at the confirmation of his worst nightmare. He'd been holding out a slim hope for the hostages and the boat based on the potential ransom. But Sanchez' words actually made more sense to him. How could there be any other outcome, he thought.

"How do you know this?" asked Chris. "How long has this been the plan?"

"Yesterday," said Raul, "you came onto the boat and found nearly everyone drunk, right? They were drinking to celebrate the great plan the captain had announced. They think they are going to be rich."

"But you don't," said Chris. "Why?"

The man looked at Chris wearily, his will to fight fading. "I am only here because of my brother, Ernesto. I am not committed like the others."

"And you're certain that they're taking the *MacGreggor* to Isabella to sink her?"

"I am."

"Is there anything else you can tell us?"

Raul paused and looked around as though he was checking to see who might be listening. "I used to work at a government building in Colombia, and I saw how badly hostage negotiations were run. Your people will not survive."

"Yeah, you said that already," said Mac, inching himself closer to Sanchez.

"Wait!" The man was clearly afraid, but it wasn't clear whether the source of his fear was Mac or someone else. "There was another reason we were in the cove at Genovesa. But I can't talk about that here."

"Why not?"

"Because there are people here who will not let me live if I do."

That's when it clicked. Something else was going on. There was no other explanation for what Chris considered the lackluster response by the authorities. "If you won't tell us anything, why are we here?" he asked.

"What the pirates did to that woman on the boat is not my way. I have a daughter back in Colombia. I don't want anyone else to be hurt or killed. So, I am talking to you."

"When are they going to sink the boat?" asked Mac.

"I'm not certain. I think they want to get the money before they kill anyone, but they may sink the boat before that."

"There is nothing else you can tell us? What about the black boat?" asked Chris.

"The *Silence*? Yes, that is the boat used by the captain."

Chris and Mac looked at each other.

"How many pirates on it?" asked Chris.

"And what types of weapons do they have?" asked Mac.

"The numbers change all the time," said Sanchez. "There are different groups on different boats, but always coming back to the *Silence*."

"Is it closer to thirty or sixty?" demanded Chris.

"Yesterday it was closer to thirty. I don't know about now."

"And what about weapons?" repeated Mac.

"Many, many weapons," Sanchez said.

They'd heard enough.

"Let's go."

Donagan was waiting for them in the hallway. He was alone.

"That pounding on the door—nice touch," said Chris.

Donagan nodded. "What do you need from me?"

30

"I'm way ahead of you," said Hendrix. Chris and Mac were standing around his hospital bed, which had been repositioned to allow Hendrix to sit up. The afternoon sun, which had found a way to briefly penetrate the storm clouds, washed the room with bright orange and red light. Despite his injuries, Hendrix radiated pure energy from his bed.

"As soon as I woke up, I contacted our South American headquarters and had a team sent over," he explained. "They arrived at the airport on Baltra Island about an hour ago, so we should see them within minutes. They're coming fully loaded, of course. What do we have in the way of vessels?"

"We've got a nicely stocked pleasure craft that should allow us to approach without inviting too much suspicion," Mac said. "It, too, is fully loaded."

"Nice!" replied Hendrix. "I'll want to hear more about that later. Where's Dana, by the way?"

"She's down the hall talking with the young woman we brought back from Genovesa," answered Chris.

"Okay. So, what's the plan, Dr. Black?"

Chris had been running and re-running scenarios in his head non-stop. There was simply too much uncertainty, but then they couldn't let uncertainty constrain them, or the mission might go very, very wrong. The authorities in the area were not going to resolve the situation quickly, or appropriately—that much was clear. Several people had already testified to the underwhelming success of hostage negotiators in South America. For all his talk, Donagan had yet to articulate a credible approach that didn't involve a rescue mission. And besides, the story the captured pirate told seemed very credible; they had very little time remaining to save the hostages and the ship.

Not for the first time, Chris found himself wishing that his dad was still around. For all his faults, Andrew Black had been a master strategist. He could see his way through crises better than anyone Chris had ever met. Andrew would be able to see through the irrelevant chaff and cut right to the heart of a situation.

Chris knew that those skills had been honed in war, where lives literally depended on decisions his dad had made. But he'd observed the same skills being put to work for more than two decades as a commercial pilot. Chris recalled the exact point in his early twenties when he woke up one morning, realized many of the benefits of his dad's stern and organized approach to life, and from then on had tried to emulate that level of methodic organization, minus the sternness.

"We think we may be on a tight clock," said Chris. "I need to find out from Peter if the pirates have contacted them again. According to our pirate source, the hostages will be killed as soon as the money is transferred. And for all we know, the *MacG* may already be at the bottom of the sea."

Chris closed his eyes for a moment to ban an image that went with this thought.

"So, I think we put a team on the *Tiburon*, go find the pirates at Isabella, and take them out while rescuing all the hostages. There's really no other option."

"Agreed," said Hendrix. "And if your source is wrong, or lying?"

"That will not be good for anyone."

Mac hunted up two more chairs so that he and Chris could sit next to Hendrix's hospital bed and plan. Nurses came and went several times as the planning session went into the early evening. A doctor came by as well, thinking that Hendrix would be resting comfortably. Finding his patient awake and animated as he discussed the maps and charts that covered his bed, the doctor was initially aghast, but ultimately said he was greatly encouraged by Hendrix's enthusiasm. And before he left, the doctor predicted a more rapid recovery as a result.

By seven that night, Hendrix's two team members had arrived, each carrying a large black duffel bag full of gear, as well as three extra bags of gear for Chris, Mac, and Dana. When Dana had returned from checking in on Beth, both Hendrix and Chris had been clear that she was not required to participate further in any of the operations.

"You've already done so much for us," explained Chris.

"Above and beyond the call of duty," Hendrix added.

The look on her face at that suggestion discouraged any of the other team members from bringing it up again. Dana was on the team. Period. Chris stepped out of the room at seven-fifteen to call Peter Lloyd. They had not really had much time to connect since the hostage situation arose.

"Ah, Dr. Black. Please hold on for a second." Chris could hear a number of voices in the background, then a closing of a door.

"Chris, are you still there?"

"I'm here. How is it going there?"

"Not well," explained Peter. "We have a number of families here. They are all understandably upset, and the rigors of international travel have not made that any easier."

"Lost bags and delayed flights?" asked Chris, knowing that both of those and more were common when connecting from any U.S. cities and the Galapagos.

"Exactly."

"What else? How has the university responded?"

"The university has done pretty well so far in my estimation," replied Peter. "They paid for all the families to come down, and they are working with the insurance company to figure out how to conduct negotiations with the pirates."

He took a deep breath as if to summon up the courage for what he had to say next.

"But the insurance company reps are not great, more functionaries than go-getters. You know the type."

"Yes, I do," said Chris. "What about the embassy and local law enforcement? I understand you met my friend Frank Donagan."

"I have. Mr. Donagan is an interesting fellow. He seems to think very highly of you."

"That would be news to me," said Chris. "Just when I think I might understand him, he takes a dramatic left turn. I'm pretty sure he's a spook."

"Donagan, a member of our clandestine services? I guess that makes sense. But we haven't received any direct support that I'm aware of from our federal agencies.

"And as to the locals," added Peter. "Not a lot of movement. I don't fully understand the inaction. Something untoward may be going on there."

Chris filed that last point away for later. "You sound beat. Are the families taking out their emotions on you?"

"I think we're all beat. But I haven't been racing around at sea in a storm chasing pirates. To your question, yes, there's been a little of that. But that is perfectly understandable. These people's children were in our care when this horrible thing happened. I think it would be strange if they weren't focusing some anger at me."

Chris felt the bottom drop out of his stomach at Peter's calm realization. It had been bothering him, and likely Mac too, every minute of the past forty-eight hours. Those students had been in their care.

Perceptive as always, Peter said, "That last bit was not for you. I'm sure you and Johnson are suffering every minute and assuming full responsibility. Don't. I'm the one who sent the boat south, and I'm the one who forced you two to join the trip at the last minute. This one is on me."

Chris was not going to let this all fall on Peter. Peter had made Chris's career possible. He owed him too much, both professionally and personally, to let him bear this alone. "We can debate that later," said Chris. "After we've got them all back alive and well."

"On that note, what can you tell me?"

Peter and Chris had worked together for years. Most of those years involved Chris or Mac getting into and out of a wide variety of challenging situations.

Over that time, Chris had learned what to tell Peter and what not to tell him. Plausible deniability was critical for Peter's role in helping from above.

"It's not good. You know about the boat we captured."

"And the hostage you rescued," interrupted Peter. "Well, done."

"Yes, well, the captain of that drunken operation decided to come clean," explained Chris, "and what he told us, if accurate, is definitely not good."

"So, where are you now?"

"We're at the hospital with Hendrix and his team coming up with a plan," said Chris.

"Is there anything I can do to help with that plan?" asked Peter.

"Thanks, but I think this falls into the category of things you should not know."

"I can't ask you and Johnson to risk yourselves to solve this. There are plenty of other people who are trained and paid to deal with these types of situations."

Chris knew that one was for the record. Neither he nor Peter had any faith in the process working itself out.

"You aren't asking, and we're going either way. I will not let those students get hurt, and we are not losing the *MacGreggor*." Letting anger creep into his voice, Chris admitted, "We know of at least seven people these ruthless pirates have already killed just in the last three weeks. They are going down."

"You're taking on too much, my boy."

"Don't worry about it, Peter. I won't be alone. Mac is easily as pissed as I am. So is our new colleague Dana. And Hendrix? Well, as you know, I've been afraid of Hendrix for years, and he is almost levitating out of his hospital bed with enthusiasm for this mission."

"I thought he was incapacitated," observed Peter.

"Oh, he is. But a major stab wound and a gunshot have done nothing but motivate him. He's not actually coming with us, but he's found ways to participate. I'll explain later."

"Okay. So, what can I do?" asked Peter.

"We need a few more hours to mobilize. We'll take satellite phones, cell phones, and marine radios with us. I need you to immediately notify me when the next contact comes in from the pirates."

"I can do that," said Peter. "Go get 'em, my boy."

31

Diegito, or 'Little James,' the tall pirate who'd decapitated his mate just for being friendly to the hostages, had earned that name by being the youngest of fourteen children back in the small town of Cali, Colombia. It hadn't helped that he didn't have a growth spurt until this fifteenth birthday.

Fourteen children had been too many for his impoverished family to support. Though there had never been any formal declaration, the children in the family all knew that they had to strike out on their own very early in order to help the family in any way that they could. Diegito had avoided anything associated with the Colombian drug trade for his first twelve years on the planet. He'd known that his father worked in the cacao fields seven days a week like so many of the men in their town, but no one in his family used drugs or talked about the drug trade. Diegito had made money selling recycled items to shop owners and periodically selling home-made bread to the few brave tourists who found their way to Cali.

All of that changed on his twelfth birthday. He'd come home from school that day so excited to see what his parents had in store for him. But immediately upon walking in the door of his small house, he could tell something was wrong. There were too many of his mother's friends in the kitchen. All were whispering, and their faces seemed so sad.

His mother circled the kids around her bed that afternoon and explained that their father had been killed earlier in the day. There had been a drug raid at the field where he was working. The government was working with the Americans. Several people had been caught in the crossfire between the army and the drug producers and were killed, his father among them. The army had buried the bodies in a mass grave, so the family did not have a body for a funeral.

His brothers and sisters had all acted out in different ways in response to their father's death. Within two years, all six of his brothers had died violent deaths themselves, two killed by rival drug lords fighting to retain a portion of the market share, two in shootouts with the police, and two due to drug overdoses. Diegito's sisters had each worked hard to keep him on the right side of the law. But eventually, when he was sixteen, the members of the cartel whom his father had worked for came to talk with him. They offered Diegito a job down along the ocean, meeting their boats at different ports or coves along the coastline to carry messages. His mother was horrified, but he took the job.

In the four years he was away from Cali, Diegito had grown eight inches and gained one-hundred and sixty pounds. He'd also made valuable connections among the many vessels that plied the waters of coastal Colombia.

When he finally came back home, he found the family once again in mourning. One of the men from the Cali cartel had beaten and killed his sister when she refused to marry him. Diegito had kissed his mother then walked down the narrow dirt streets to the bar where he knew the man would likely be at that time in the afternoon.

Finding the man sitting among more than a dozen of his colleagues, Diegito approached the man from behind as he sat drinking a beer. Before anyone realized what was about to happen, Diegito grabbed the man's head and twisted it quickly, instantly breaking the man's neck and killing him.

Guns had come out from all directions, but an older man sitting at the bar had yelled, "Stop!"

He'd looked at Diegito and said, "You get this one for free my boy, because this man deserved it. He should not have touched your sister. But leave this town and do not come back, or we will be forced to deal with you too."

Newly encouraged by his penchant for killing, Diegito briefly considered taking out as many of the men as he could right there. But he'd decided not to die that day, and fled Cali never to return. It hadn't taken him long to find work on one of the boats he'd dealt with for the cartel. His long-simmering enthusiasm for violence had served him well and his 'career' in piracy had taken off.

Now in a position of authority within the pirate empire commandeered from the *Silence,* Diegito stood on the bridge, high above the waterline. Looking out past the bow through tinted windows, he used a satellite phone to call his contact in the police department on Santa Cruz Island.

Without preamble, Diegito said, "You can tell them that the number is now fifteen-million dollars." He did not expect to receive that much money, but he liked the idea of making the Americans sweat. And perhaps they would come out of this with more money than he expected.

"We want the money transferred to this account within twenty-four hours," he continued and read off the numbers for the account in the Cayman Islands. "At twenty-four hours and one minute, if the money is not there, we will kill one hostage. And one after that every hour. Until the money arrives."

The contact, Arturo Lopez, a young lieutenant whose older sister had become entangled with the pirates on the mainland, responded, "I will relay this message, but
the negotiators are going to want to talk with you directly."

"Fine."

"And you realize that they are going to need more time?" asked Lopez.

"Your job is to relay our messages. Do so now."

Ending the call, Diegito realized that he didn't care whether the money came or not. He knew that keeping the members of their group employed cost a great deal of money, but he simply did not care. No matter how this situation would resolve, he was going to kill more people. If that meant Americans, fine. If that meant other pirates, well, he could do that too.

32

After a brief taxi ride back from the hospital, Chris, Mac, and Dana walked into the lobby of the Hotel Déjà Vu, simultaneously exhausted and ready for the next mission. Chris had felt the collective energy of the group peak as the final details of the plan came together. But that peak was followed by a wave of fatigue rolling over the trio, none of whom had had enough sleep for days.

Preoccupied with the goal of getting a few hours of rest before disembarking for Isabella Island and a potential encounter with the pirates, Chris almost missed them as he passed through the hotel's small lobby en route to the main staircase.

Immediately adjacent to the front desk was a small lounge area populated by comfortable, if well worn, sofa-like chairs. Sitting in two of those chairs, among several other hotel guests, were Abby Wilson's parents.

Chris had only met the couple once and would likely have walked right on by had they not been so obviously staring at him. To Mac and Dana, he said, "I'll meet you guys upstairs. Just leave the couch open for me and set your alarms for five."

Dana continued up the stairs. Mac looked past Chris to the older couple who were now standing and conspicuously looking his direction.

He did not recognize the people, but they had the look of concerned parents. "You got this?" he asked Chris.

"I do," said Chris. "Go get some sleep."

As Mac continued up the stairs, Chris walked over to meet them. The resemblance between Abby and her mother was uncanny. But he could also see how Abby took after her father as well, both of them sharing the same athletic build. "Mr. and Mrs. Wilson," Chris said, offering his hand.

Mrs. Wilson accepted the hand graciously, while Mr. Wilson used his strong grip to pull Chris in for an unanticipated hug.

Chris motioned toward the lower level of the lobby, where the empty chairs would give them some privacy.

"How are you doing, son?" asked Mr. Wilson.

"I'm okay, thanks."

"Was that Mac Johnson with you when you came in? His face looked like he's seen some action recently." Like Chris's father, Randall Wilson had fought in the Vietnam War. While Andrew Black had flown jets above the jungle, Randall Wilson had led a company of rangers down deep within the forests for two tours of duty.

"Yes, he has," said Chris. "But it isn't anything that Mac isn't used to."

The Wilson's exchanged a knowing glance. "Look, Chris, we don't want to take up too much of your time," Mr. Wilson said.

"We've already spoken with Dr. Lloyd several times, and he has given us as much information as he can," Mrs. Wilson added.

Chris nodded. "So how can I help you?"

Mrs. Wilson reached across and rested her hand on Chris's thigh. "We know that things haven't been easy for you and Abby."

"We know what you did to protect her back in Carmel," added Mr. Wilson. "And we know how she responded to that situation; that she never wanted to find herself in a similar situation."

"We could see how much she cared for you," Abby's mother said. "And still cares for you—"

Chris inhaled deeply. Even approaching forty years of age, thousands of miles from home, talking to someone else's parents, he could feel the protective envelope of parental concern.

"You know that Abby is all we have," Mr. Wilson said, his voice cracking and his eyes welling up with tears. "She's all we've got."

Watching Mr. Wilson struggle to keep his composure, Chris fought to hold back his own tears. A montage of complicated memories and emotions, many of which had nothing to do with the current situation stirred deep feelings. He thought of his unresolved issues with his father, the pain at the loss of his colleague and friend Gretchen, and the extraordinary loneliness that he'd felt since Abby had left him.

"How . . . how can I help?"

"Oh, my dear boy," Mrs. Wilson said. "Just by being yourself."

Chris looked up at that, making eye contact with both of Abby's parents.

"We know that you and Mac won't take this abduction sitting down," Mr. Wilson said.

"We have absolutely no right to ask this of you, Chris," Mrs. Wilson added. "But . . ."

". . . we want you to bring our girl home." Mr. Wilson reached into the interior pocket of his sports jacket and produced what Chris recognized as one of Abby's many swimming medals.

"Abby won this at the first meet she ever swam in. It was her freshman year in high school. The fifty-meter free. She demolished the competition. We were all so surprised by her victory that we laughed all the way home from the meet. Over the years, this medal took on new significance. When I was in the hospital with lung cancer, she gave me this medal to keep by my bedside. Since then, the three of us have passed it around a number of times, for a number of reasons."

He put a shaking hand to his eyes to wipe away an errant tear.

"I'm giving it to you now. And when you find our girl, which we know you will, I ask that you pass it back to her."

Chris opened his palm to accept the medal. It was much heavier than he expected, and cool to the touch despite having been in Mr. Wilson's pocket for an unknown length of time.

The Wilsons both stood, so Chris rose as well. Mrs. Wilson reached out and hugged Chris tightly, ending with a kiss on his cheek. Mr. Wilson hugged Chris much more fiercely, showing the considerable strength he still retained.

"I was a tough bastard once upon a time," he said as he released Chris. "And I can spot another one a mile away. I would feel even more guilt for asking this of you if I wasn't certain that you were going to go after her anyway. Bring her back to us, Chris."

"I will," said Chris, despite his concerns about being able to deliver on that promise.

The Wilsons walked up the short flight of stairs to the main lobby, then disappeared out the front door of the hotel.

Chris plopped back down in his chair and looked at the gold medal in his hands. He let it slip into his lap as he bent down and rested his face in his hands. And then, he wept.

33

The sun was barely over the morning horizon as Chris sat quietly on a bench along the waterfront. With all the supplies loaded aboard the *Tiburon*, the departure had been delayed by one of Mac's 'vital' last-minute errands. So, Chris had a few precious moments to just sit and wonder at the magic of the Galapagos. Even here, in the most populous place in the entire island chain, the rich ecological diversity that made the place so compelling found a way to express itself.

Laying spread out on the sidewalk before him was one of the Galapagos' most charismatic ambassadors, the marine iguana. Looking very much like much smaller versions of the *Godzilla* monster from his childhood, these peaceful vegetarian beasts were the only species of marine iguana in the world. In the water they appeared to swim with reckless abandon. On the beach, they were far more judicious in their use of energy, spending most of the time lying spread out on a rock, the sand, the sidewalk, or the road.

While Chris contemplated how cool he thought the iguanas were, a gull floated down in the morning breeze and alighted right on the iguana. The swallow-tailed gull, also endemic to the Galapagos, briefly looked down to assess exactly what it had landed on. But then it settled down and made no effort to move. The iguana also made no effort to respond to the gull's presence. From his seat, Chris was watching compounded Galapagosian endemism right before his eyes.

He was reminded of his last research trip to Israel. A colleague had taken Chris on a side trip to Jerusalem one day when the weather off-shore had prevented their dive operations. Chris had explained to his mom later that he'd been utterly unprepared for the experience. A conspicuously non-religious person, Chris had nevertheless been overwhelmed by the history captured within the city. Historical moments dating back thousands of years, things he'd only read about, had all taken place on the grounds he now tread. It was overwhelming.

Chris smiled, recalling his words to Mac, "I walked the twelve stations of the cross! I saw where Jesus fell to one knee as he labored up the hill with the crucifix, and where he was helped by a man from the crowd. I walked in Jesus' footsteps, for god's sake!"

"An interesting choice of words," Mac had replied.

His Israeli colleague, Aviad, had explained that his reaction was not unique. In fact, the emotional response to Jerusalem's religious significance was often so powerful that it had actually been designated a 'syndrome' in mental health manuals. People suffering from 'Jerusalem Syndrome' were known to spontaneously change into flowing white robes and speak in languages that hadn't been spoken in a thousand years or more. Some people recovered, some did not. And it was clear from the mental health manuals that underlying conditions could exacerbate the syndrome.

Sitting there, watching the iguana and the gull, Chris was reminded of his first trip to the Galapagos, and the power of the effect the islands had had on his psyche. He'd snorkeled within hours of arriving on San Cristobal Island in the very spot where Charles Darwin had first landed in the Galapagos on the voyage of the *Beagle*. He'd literally lain on the seafloor looking up at the very spot where the Beagle had moored.

The power of that moment had led Chris to coin the new term, 'Galapagos Syndrome,' to describe the effect of the islands on biologists from around the world. At least in his case, the syndrome had endured. For as crazy as the last three days had been, he was still aware of his presence in such a special place.

Mac appeared at his side and sat down. He was followed by Dana and one of Hendrix's men.

"Did you get what you needed?" asked Chris.

"I did, but more on that later. What are you doing?"

"Reflecting," explained Chris.

"Reflecting? On what exactly?"

"Last night."

"Right," said Mac. "The people in the lobby. Who were they?"

"Abby's parents," answered Chris.

Mac looked down and slowly shook his head. "Not your fault, man."

"What did they say?" asked Dana. "Did they blame you?"

"Not in so many words," said Chris. "They were actually very comforting, but at the same time they were asking me to find Abby."

"Jesus," Mac said.

He took the medal out of his pocket. "They gave me one of Abby's medals, for luck, I suppose. I am supposed to give it to her when we find her."

"What did you say?" Dana asked.

Chris looked up. "I told them we would."

34

Tonya Gordon was locked in a room on deck one of the *Silence*. She'd seen the name on the stern as they'd approached, her only connection to the outside world once again a single porthole located just above the waterline. The pirates had left her alone since moving her over to the larger ship. In her isolation, Tonya's concern for her daughter's welfare had overwhelmed any physical pain she'd endured. Her emotions constantly cycled, from worry to outright fear, then sadness and resolution, before returning to worry.

Tonya knew that the magnitude of her concern for Beth made Tom and Ben's deaths feel like distant memories, even though they'd only happened days ago. She tried to determine exactly how many days ago her horrible saga had begun, but she couldn't make much headway. She knew she'd been on this new boat for one night. But the number of days she'd been captive before then was hazy—it could have been anywhere from four days to a week.

Unlike the previous boat she was on, the walls of the *Silence* were insulated well, so she could not hear anything other than the rare conversation outside the stateroom's door. The porthole, and to a lesser extent the peephole in the door, provided her only means to accumulate any information at all. She had positioned the only chair in the stateroom in front of the porthole so she could watch nearly continuously. On the wall to the left of the porthole, Tonya used a pencil she'd recovered from a desk drawer to note the passage of any boats or landmarks as the *Silence* moved around. All observations were listed by day dating to her first day on the ship.

Much to her growing consternation, Tonya had allowed her brief co-captive to convince her that giving up the emergency money that she and Tom had hidden in the galley of the sailboat was a good idea. Maria had made what felt like a compelling argument at the time. She would use her Spanish language skills to lead the pirates to the money in exchange for their release.

As the hours piled up, Tonya doubted more and more whether she'd ever see Maria again. For all she knew, the woman had taken the money herself and somehow gotten away. Or, more likely, she'd used the money to buy her own freedom. By forsaking Tonya, Maria had forsaken Beth. And that was extremely difficult to accept.

Returning her thoughts to the porthole in front of her, Tonya could clearly see land very close by. She could not hear the sounds of the breaking waves, but given the proximity, she could virtually feel the waves' impact on the shore.

The sun was low on the horizon, but it was still making the glass of the porthole very hot to the touch. When the bow of a large white boat appeared in front of the window, about three hundred feet out from where she was sitting, Tonya could not believe it. She screamed out for help knowing full well that as she pounded on the glass, there was no chance that the boat would either hear her or stop for her.

The 'mega-yacht,' as Tonya thought of it, thinking back to boats she'd seen on TV shows she'd watched with Beth when she was younger, struck her as huge given the time it took to pass by her window. It also appeared to be slowing down, which gave Tonya great hope.

She could clearly see the staff piloting the large vessel from the uppermost deck. The two men were in uniform and carried themselves like military, or former military, confirming for Tonya that it was indeed a 'mega yacht.' As the stern of the vessel passed slowly by, she could see what looked like the words *Tiburon*.

"I think that means 'shark,'" Tonya mumbled to herself.

On the stern of the middle deck, she could see a couple sitting in a Jacuzzi or hot tub, laughing. The woman had shoulder-length brown hair and was very tan. The man had short dark hair, some grey visible at the temples. He turned toward the boat and appeared to be looking right at Tonya with a brilliant smile.

35

Standing in the corner of the captain's cabin, which was situated just aft of the bridge on the *Silence*, Diegito watched through tinted glass as the *Tiburon* moved past. He was not focused on the boat or its occupants. Few things in his violent life concerned Diegito any longer and he did not perceive any threat from gringos on a fancy gringo yacht. The focus of his concern was right there in the room, on his own well-being and that of his comrades.

Diegito did not have friends. But he had worked alongside many of the pirates on board for many years, and he didn't despise all of them. Santiago, for instance, had once saved Diegito from jail by bribing two Ecuadorian coast guard officers after they'd been caught stealing a boat in Guayaquil. Diegito had appreciated that, even if he'd never shown that appreciation. He was concerned now that he would never have the chance.

Santiago was kneeling on the floor in the middle of the room, directly in front of the captain's desk. Diegito was familiar with what might happen next. As he watched the scene unfold before him, he could see Santiago's body shake visibly.

"Santiago? Santiago," said the captain, getting up from the desk to walk the room. "Are you paying attention? Your job was a simple one:

take the *Innovator* to the meet with the Coast Guard and deliver the contents in the hold.

"But you did not do that, did you? No. You chose to assign it to that idiot Raul Sanchez and his crew of drunks. And now what do I hear? The boat was captured. And how was it captured? With NO LOSS OF LIFE! Those idiots didn't even put up a fight."

Pointing in the general direction of Puerto Ayora, the captain continued, "They didn't put up a fight, and now they are in custody. Custody!"

Santiago cringed under the verbal onslaught from the captain.

"Do you know what was in the hold, Santiago?"

Santiago shook his head.

"No? Well, I'll tell you, cash and merchandise worth a half-million dollars. And do you know why it was in the hold of that boat?"

Santiago whimpered; his response inaudible.

"What? Was that a 'no,' you worthless piece of filth?"

The captain turned towards Diegito. "Your knife, please."

Without hesitation, Diegito handed the captain the knife.

"I'll tell you why, Santiago," continued the captain. "It was a payoff to keep the Ecuadorian authorities off our backs."

The captain circled the man kneeling on the floor.

"So now, due to your idiocy, we have lost all the money I sent on the *Innovator*, and we may have lost our contact in the Coast Guard," the captain said. "That contact was not easy to establish. And it may take years to make it possible again. Years we don't have."

Diegito smelled what he thought was urine coming from Santiago.

"What should I take from you, Santiago?" asked the captain, patting Santiago on the top of the head with the flat side of the knife. "What do *you* suggest I take? I could take a finger, I could take your head, or I could take something in between."

Santiago started to cry, his shoulders vibrating with every whimper.

The captain looked down at Santiago with an expression that Diegito could not read.

After several moments, using the tip of the knife to lift Santiago's chin, the captain said, "Maybe I'll let you go this time. I think you've learned your lesson."

Santiago's shoulders seemed to relax for a brief second and Diegito contemplated that perhaps Santiago was going to make it out of the room alive.

Suddenly, the captain reversed the knife and slashed across Santiago's throat. Blood poured out onto the carpet from between Santiago's fingers, which had instinctively reached up to stop the bleeding. In seconds he had lost too much blood to maintain his kneeling position and dropped to the floor.

"Take this waste out of my sight," the captain demanded. "And get the woman in here."

36

Two decks above Tonya Gordon's stateroom, and two decks below the captain's office, Abby Wilson stood in an empty storage room watching out the window. She had been taken from the lab on the *MacGreggor* some time before with no explanation. She could hear guards talking outside her door.

Oliver Chumley-Smith had regained consciousness earlier that morning and tried to talk to her.

"I'm sorry that I wasn't able to help, Abby." Oliver's words were barely audible despite the relative quiet of the room.

"Nonsense, there isn't anything that you could've done," Abby had responded, wiping Oliver's forehead. "These people are vicious."

"Perhaps, but I don't imagine Chris and Mac are going to take this sitting down." He tried to adjust his position but could not summon the strength to lift himself up.

"No," Abby had said, "I don't imagine that they will. And I hope for our sakes that they don't."

"I wish . . . I wish—" Oliver had passed out again without completing the sentence.

Abby had begged the pirates to allow her to stay with the wounded man, but they'd paid her no heed and dragged her away and onto another vessel.

Suddenly the door to the storage room opened again, revealing the large dreadlocked pirate. Abby instantly recoiled at the sight of the violent man, recalling his threat about 'visiting' her. She moved as far away from him as the room allowed.

The man ducked his head as he entered and quickly crossed to Abby. He grasped her upper arm in his huge hand, which easily encircled her bicep. "We are going to meet the captain. You are to shut up and do as you're told. Speak only when you are asked."

Just being in the presence of the brutal man made it difficult for Abby to focus beyond her fear.

"Do you understand me?"

"Yes," Abby replied, unwilling to make eye contact with the man.

He propelled her out the door and up two flights of stairs. Then the pirate opened a door on the right, pushing Abby into the room, "Here she is, Capitan."

As Abby stumbled in, she immediately noticed the large pool of what looked like fresh blood spread on the floor at her feet. Someone had obviously been killed right where she was standing, and very recently.

She did not dare look up, but her mind processed the information rapidly. The only member of their group she hadn't seen since the beginning of the attack was the *MacGreggor's* Captain Dennis. Was it his blood? Of course, she'd also seen them kill one of their own right in front of her.

A voice in front of Abby commanded her to look up. When she did, she stared right into the burning grey eyes of a woman. She instantly recognized the tattooed woman she'd met earlier. Abby could now see that the tattoos contained several variations on the skull and crossbones so common in pirate lore. Her heart filled with despair when she realized that Maria, the woman she'd thought was a fellow captive, was the captain commandeering the pirate ship.

The woman's eyes betrayed nothing but hate. In that moment, Abby gave up all hope. Chris and Mac were not coming to save them. Why would they? She'd responded with nothing but disdain the last time they had risked their lives to ensure her safety.

"It's Abby, is it not?" said the captain.

Abby nodded.

"Good." Motioning toward the floor around Abby, the captain continued, "As you can see, we've already had a troublesome day. I recommend that you do not contribute to my irritation. Do you understand?"

Abby tried to recall what she'd told the woman but couldn't remember much of the conversation. She hoped she had not betrayed any information that would now be used against her and the students in her care.

"Yes, I understand."

"Fine. Now, where is the phone?"

"Here, Capitan," said Diegito as he handed the captain one of the several satellite phones on board. He then forced Abby down onto her knees amidst the blood.

Abby felt the blood soaking through her pants and struggled against her desire to scream.

"Is it going to work this time?" asked the captain. "If it does not work . . ."

"It should work, Capitan," said Diegito, looking down at his hand. "We tested it just a few minutes ago." Satellite phones were designed to function nearly anywhere on the earth's surface, but despite that promise, they frequently failed to perform.

The captain took the phone, looked at a piece of paper on the desk, and punched in a phone number.

Abby could hear a garbled male voice answered the call on speakerphone.

With no preamble, the captain said, "Where are we on the ransom?"

"We are working on it," said the man. "Fifteen million dollars is a lot of money. We need more time."

"You've had more than enough time," said the captain. "I expect a call at this number by sundown; in one hour. And I want to hear that the money has been transferred to our account. "If the call doesn't come or we don't have our money, I'm going to kill the woman in front of me first, and then follow shortly after with her weakling friend."

The voice on the other end of the phone could be heard speaking to people in the background. Then he turned back to the phone. "We want to speak to the woman."

"Fine," said the captain. She came around the front of the desk and held the satellite phone out toward Abby. "Speak!"

"Hello?" Abby said.

"Who is this?" asked the man on the phone. Abby did not recognize his voice.

"My name is Abby Wilson. I'm one of the instructors on the *MacGreggor*."

"Ms. Wilson, my name is Frank Donagan. Are you hurt?"

"No," replied Abby. "But Oliver Chumley-Smith is in very bad shape."

"What about the students?"

"That's enough!" interjected the captain. "No students have been hurt . . . yet. Go find our money and make the call."

"Satellite phone calls are not reliable out here in the islands," Frank Donagan said. "We don't want someone killed due to a dropped call. We propose that you start calling us in an hour and keep calling until you get through."

The captain's eyes surveilled the room as she exhaled loudly. "Fine. But you'd better have our money."

Diegito effortlessly lifted Abby off the floor and returned her to the storage room. Hearing the door close behind her, Abby tensed her upper body against the assault she knew was coming. She could feel a scream building in her throat. It took several moments for her to realize that she was alone in the room. No attack was coming.

Briefly relieved of the immediate need to defend herself, she moved over to the window, bracing herself on the windowsill as stress drained from her. Staring out the window, Abby estimated that she was at least twenty feet above the waterline. She watched the ocean below, allowing herself to become transfixed by its undulating movements. The storm-driven rains had stopped briefly, and the light that danced over the waves took her mind far from her current situation to her home back in Monterey.

When she'd moved to California, from the east coast, one of the first things Abby had done was purchase a sea-going kayak and a rack for her car to carry it. At first, getting the kayak onto the roof rack had been a formidable challenge. But Chris and Mac had taught her a few tricks that ultimately allowed her to do it alone. And despite her considerable workload at the CMEx, Abby had been able to spend many hours on the Monterey Bay surrounded by whales, otters, sea lions, and even a white shark from time to time, all within an easy paddle from shore. It was easily as extraordinary as these Galapagos Islands, she thought. Just more familiar, and thus less exotic. It was home, and that's where she desperately wanted to be.

Abby slowly became aware of the bow of a large white yacht coming into her peripheral vision. As she watched it slowly cruise along, she assumed that it was yet another conquest by the pirates. But as the bridge passed by, she noticed that the men at the helm did not look like pirates at all.

Abby scrutinized the boat as it slowly moved past her. When the back deck and the couple luxuriating in the hot tub came into sight, she first thought she was hallucinating. She had to reach out and place one palm on the glass to steady herself. She didn't recognize the woman, but there was no mistaking the man who was holding up a glass of wine as though he didn't have a care in the world.

It was Chris Black. And he was coming for them.

37

Steaming past the large black vessel in such close proximity that it briefly blocked out the sun, Chris Black reflected on the outsized role the ship had taken in his mind. He'd begun to fixate on the ship as an omnipresent phantom lurking along the horizon like a predator. However, while the ship now represented an even greater immediate threat, seeing it up close also demystified it for Chris. As he took in details of the hull and its upper decks, the reality of the challenge before them became more tractable.

As they passed the stern of the black ship, the *MacGreggor* became visible on the other side. He could feel his muscles tense in anticipation.

"The *Silence*?" said Mac from a crouched position below the window on the upper deck of the *Tiburon*. "You've got to be kidding me."

"What?" asked Chris. He'd exited the jacuzzi and was now sitting at a table with Dana three feet away from Mac. Unlike Mac, they were conspicuously visible, drinking apple juice from wine glasses and going through the motions of playing backgammon.

"It's a pirate ship, for god's sake," said Mac. Making air quotes with his fingers as he explained, "Dead men tell no tales, and all that."

"Ah, right."

"I wonder," added Mac, "if they've got a 'jolly roger' up there too. And maybe some swords."

The *Tiburon* was anchored approximately twelve-hundred feet from the *Silence*, close enough inshore that from their anchorage, the team could also see the *MacGreggor* tied up to the larger ship's starboard side. They were also close enough to shore to see the marine iguanas coming and going from the rocky intertidal area into the sea.

"It's a big ship," noted Dana as she rolled double sixes. "I estimate a full crew complement of thirty for a vessel of that size, with room for another sixty."

"Right," said Chris as he rolled a one and three. "That syncs with what the captured pirate told us. But I doubt that they're following regulations. Do we think they'll have more or fewer than thirty?"

"My bet is fewer," said Mac.

"I agree," said Dana, taking a sip of her apple juice. "But even half that number is still an awful lot of hostiles in a relatively small area."

"I didn't see much activity during our earlier 'fly by,'" said Chris. "Neither on the *Silence* nor on the *MacG*. It's difficult to know what is going on over there."

"They're almost certainly watching us now," observed Dana, rolling double sixes yet again. "I wouldn't be surprised if they are considering how to capture this boat too. It would make a great prize for them."

"Yeah, I'll bet there are more eyes on us than we can see," Mac added. "The approach here is going to be more challenging than it was on Genovesa."

At that moment, Frank Donagan stepped out onto the back deck wearing an attendant's uniform. "I agree with Mr. Johnson. But there is now some urgency."

Chris had been stunned when Donagan had appeared at the dock back in Puerto Ayora dressed and geared up for a fight. His experience with

Donagan in Cape Town had suggested that he preferred to work behind the scenes. But Chris had realized that Donagan was not at all predictable.

Chris accepted a cheese plate from Donagan and asked, "Do we have word from Peter about the ransom demand?"

"Not exactly," said Donagan, going through the motions of collecting used wine glasses from the table.

"Not exactly?" asked Chris and Mac simultaneously.

Donagan explained as he poured apple juice from a wine bottle into Dana's glass. "The pirates did indeed contact the negotiators again. And they've articulated further demands. But I didn't get the information from Dr. Lloyd."

"You're tapping their line?" Mac asked.

"No, I spoke to them directly," said Donagan. "We had the call routed to the mobile communication unit I brought with me down in the galley."

Chris watched the sun disappear below the horizon that was now increasingly clear of clouds. "What did they demand?"

"They want the money transferred within an hour . . . actually now fifty minutes . . . or they're going to start killing hostages." Donagan busied himself, wiping imaginary crumbs off the table. "I also spoke directly to Ms. Wilson."

"You spoke to Abby?" asked Chris, his mind racing. "How was she? What did she say?"

"She indicated that she is uninjured. But apparently, Mr. Chumley-Smith needs medical attention."

"What about the students?" asked Chris, feeling immense relief at the knowledge that Abby was still okay.

"We were cut off before I was able to learn anything else."

Chris fought the urge to jump into action. "I think we need to put plan B into play immediately." Glancing back at the horizon, he added. "The light is going fast, so we should have some cover pretty quickly."

"I concur," said Donagan.

"Dana, Mac, and I will take one of Hendrix's guys and swim over to the *MacG*," said Chris. "If the students are still there, we'll get them off. If they've been moved, we'll use the *MacG* as a staging point to board the *Silence*."

"Why not take both of Hendrix's guys?" asked Mac.

"Because, to Dana's earlier point, we know from our previous experience that these pirates have other boats around, and they're not afraid to attack vessels like this one, particularly if they think it's an easy target."

"Good point," added Donagan. "In fact, we learned just before we left port that the hold of the vessel you captured, the *Innovator*, was full of money and merchandise."

"So, the captured pirate actually gave us accurate intel," noted Mac. "That's interesting."

"Yes, that appears to be the case," answered Donagan.

"Okay, let's do it," said Chris as he conspicuously leaned over and kissed Dana on the cheek.

"You know . . . in case we're being watched. Needs to look authentic." Dana looked back at Chris, the edges of her mouth hinting at a smile. "If that was for the sake of the pirates, we should probably give them a better show next time."

38

Diegito stuck his knife into the starboard rail of the *Silence* as he stood watching the three pirates he'd hand-picked to sink the captured vessel lower themselves down onto the *MacGreggor's* back deck. Personally, he thought the boat was too valuable to sink; it could serve as a useful complement to the larger and less maneuverable *Silence*. But the captain had indicated she wanted it sunk, and Diegito was in no mood to challenge her, for now.

Maria del Carmen was neither a doctor, as she'd told Tonya Gordon, nor a lawyer, as she'd told Abby. She was the daughter of a politician from Mexico City. Maria had grown up in a gated community high on a hillside above the city. She'd told Diegito on many occasions how much she loved her parents, but that she'd been raised by one governess after another as her parents traveled continuously for her father's job.

When Maria had reached the age of eighteen, she'd moved to the United States to get a bachelor's degree in business at the University of Pennsylvania.

It was in her junior year at Penn that her life took a major turn. That year her father was indicted, along with several other members of the administration, on bribery and racketeering charges. Maria never knew whether the charges were legitimate or not, but she learned that it didn't matter. In the dark world of Mexican politics, her father was cast aside, stripped of his office, and ultimately jailed.

With the patron of the family in jail, the financial status of the family declined precipitously. Although from a different social class altogether, Diegito could relate all too well. Like Diegito, Maria had been forced to alter her life. She took up with a man she'd met in Puerto Vallarta in the hopes that something good would come from it. He, in turn, had introduced her to the life of modern piracy. Initially, she'd been appalled and horrified by the activities of the man and his crew. But over time she began to see it less as violent and perverse and more as an opportunity. Once Maria had tapped into her business acumen she'd acquired in her years at Penn and applied it to piracy, everything took on a new light for her. And she also learned that she had a penchant for violence when it was necessary. Another point Diegito understood intimately.

When her partner's crew had sought to turn on him after months of failed raids, Maria had recognized the impending mutiny before it happened. When the crew came to confront the captain, with Maria standing at his side, she'd made a choice. Drawing a knife from under her jacket, she'd killed the captain before the crew had a chance to do so. She then took the opportunity to lay out a new set of rules and an ambitious plan for growing the pirate business.

The pirates, many of whom lacked any formal education, were completely caught off guard by Maria's actions. Faced with a choice, they chose to join her rather than kill her. Since that moment, two decades before, Maria had strategically nurtured the mythology around her ascendance to the captaincy. She'd taken every opportunity to violently advance that mythology: cutting off fingers, limbs, and heads whenever necessary.

Maria's approach to piracy was bolstered by her enthusiasm for history. She'd learned that the most prolific pirate of all time was not some European male with a colored beard wreaking havoc in the Caribbean, but a quiet Chinese woman named Ching Shih. Ching Shih had commanded hundreds of vessels and literally tens of thousands of men during the nineteenth century. She'd terrorized China's seas for decades and profited considerably.

Maria's empire, by comparison, was small, numbering in the tens of vessels and hundreds of men. And after peaking a decade ago, the volume of incoming wealth had steadily decreased. That decrease had necessitated an increasing number of raids of negligible utility that were designed primarily to keep her men busy. The concept of a raid on a large vessel and the subsequent plan for a ransom had been suggested to Maria by a contact in the Colombian Navy. He'd suggested she contact a colleague in Ecuador, who, in turn, had told Maria of the forthcoming trip south by the *MacGreggor*.

Another key element of Maria's approach to piracy had been the inclusion of large, conspicuously tough-looking guys in her inner circle. During the first two days that she'd worked with Diegito years earlier, she observed people assuming that he was the captain.

Far from irritated, Maria had instantly recognized the opportunities provided by playing to people's assumptions. Diegito had been her first mate since then.

Looking at the knife, standing tall with nearly an inch of its razor-sharp tip embedded in the rail, Diegito wondered what it would be like to assume command of the pirate empire. He had no doubt that he could match the captain's ferocity and her willingness to kill. No doubt at all. But he also knew that keeping the business going required more than just violence. Having closely observed both the cocaine trafficking industry as well as these pirates for most of his life, Diegito wasn't sure if he had that in him. He had never shared that concern with anyone because there was no one to share it with. Perhaps someday, he reflected.

Taking in the view from his position on the upper deck, Diegito was confident in the night's operations. The sun had set an hour earlier, and with only a few visible lights from the *Silence,* and the yacht off to the right, the night sky was pitch black. The stars were coming out, but with no moon it was going to be a dark night. Perfect, he thought, for what had to happen next.

They would sink the boat and collect the ransom. After that, they'd dispose of the captives and leave the Galapagos before the authorities would discover them. He knew that the captain had invested enough money in bribes to the right people to ensure that there would be no surprise raids on the *Silence* this night. She was very good at that.

39

From the shadows of the *MacGreggor's* back deck, Chris, Mac, Dana, and H1, which is how Chris and Mac referred to the man who'd joined them from Hendrix's team, watched as the three pirates climbed down a rope ladder from the *Silence*. Two pirates disappeared down through hatches on the deck into the engine room below, while the third made his way forward, entering the door into one of the labs.

Chris could see a fourth man looking down from the rail above. Even in the dark, the man's large size was evident. Once he moved away from the rail, Chris signaled to his colleagues, and they split up.

Slowly moving past the ROV toward the door of the external lab, Chris could discern a large dark spot on the deck that looked very much like blood. As he moved into the lab, he heard Mac's voice in his earpiece. "Target 1 down."

Seconds later, H1 reported, "Target 2 down."

The limited moonlight streaming in through the open door illuminated a chaotic scene in the lab. Chris noted PFDs and gumby suits spread out around the floor. As he crept through the cluttered room, he came upon a pile of what looked like used dressings. Was this where Chumley-Smith was cared for?

Dana announced on the radio, "Target 3 down."

Chris breathed a sigh of relief. "Let's rendezvous on the bridge in five minutes, over."

"Copy that," came three replies.

Meeting at the bridge after a quick search of the *MacGreggor's* main deck, Chris explained to the group, "No one is here. I checked everywhere. They must have moved everyone to the *Silence*. Did anyone catch those large stains on the back deck?"

"I did," whispered Mac. "Not good, but we don't know what happened. Let's stay positive."

"Right," replied Chris, looking at the luminescent dial on his dive watch. "Time to go to plan B."

"Actually, I have a new idea on that," Mac replied. "When was the last time you saw *The Wizard of Oz*?"

"Hold that thought, Mac," said Chris, looking at the pirate Dana had tied up and adjusting the plan on the fly. "We've got a chance to get some intel first."

"Good idea," said Mac, quickly grasping what Chris was suggesting. "We get their intel, then we get their clothes."

"Their clothes?" asked Dana.

Chris could see where Mac was going. "Copy that."

H1 agreed. "Mac and I will head back to the engine room. We'll report back shortly."

Fifteen-minutes later, Chris keyed his mic to speak with Donagan back on the *Tiburon*. "The *MacG* is secured. She's ready to move, but we need to keep her here to offload the hostages, all of which appear to have been moved to the *Silence*."

"Copy that," replied Donagan.

"We're moving forward with plan B," said Chris. They'd removed the clothes from the three captured pirates and then revived each of them for interrogation.

Mac chimed in from down in the hold. "My guy down here was not cooperative at first, but I think we understand each other better now. He says he has personally observed all the students jammed into one suite on deck two of the *Silence*. For what it's worth, I believe him. He thinks Abby and Chumley-Smith are with the captain. He was not nearly as confident in this information."

"My guy says the same," added Dana, who was standing next to Chris. "At least about the students. He didn't indicate anything about the whereabouts of anyone else."

"That's confirmation of sorts, at least for the students," Chris said.

"My guy doesn't know where the hostages are," H1 explained. "But he says he works for one of the leaders, a man named Diegito. He says we can expect up to twenty pirates on board the *Silence*. It would've been more, but you three culled the herd over the past few days at Darwin and Genovesa Islands."

Using the night vision goggles aboard the *Tiburon*, Donagan, and H2 had seen no movement above decks on the *Silence* and reported as much over the radio.

"Any other vessel traffic of any kind on radar?" asked Chris, wondering about any other pirate boats that might rendezvous with the *Silence*.

"Negative," replied H2, Hendrix's other guy on the *Tiburon* with Donagan. "The pattern is clear."

"Donagan, we're going in," Chris announced over the radio. "They left a rope ladder down to the *MacG's* back deck. We'll use it to get on board and then spread out from there. Also," he added, "though the *MacG* is completely powered down, the *Silence* is running its generators while at anchor and they're pretty loud. Given the darkness and the generator noise, you should have good cover. As soon as we're on board, you two take one of the inflatables from the *Tiburon* and motor over here to the *MacG*. Power her up and be ready."

"Copy that," H2 said.

"Good hunting," Donagan added.

Mac's plan involved sneaking on board the *Silence* wearing the captured pirates' clothing over their own a la *The Wizard of Oz*.

"I'm the Tinman," Mac announced as they were meeting at the rope ladder on the stern.

"Oh, I don't think so. You're definitely the Lion."

'If I'm the Cowardly Lion, who are you?"

"I am the Storm," said Chris.

"What?"

"Later. Now shut up and let's go."

They quietly climbed the rope ladder. "Nocturnal assault number three. We should have knives in our teeth for this."

"That's a great idea," whispered Chris. "Less talking that way."

Chris, Mac, and H1 safely ascended the ladder one at a time and boarded the *Silence* without being noticed. Dana covered them from down on the *MacGreggor*. Once they confirmed that the coast was clear, they signaled for Dana to join.

Looking over toward the *Tiburon*, Chris could not see or hear Donagan on the inflatable, but he knew it was coming. He looked briefly overhead as well but could see nothing but stars.

Dana was still climbing the rope ladder when a nearby door burst open. Two pirates emerged, bathed briefly from a light source inside the ship. H1 was able to slip behind a lifeboat station, but Mac and Chris were completely exposed with no place to go.

The door closed and the deck returned to darkness. It took the two pirates several seconds to adjust their eyes. In that time, Chris and Mac closed the distance.

"Hey! You heard the captain's orders, nobody on the outer decks," yelled one of the pirates, in Spanish. "Get back inside!"

"Si, si," said Chris as he stepped to within range of the nearest pirate. Slipping on the brass knuckles he'd found on the *D-fens*, Chris jabbed out at the man's throat, crushing his larynx. The pirate uttered a raspy gurgling sound, grabbing the railing with one hand to steady himself. Chris followed the jab with a punch to the pirate's gut, doubling him up. With the pirate bent partially over the rail, Chris knelt down, grabbed the man's legs, and tossed him over the side.

The splash below was barely audible

The second pirate, while still trying to process what he'd just seen happen, moved to the rail and looked over. Chris could hear a brief pop as the pirate's head snapped back from the force of Dana's bullet.

"Dana, I'm at the rail. Don't shoot."

"Copy that."

Chris looked over the side. Dana was ten feet down. Her left arm was woven into the rope ladder, supporting her weight, while her right hand, holding her automatic pistol, pointed upward and swept back and forth as she looked for additional targets. Each member of the team carried a variety of weapons, including automatic pistols equipped with silencers. Dana had explained that the silencers weren't actually very silent, but the large ship's generators should help considerably. "Silencers work best against a backdrop of other ambient noise."

"Come on up," urged Chris, while Mac lifted the body of the other pirate and tossed it over the side.

Dana crested the rail as H1 rejoined them. All four knelt, covered in the darkness.

"That was close." Mac wiped his brow.

"Okay, split up," said Chris. "Students first. We find and secure them, then the others. Keep your coms live."

Mac and H1 moved off toward the bow. Chris and Dana ran aft several feet to a staircase and ascended to the next deck up.

JAMES LINDHOLM

Chris tested the knob on the first door they encountered. The blackened windows made it difficult to know if they were going to step into a fully lighted room full of angry pirates or an empty passageway.

Determining that the door opened in, Chris signaled three-two-one and then pushed open the door.

Dana moved in, her gun out. Two pirates were walking down a passage toward her; with two bullets she dropped both men where they stood.

"Two more down," whispered Chris into his radio as he and Dana moved forward silently. Dana opened a door to a storage room, and Chris dragged each dead pirate inside.

"Okay, passageway ahead to the right."

Chris poked his head around the corner. A narrow corridor extended forward toward the bow. Illumination came from a few functioning overhead lights that were distributed unevenly down the corridor. Taking in the number of rooms they might have to search, Chris was not happy. This could eat up a lot of time.

He motioned forward, and they slowly passed by the first four doors, listening for any sound of activity inside. At the fifth door on the port-side Chris, signaled a stop with his fist. He thought he heard a woman's voice inside.

Mac's voice came over the radio. "Two more down. No sign of the students."

"We're on board the *MacGreggor*," Donagan joined in. "Proceeding to the bridge."

Chris and Dana listened at the door and decided to go in. Chris twisted the doorknob and found it unlocked. In seconds they were in, Chris leading the way.

The room was illuminated by a small reading light on the headboard above the bed. On the bare mattress was a woman lying in the fetal position. Chris didn't recognize her. He was about to speak to her when the bathroom door to his right opened. A very large, dreadlocked man began stepping out. The mutual surprise was self-evident, but Chris was faster to respond. He struck out with the side of his pistol, hitting the man right between the eyes. The man fell backward onto the toilet, unconscious.

Chris checked the pirate for weapons, noting a tattoo on the man's forearm that read 'Diegito.' He found a large knife strapped to the man's thigh, and a pistol jammed in his belt. Chris removed the weapons, pushed the man's legs out of the way, and closed the bathroom door.

Dana moved past Chris to speak to and comfort the woman who was staring at them, her eyes wide open in shock. "It's okay. We're here to help. My name is Dana and this is Chris. Can you sit up?"

The woman was clearly disoriented and struggled to sit up. "They . . . took my daughter . . . killed my friends."

"Can you tell me your name?" asked Dana, using one hand to support the woman's back and the other to hold her left hand.

"Tonya. Tonya Gordon."

Dana caught Chris's eye. She gently squeezed the woman's hand as she reached a sitting position and said, "Tonya, what is your daughter's name?"

"Elizabeth. But we call her Beth."

"Tonya," said Chris, as he kneeled down by the bed. "We found Beth on a boat called *Innovator* two days ago. She's safe back on Santa Cruz Island."

Instantly Tonya was alert, her wide eyes looking back and forth between Chris and Dana. "Beth . . . Beth is safe? What are you talking about? How did you find her? Were you looking for us?"

"We're searching for our friends. They were abducted on our research vessel several days ago. We tracked them to an island but found only the *Innovator.*"

Tonya grabbed Dana's upper arm as tears welled up in her eyes. "You're certain she's safe?"

"She is," said Dana, smiling. "I spent time with her in the hospital. She's a strong young woman."

"Yes, she is," replied Tonya, smiling for the first time in days. "Much stronger than her mother."

"I don't know about that." Dana smiled as she embraced the woman's shoulders.

Chris took in the surroundings. By the window he found a wall covered with what looked like observations scrawled in pen. He pulled out a GoPro camera from his left thigh pocket and took several photos of the notes on the wall.

"I made those notes," Tonya said. "I've written down everything I've seen go past my window for days."

"Have you seen any other hostages on board? Did anyone come on board within the past few days?"

"Not on board this boat," she replied. "But there was another woman locked up with me briefly on another boat. I think that was several days ago."

"What did she look like?" asked Chris. "Was her hair auburn?"

Tonya furrowed her brow as though struggling to remember. "No. This woman's hair was bleached blonde."

Chris moved toward the door, listening for any activity in the passageway. Hearing none, he keyed his mic. "Mac, we've just found Beth's mother. We're continuing toward the bow."

There was no reply.

"Mac?"

Moving quickly now, the trio moved up the passageway. Chris estimated that they were halfway to the bow when the jarring klaxon sound of the fire alarm erupted all around them.

Dana turned to see the large pirate standing in the hallway behind them with his hand on the fire alarm. She lifted her weapon and fired twice. The second shot hit him in the upper chest, and he went down.

"Damn! We've got to move," she said.

40

Running down the hall of the darkened pirate ship, trailing one rescued hostage, looking for twenty more, and wondering about his friend Mac who wasn't responding to radio calls, Chris felt anxiety building in his chest. But as he reached the staircase at the bow, he recalled one of his father's many lessons.

"Chris, at some point, you're going to find yourself in the midst of a crisis. It will seem as if everything is spiraling out of control. But if you remain calm, if you avoid letting everything around you become conflated, you can find your way out of any situation."

Chris smiled at that recollection and took a deep calming breath.

"What?" asked Dana from behind him.

"Nothing. I'll tell you later."

The fire alarm stopped. It took Chris's ears a few seconds to adjust to the quiet. He could hear distant voices coming from the direction of the bow.

"Tonya, we need to keep you safe. We're going to give you a weapon." Motioning to the door at his right, Chris continued, "You should hide in this stateroom until we come back for you. And we *will* come back for you."

"Okay," said Tonya. "Be careful. They're horrible people."

"We know," said Chris, looking directly into Tonya's eyes. "But they don't know what they're up against this time."

Chris handed Dana the gun he'd taken from Diegito. She expertly ejected the magazine from the handle and cleared the chamber of any bullets. Slamming the magazine back, she said to Tonya, "Have you ever used a gun before?"

"Yes, many times," replied Tonya. "My ex-husband was a fanatic."

"Okay, good," said Dana, handing Tonya the pistol. "Here you go. Now please lock yourself in and wait for us to come get you."

Chris grabbed a Sharpie out of his vest pocket and wrote down the number of the room on the inside of this left forearm.

"Good idea," noted Dana.

With Tonya secured out of sight, Chris and Dana were free to quickly move toward the bow. According to what the captured pirate had said, the students should be immediately in front of them, one deck above.

"Mac, if you can hear me, we're on our way."

"I think Mac's radio's out," H1 responded. "The hostages are indeed one deck above you, in a salon just aft of the bridge, on the port side. We were about to move on them when we started taking fire. We pushed the firefight to the upper decks, away from the students."

"We found a hostage, but no sign of Abby or Chumley-Smith yet. Do you need assistance?"

"Negative. Go for the students."

H2 chimed in via the radio, "Donagan and I are now on-board. We'll find our way to you to help with the students."

"Repeat. You're on-board the *Silence*?" asked Chris as he pressed his finger to his earpiece. That was not part of the plan.

Donagan responded, breathing heavily, "That's affirmative. We secured the *MacG*. But when the alarm bells sounded, we figured you guys might need a hand. So, we climbed on-board."

"Roger that," said Chris.

Chris and Dana continued up the forward staircase, stopping one deck below the bridge.

"Do you think that big guy back there was the captain of this bunch?" Chris whispered to Dana.

"Hard to say what passes for leadership around here," she replied. "If he is, then perhaps the rest of them will lose their motivation now that their leader is down."

"Or they'll panic and lose it. We'd better hurry. Now that we've lost the element of surprise, we don't know what the pirates will do with the hostages."

41

Abby and Dennis bumped shoulders as they were pushed at gunpoint into a cabin by the captain and another pirate.

"Who is attacking us?" the captain screamed over the clanging alarm.

Abby turned to see Roberto and Terra sitting on the floor, administering aid to Oliver Chumley-Smith amongst the other sixteen students huddled around the bed on the floor. The fire alarm continued to sound in deafening bursts from the hallway beyond.

Closing the door, the captain screamed again over the clanging alarm, "Who is attacking us?"

"What?" replied the other pirate, leaning closer and cupping his hand to his ear.

The captain moved across the room to check the window.

The alarm ceased and was immediately replaced by muffled sounds of gunfire and men shouting.

The captain repeated her question a third time, this time directly addressing Abby and Dennis. Her gun was down at her side. She tapped it repeatedly against her thigh as she spoke.

"The military? The police? How should we know?" exclaimed Dennis, cradling his right arm as though injured. "You're the ones who took us hostage. What did you expect?"

"Do not think me a fool!" the captain said to Dennis. "We have contacts with the Ecuadorians, and they would have alerted us of an assault. This is *not* the authorities."

"Whatever you say," replied Dennis. "But how are we supposed to know anything?"

Turning to Abby, the captain said, "When we took your boat, we lost five men. Whoever killed those men left a note. The police and the military, they don't leave notes." The captain stepped closer to Abby until she was an inch from her face. "Who is it?"

"We don't know!" Dennis shouted as he reached out for Abby to pull her away.

The captain raised her pistol and shot Dennis in the face without ever losing eye contact with Abby.

The report from the gun was deafening in the enclosed space. The smell of gunpowder spread quickly throughout the room. Dennis's body collapsed to the floor as several students screamed.

"I ask you one last time: Who is it?" The captain put her gun to Abby's forehead. Abby remained silent.

"Capitan, the attackers have been cornered on the upper decks. They are trapped, and we will get them. But we must move," said the pirate, his eyes darting around the room.

More gunfire erupted outside the door. The captain lowered her gun and looked towards the door.

Abby reacted instantly and lunged for the captain's gun. With one hand she grabbed the gun, and with the other, she locked on to the captain's wrist.

Struggling to keep the weapon under control, the captain accidentally squeezed the trigger. A second report filled the room as the shot hit the prone Chumley-Smith in his left thigh.

The pirate behind Abby struck her on the side of her head with his weapon, sending her to the ground, but still conscious.

Eyeing the second door to the room, which opened out to the deck, the captain said to the pirate, "Where's Diegito? Have you seen him?"

"No, Capitan."

"Fuck. I'm going out that door. If this is not the authorities attacking us, then there's still a chance that we can get our money. You stay here and block the other door. Keep these prisoners here until I return."

"Yes, Capitan."

The captain grabbed Abby by the hair and pulled her to a standing position. "You're coming with me. Let's go." The pair disappeared out the door.

42

Chris Black, weapon drawn, kicked in the third door in a series of staterooms one deck below the bridge and stepped in. Dana, Donagan, and H2 followed. He rapidly assessed the scene before him and went straight after the only pirate in the room. The man had been knocked down by the opening door but was now getting up. He'd drawn his knife.

The view of Captain Dennis dead on the floor, Chumley-Smith with a new and potentially mortal injury to his leg, and eighteen terrified students jammed into a small room, triggered in Chris what Mac often referred to as 'his inner caveman:' primal instincts that, once unleashed, were not easily turned off.

Holstering his pistol, Chris slipped on both sets of brass knuckles he'd grabbed from Hendrix earlier and moved in. The pirate, who was the same height and general size as Chris, struck out with the knife expertly, cutting into Chris's left shoulder and drawing blood. But that was the last blow the man would land.

Pumping his fists as though to launch a punch, thus drawing the pirate's attention up high, Chris struck the pirate with a savage front kick to his chest, lifting the man off his feet and tossing him against the far wall. Setting his jaw and gritting his teeth, Chris then waded in with the brass knuckles, pummeling the man's face with multiple blows. He felt someone from behind him put a hand on his shoulder, but he brushed them off and kept punching.

"CHRIS!" yelled Dana.

Donagan and H2 moved into the room and helped pull Chris back. The pirate, who'd been held up against the wall by the force of Chris's punches, slid down the wall and collapsed on the floor, his face decimated.

The room was absolutely quiet; the only sounds coming from the battle being waged overhead. Chris shrugged off Donagan and H2 and knelt down by Chumley-Smith.

"What happened?"

Roberto watched as Chris first removed the bloodied brass knuckles and put them in his pockets and then wiped his bloodied hands on his pants. "Roberto?"

"Sorry. Oliver . . . I mean, Dr. Chumley-Smith was already hurt from several days go. But just before you came in, Abby . . . I'm sorry, I mean Ms. Wilson—"

"First names are fine," interrupted Chris.

"Abby was here just before you came in. Captain Dennis was shot in the face. Abby tried to get the gun, and it went off, hitting Oliver in the thigh."

"What happened to Abby?" asked Chris.

Pointing at the downed pirate, Roberto said, "A woman. He called her captain. She and Abby left through that other door."

Chris reached out and rested his hands on Roberto and Terra's shoulders. "Thank you both for your efforts."

Looking around at everyone else, making direct eye contact with as many of the students as he could, Chris spoke, "Team, we need to get you all off this boat as quickly as possible. My two friends here will help you get back to the *MacGreggor*. Can all of you pull that off?"

One by one, the students nodded and stood up.

Chris turned toward Donagan and H2. "If you guys can get them all onto the *MacGreggor* and pull away from this ship, Dana and I will go help Mac and H1."

"Roger that," H2 said.

"We can do that," Donagan agreed.

"Dr. Black?"

Chris turned in response to the question from Terra. "Yes?"

"The pirates. That one, over there, said that the attackers were trapped on the upper deck. He said they were cornered with nowhere to go."

"Well, we'll see about that," Chris replied, motioning to Dana to follow him out the door.

43

Only a single flight of stairs separated Chris and Dana from the bridge. "H1, what's your status?" Chris said into his radio.

"We're . . ."

Explosions cut off H1's reply.

"We're engaged on the deck just aft of the bridge!" H1 yelled over the din of battle. "Multiple targets. We could use some assistance."

"On our way."

At the top of the stairs, the duo encountered a massive steel door. It was locked from the other side.

Dana placed a small charge on the locking mechanism while Chris covered the stairwell. The sounds of an intense firefight reverberated through the door.

"Take two steps forward and turn your back," directed Dana. Chris complied, and a small explosion destroyed the lock.

Chris followed Dana onto the bridge with his weapon drawn. He surveyed the damage as he moved. The bridge was the heart of any ship, and the *Silence's* heart had been obliterated.

The windows were blown out in all directions, and the control consoles, destroyed. The large glass partition that separated the bridge from the deck behind was gone.

The upper deck aft of the bridge was wide open. There was no water in the pool and no lounge chairs on the deck, just debris.

Stepping out through where glass doors had once stood, Chris and Dana immediately began to take fire. Finding cover behind a bar, Chris leaned close to Dana.

"Cover me. I'm going to see if we can level the playing field."

"Got it," she replied, before kissing him hard on the lips. "Just in case anyone's watching. Needs to look authentic."

Chris did a double-take, before arching his eyebrows.

"What?" asked Dana.

"Putting on a better show, are we?" He leaned in and kissed her back.

Still sitting next to Dana, Chris removed what looked like a radar gun from a large pocket on his outer right thigh.

Calling H1 on the radio, he asked, "Where are you guys?"

"We're back behind the Jacuzzi," came the reply. "About 30 feet back from your position, dead center of the deck."

"Okay, hold tight guys. Now, Dana."

Dana pulled a semi-automatic machine pistol from her bag, stood up behind the bar, and began spraying the deck with fire.

Chris stood up next to her and pointed his weapon slowly and methodically at each of the locations where he could see bad guys hiding.

The bar was bombarded by a fusillade of bullets, forcing both Chris and Dana to duck back down.

"Did it work?" asked Dana.

"We should know in a second," said Chris. "If it didn't, I think we're done."

Hendrix had provided Chris and the team with a variety of options for the assault on the Silence. But the laser tagging gun was, Chris thought, without a doubt the coolest. Each of the places that Chris had just illuminated with the gun was now being actively targeted by a drone flying overhead. A drone being operated by Hendrix himself back in his hospital room in Puerto Ayora.

"I may not be able to join you myself this time around, Dr. Black," Hendrix had said. "But I'll be there in spirit."

"In spirit?" Chris had asked, thinking that a strange turn of phrase coming from Hendrix.

"That's right," Hendrix had replied. "Boys, show Dr. Black and Johnson *The Spirit*."

The Spirit Hendrix had been referring to was actually a very sophisticated new drone armed with more firepower than any ten men could carry. The drone brought awesome power to the assault, and it offered Hendrix a way to remain an active part of the team. Hendrix had placed a GPS tracker with Chris's gear, which gave him a constant update on the team's whereabouts.

Within seconds, the drone struck. Chris instinctively covered Dana as multiple explosions rocked the ship. In two minutes, the assault was over.

Carefully extending their heads around the edge of the bar, Chris and Dana both surveilled the damage. Most of the upper deck between them and the Jacuzzi was gone.

"H1, do you read me? You and Mac okay?"

"Copy, we're here. Breaking cover now."

"Donagan, what's your situation?"

"We are getting the last of the students down onto the *MacGreggor*. That was quite a show you just provided."

"Thank Hendrix for that."

Mac and H1 approached from their hiding spot amidships, stepping around the empty pool, which was now filled with more debris.

Dana walked back to meet them.

Chris spotted the drone doing a close fly-by and gave it a salute. As he bent down to pick up a piece of debris in front of him, shots rang out from behind. Chris saw Mac go down, hit in the chest. He was followed immediately by Dana, who was hit in the back.

Turning toward the threat, but with no weapon in hand to respond, Chris saw the dreadlocked pirate he'd found in Tonya Gordan's cabin standing tall and pointing a gun right at him.

44

"Hey, cabrón," said Diegito as he slowly walked toward Chris. "You broke my nose. And your bitch shot me in the shoulder."

Chris could see the man was favoring the shoulder, and his nose looked bad. But he was a very big guy, and Chris knew he couldn't underestimate the guy's power, even when he was wounded.

"I guess she missed her target," said Chris, his eyes scanning the back deck for options. "I'll have to talk with her about that later."

"Later? I don't think so, cabrón. No, I don't think so."

"You're right, of course," said Chris, tightening both fists. "I'm going to kill you long before later gets here."

Chris calculated that at this point, the man called Diegito would not shoot him. The vessel was in tatters, the majority of the crew dead. This tough guy's last option for any victory would be the manly satisfaction of hand to hand combat.

"Perhaps, cabrón. Perhaps, not," said Diegito, as he put down his gun. "Maybe you'll kill me, maybe not. But I'll tell you this, if you don't kill me, it isn't going to go very well for you. Because I'm not going to kill *you*. No, you're going to get a chance to visit a place we have below decks; a place that will make you wish you were dead."

The two men began to circle each other, stepping over debris without breaking eye contact. In the midst of the circling, Chris was able to see both Mac and Dana in his peripheral vision. Like him, they'd both been wearing Kevlar vests when they were shot.

"Were you talking just then," said Chris as he planned his first move. He also was wondering if Hendrix was seeing any of this from above. "Because all I heard was blah, blah, blah, bullshit, bullshit, bullshit."

"Maybe I *will* kill you, cabrón," snarled Diegito. "It will be a pleasure to shut your fucking mouth."

"I don't think so," replied Chris. He judged his best option was going to be to hobble the larger man early. He'd have to break the knee first. Then he'd see how tough this guy really was. "I'm not meant to die at the hands of someone who calls himself 'Little Diego.' What happened there? Was 'Medium Diego' already taken? No, you're definitely the one going down, *cabrón*."

Diegito reached behind him and pulled a large hunting knife out of his belt.

"You found another knife, Little Diego," said Chris. "Nice work. You must be wearing your big boy pants today." He reached into his pockets and pulled out the brass knuckles one more time. He'd never imagined ever wearing a pair, but now he couldn't imagine going anywhere without them.

Diegito smiled. "Let's get this over with, cabrón. I—"

Diegito's last thoughts were interrupted by an explosion of gunfire. Hit in the back, he spun around to see Tonya Gordon standing behind him. Chris dove for cover as more shots rang out.

Tonya stood over Diegito's body firing shots until the clip was expended.

45

Chris looked up from his prone position on the deck. Tonya Gordon's energy had gone with the last bullets she fired into Diegito. She collapsed on the deck next to the body and wept quietly, her head in her hands.

After confirming that Diegito wouldn't be getting up to challenge them again, Chris checked on Dana. She was nursing a sore spot on her back where Diegito's shot had hit her vest. She suggested, "I'll take care of Tonya. Go."

Chris walked over to Mac, whose earpiece had been dislodged early in the fighting. "Abby's still MIA. I've got to find her."

"Room to room?" Mac asked.

The ship was large, with a lot of places to look. "I don't see any other way."

"Let's go." Mac tossed Chris a weapon and picked one up for himself. "We don't know who else is down there."

"Donagan," Chris bellowed as the followed Mac, "tell Hendrix to keep the eye in the sky, or *The Spirit*, or whatever he calls it, on-site. We might still need him."

Most of the deck immediately below the bridge was damaged or burning from the drone strike above. Moving down the stairs to the next landing, Chris was about to turn to the right when he heard an ominous voice from the open bow immediately ahead of them.

The sliding glass door that had once welcomed visitors to the bow had been spray painted black. Half of it had shattered, allowing Chris to see out into the dark beyond. There was Abby, a bleached-blonde woman standing next to her, one hand on the back of Abby's neck, the other holding a large knife.

"Donagan, the captain is a woman. She's on the bow holding Abby at knifepoint."

"Roger that."

Chris and Mac stepped through the broken glass door, guns out. They were fifteen feet away from the pirate and Abby.

Abby looked terrible. Chris could see that her clothes were covered in blood, her arms and face covered with bruises. But in her eyes, he saw the most damage. Abby was the eternal optimist, always ready to put a positive spin on things to brighten the days of those around her. But now the only thing he saw in those eyes was defeat. His stomach tightened as he imagined the horrors she had experienced the past few days.

"Drop the weapons, Yankees. Now." The woman brought the knife to Abby's throat, drawing blood. "*Now.*"

Chris tossed his weapon to the side. Mac followed shortly after.

"What now?" asked Chris.

"Now, either I leave or we all die." As she spoke, the woman moved the knife to her left hand and removed a grenade from her right pocket.

Mac whispered out of the side of his mouth, "She hasn't pulled the pin."

"Diegito's dead," explained Chris.

"I figured that," replied Maria. "You killed him?"

"No. I surely would have," said Chris. "But Tonya Gordon beat me to it. Killed him with his own gun, in fact. There's a nice symmetry to that, you have to admit."

"Who are you, exactly?" asked the woman, her curiosity overwhelming her desire to escape for the moment. "A soldier?"

"You first," Chris said, hoping to buy time.

"Okay," replied the woman. "Why don't you tell me who I am?"

"I'm assuming that you must be the captain of this horror show, but I don't know your name."

"What the hell? You'll all be dead soon. My name is Maria del Carmen. And you are?"

"Chris Black."

"A soldier, then?"

"Nope. Just a simple marine biologist, I'm afraid."

Maria shook her head in disbelief. "A *scientist* did all this? I don't think so."

"Oh, it's true," clarified Chris. "And I'm not done yet. You should've stuck to smaller prey. You could have kept doing that indefinitely, I imagine."

"Perhaps, but times change. Increasing fixed costs. Employees with expectations of higher wages. I am a business-woman."

"A business-woman? Ha! You've murdered an untold number of people and stood by when your people viciously abused your prisoners. You're a monster."

"Don't you dare lecture me! You have no idea what I've been through. You have no right to judge me."

"Yeah, whatever," said Chris. "I'm sure you've got a story, and I'm sure you think your story's important. But it isn't. And it ends here."

And then he said. "Now, Donagan."

From above and to the left, Hendrix's drone swept down toward the deck. As it passed directly over the pirate captain at ten feet up, it discharged defensive flares. The resulting light show was blinding. Both Abby and Maria instinctively covered their eyes. In that instant,

Chris charged forward. He had no weapon. But Chris knew he had one advantage; once they were in the water, they would be in his element.

Maria lowered her forearm just in time to see Chris lunge right at her mid-section. Chris's momentum carried both of them over the rail. Maria was able to grab enough of Abby's sweatshirt before she went over, drawing her over the side as well. Chris estimated the drop to the water to be fifteen to twenty feet. He caught sight of Abby coming over the rail as well, but his only concern at that moment was to maintain contact with the pirate when they hit the water.

The three hit the water in a tangle of arms and legs. The height of the drop pushed them deep. Chris could feel the pressure in his ears. He could also feel Maria struggling in the chilly water. In seconds they would start floating back up toward the surface.

Chris felt long hair brush his right hand. He grabbed and pulled Maria's head toward him. He then wrapped his legs around her head and locked his legs in a vice.

Maria let go of Abby and grasped at Chris's legs, but her movements were panicked. She must not have held her breath when they hit the water, Chris realized. His main job now was to hold on tight with his legs and to flare out the rest of the body to slow their rate of ascension.

Maria switched from grasping to punching. The blows even diminished underwater, were still powerful. But Chris held tight.

Chris could tell from the pressure in his ears that they were passing twenty feet. He knew that the rate of ascent would increase from there. Tightening his legs further, he torqued back and forth.

As they passed ten feet, the pirate's struggling slowed. At five feet, Chris could see lights from the ship shining above. He was starting to worry about his own air supply when the pirate's struggling stopped. Chris opened his legs and released the woman. As his ascent continued, Maria del Carmen's body sank in the other direction.

Chris broke the surface gasping for air. Abby, the former collegiate swimmer, was treading water comfortably nearby. He leaned back and inflated his chest so that he could float at the surface without making any effort while he recovered from the fight.

Through the pulse pounding in his ears, Chris thought he could hear the outboard motor from the *MacGreggor's* inflatable approach.

46

Chris looked across the table at Mac. They'd sat in silence at their favorite restaurant along the waterfront in Puerto Ayora for fifteen minutes. Their table bordered the restaurant's open front, separated from the busy sidewalk by a short wall. On the table were scattered fish identification books as well as the yellow waterproof data logbooks into which they'd recorded everything they'd observed prior to the assault on the *MacGreggor*.

Chris saw Mac's eyes enlarge and turned to see what was going on. He spotted Peter, but behind Peter came the real object of Mac's surprise. Rolling down the street was the giant mechanized caterpillar that they'd seen days earlier, lights once again aglow and calliope music blaring.

Chris watched Peter do a double-take as the beast passed within two feet of him. His eyes still fixed on the strange procession, Peter sat down at their table and ordered a beer.

"Is it going to come back again?" he asked once the waiter had gone back inside.

"We don't really know," answered Mac. "We don't know where it comes from, or where it goes."

"And we don't know where anyone gets on, gets off, or how much it costs to ride."

"Fascinating," observed Peter. "I think I'm going to be here for at least another week, so perhaps I can get to the bottom of that for you boys."

The trio just sat without saying a word, enjoying their beers and watching the people stream past on the sidewalk. It had been a rough couple of weeks, and they were still struggling with the aftermath. Once Chris and Abby had been pulled from the water after their final altercation with the pirate captain, Chris and Mac had escorted Oliver Chumley-Smith and Abby to Santa Cruz in the helicopter. Dana had stayed behind with H1 and H2 to prepare the *MacGreggor* to steam back to Santa Cruz. Donagan had been dispatched to interface with the Ecuadorian Navy, who had arrived on the scene two hours after sunrise.

Donagan had returned to shore on the second day just in time to run interference for Chris and Mac with the Ecuadorian authorities. Chris couldn't be sure, but he thought he might've observed a little more enthusiasm in Donagan than he'd seen before. Perhaps, Chris thought, being in the thick of things had changed Donagan's perspective.

Three more days had passed, during which time nearly all of the students and their families had fled the Galapagos 'never to return in this lifetime.' Hendrix had checked out of the hospital the day before in fine spirits. He, Dana, and the two H's were holed up at an undisclosed location working on things Chris could only guess at. Oliver Chumley-Smith was still in intensive care at the nearby hospital. He was expected to live, but the extent of the damage he took from the brutal beatings was unclear and the amount of blood loss from the gunshot wound to the leg was considerable.

And then there was Abby. The moment they'd been safe on the *MacGreggor's* inflatable after plummeting from the bow of the *Silence* and fighting for their lives, Abby had given Chris the firmest hug he'd ever received. She'd hugged him tight and not let go for several minutes.

He read many things into that hug—fear and joy, maybe gratitude. He imagined in that hug a reassessment of everything that had transpired between them over the past two years. He'd felt hope, but he also knew that in the midst of a crisis was not the time to discuss it. When she released him from the hug, he'd remembered the medal he was carrying in his pocket. He'd handed it to her, prepared to give an explanation, but she didn't need one. She'd simply folded her hands over the medal and begun to cry, her tears matching the intensity of the earlier hug.

This had been mere days ago. According to Alex, who happened to be staying at the same hotel as Abby and her parents, Abby had seen her parents off and then returned immediately to the hospital to stay at Oliver's bedside. She had not reached out to Chris or Mac since they'd stepped off the helicopter.

"How is Oliver doing?" asked Chris, casually sipping his beer. "He was in pretty bad shape on the helicopter flight back from Isabella. They almost lost him a couple of times. Mac actually assisted the paramedics with CPR."

"I heard about that," answered Peter. "He is recovering. Slowly. I think it will be some time before he is ready to fly back to the states."

Peter paused, then added, "You should know that he apologized to me about his handling of the ROV situation."

"He apologized?" asked Mac. "Really?"

"Indeed," replied Peter. "I visited with him in the hospital yesterday."

"Was Abby there?" asked Chris.

"She was," noted Peter. "I understand she is spending much of her time there."

"He wasn't wrong," admitted Mac. "The ROV should've been working better."

Chris raised his eyebrows. "That rest has really done wonders for your attitude. Maybe we should hang a hammock back in the lab."

Chris and Mac had spent much of the past forty-eight hours in the hammocks at the Hotel Déjà Vu sleeping, reading, and swimming in the pool nearby. When the hotel's wireless functioned, Chris also played word games on his smartphone, competing with people from all over the world for gold coins that, as Mac noted, were completely useless outside of the game.

"The impression I got from our conversation," explained Peter, "was that your efforts to rescue the hostages was not lost on Oliver and Abby. Perhaps you'll have a chance to talk about it with them at some point when we're back in Monterey."

"Perhaps," said Chris, as he picked at the label on his beer bottle.

No one spoke for a while.

Eventually, Peter observed, "You did well with the interviews."

There had been no way to avoid the media onslaught that followed their return to Puerto Ayora. As the medevac helicopter had approached the hospital, Chris had been able to see the bright lights of news crews stationed outside the hospital's entrance.

Chris was grateful for the fact that he and Mac were largely shielded from the reporters' inquiries. He knew this was more for liability purposes than for his own mental health, but the net effect was the same. However, they weren't able to completely avoid talking with reporters.

The morning after they'd returned, Chris had been strongly encouraged by Peter to sit down with reporters from CNN, Telemundo, MSNBC, and Fox News, in that order, for live interviews. Peter had explained that the range of questions would be narrow and generally 'safe.'

"Thanks," said Chris. "It was pretty clear the reporters wanted to go off-script. The guy from CNN cornered me after we finished and gave me his card. He wants the real scoop, with 'no bullshit,' when we get back stateside."

"I'd be very careful there," Peter observed. "The liability minefield is treacherous. I'd hate to see you step on any metaphorical mines."

"I think I've already encountered one of the 'mines' you're talking about," Mac threw in. "The woman from MSNBC pulled me aside while Chris was talking to Telemundo to ask about our interaction with the authorities. She was working the angle that we didn't get the support we needed in the field."

"An understatement of epic proportions," interjected Chris.

"I think heads are going to roll at the Ecuadorian Navy," Peter said. "Not literally, of course."

"How so?" asked Mac.

"Well, you were both unambiguous about the lack of timely responses on several occasions once this incident had started."

"Right," replied Mac, "if by 'lack of timely responses,' you mean no response at all. But I'm sure that'll be conveniently covered up."

"Fortunately," continued Peter, "Chris had the peace of mind to take pictures of that poor woman's scribblings on her stateroom wall of the *Silence*. By the way, she and her daughter are already on their way home."

"Yes," said Chris. "We both received a very nice email message from them." He'd given both of them his address back in Carmel and strongly encouraged them to come visit any time.

"Good. Well, the students described the pirate captain's admission that they'd had informants within the Ecuadorian authorities. And the notes you photographed confirmed a visit to the *Silence* by one of the two naval ships in the vicinity. Apparently, the booty that was recovered on the *Innovator* was not the first instance of the pirates paying off key people. Not enough apparently, because nobody was willing to intervene to help the pirates, but some of the officers were willing to find convenient excuses to stay out of the action."

"Fuckers," observed Mac.

"No argument here," said Peter.

"Perhaps Donagan can make himself useful in trying to root out bad elements," suggested Chris.

"Perhaps," agreed Peter.

"How many victims did this group terrorize?" asked Chris.

"I don't think we will know that for some time. There were records on board the *Silence*, but it will take time."

"What kind of 'records' do pirates keep?" asked Mac with obvious incredulity.

"I'm not fully briefed on all the details," said Peter, "but it sounds like the captain, Maria del Carmen, was actually a business major from the University of Pennsylvania. She apparently recorded everything the pirates did. Unfortunately, the stateroom where she kept those records was damaged in the drone attack. So again, it will take some time."

"And who's going to do that? The Ecuadorians?" asked Mac.

"They'll certainly be involved," answered Peter. "But Donagan will no doubt lead the investigation."

"Before we came down here," Chris said, "Tony set me up with this woman, a lawyer working for the United Nations."

"He's never set me up with anyone, period," said Mac before taking a sip of his beer.

"Yes, and we'll want to get to the bottom of that at some point," said Chris raising his eyebrows at Peter. "But to the point we're discussing here, we had this fascinating conversation about the lawlessness of international waters. It really is like the wild west out there. These pirates are probably just the tip of the iceberg."

All three sat in silence and drank their beers.

"What's next for the *MacG*?" Chris finally asked.

"Captain Williams just flew in from Arizona, where he was staying with his ailing mother. He and Alex are both back on board," Peter said.

"I offered to fly Alex home days ago, but to his credit, he wants to stay with the ship and sail her home."

"Alex is a dude," observed Mac, leaning back in his chair.

"Yes, he is," said Chris. "And I'm glad to hear that Bill was able to fly down to help. We need to figure out how we can honor Dennis. I'd like to see if there is something we can do for his daughter."

"That's a very good idea, Dr. Black," said Peter. He pulled a small notebook out of an interior pocket in his jacket and wrote something down. "I'll have someone start looking at options right away and get back to you."

"Thanks."

"How is the university reacting to all of this, now that it's over?" asked Chris.

"I don't think there'll be any international trips for the *MacGreggor* anytime soon," answered Peter.

"That's ridiculous," observed Mac, sitting forward and slamming his beer down hard enough to attract the attention of people at nearby tables. "What are the odds of something like this happening again?"

"That's the academic bureaucracy for you," noted Chris. "What about broader concerns? Are you taking any heat from above, Peter?" He was certain that the university administrators would not be happy about another incident involving the *MacG* in such a short period of time.

"That's the job. I'm paid to take the heat," replied Peter.

"Sure," said Chris. "But how much heat are you taking?"

"You let me worry about that for now. We'll talk when we're all back on campus."

Chris was concerned. It was true that Peter's job as Director of the CMEx was to work with the university administrators—a job that Chris had seen Peter handle with aplomb on more than one occasion. But as the 'incidents' had piled up over the past two years, Chris was increasingly worried about the impact of that pressure on his friend.

"Is it that bad?" asked Chris, reading between the lines.

"Look," said Peter. "I was in the trenches for years and old Dick Cooper kept the heat off of me. Now you guys are in those trenches, and it's my job to do everything I can to keep the heat off you. It's just the way it works."

Chris and Mac exchanged a glance. It must be getting ugly; they both knew. But they also both knew better than to press further right then.

"You two have outdone yourselves once again," suggested Peter. "When I think of what you've been through these past couple of years, it boggles my mind."

Not used to this type of praise from Peter, Chris observed that Mac was conspicuously silent.

"Plus," Peter continued, "I'm the one who sent you two down here with such urgency. This is all on me. You deserve some time off."

"You obviously couldn't have known," said Chris. "But thanks, Boss."

The three touched bottles, and then Peter added as he looked up the street, "Do you think it's coming back again?"

47

"And now, we surf," explained Mac as he walked out of a small surf shop at the edge of town with two rented surfboards under his arms.

After collecting their gear from the *MacGreggor*, Chris and Mac had returned to San Cristobal Island to catch a flight back to the mainland the following day. That had left six hours of daylight for them to kill. Given the twenty-four-hour no-fly rule for SCUBA diving, which suggests divers not fly for twenty-four hours after their last dive to avoid getting 'the bends,' there was no time to explore some of the world-class dive sites they hadn't visited this trip.

During his previous visit to the island, Chris had found a spot across the leeward side that offered reliable waves for surfing in a beautiful setting. It hadn't taken him long to convince Mac that surfing was going to be the best use of their remaining hours on the islands.

Thus, only minutes after checking into their hotel rooms, Chris and Mac loaded up, rented boards, and hopped into one of the many white pickup trucks that served as taxis on the island.

The little embayment of Puerto Chino resided on the southeastern edge of San Cristobal. Chris had visited it frequently on his previous trip to the Galapagos. The drive out to Puerto Chino took forty-five minutes, with another twenty minutes required to walk down the narrow pathway from the parking lot to the beach. With so much natural scenery to take-in during the drive, Mac was uncharacteristically quiet for entire the ride out, giving Chris a chance to calmly watch the foliage and wildlife pass by in peace. Once on-site, the path down to the beach terminated at a dense copse of trees. Emerging from under the dark canopy, the wide expanse of the bay opened up before them, with crystal blue waves crashing against dark, volcanic rocks to either side of a small sandy beach.

"This definitely does not suck," observed Mac, not wasting any time slipping into his wetsuit.

"No, it doesn't," replied Chris as he used his smartphone to snap a panoramic picture of the beach from one end to the other. "Just don't get in my picture."

Paddling out into clean, three-to-five-foot surf, without another human being to be seen, provided the pair with a relaxing counterpoint to the horrors of the past several weeks. After more than an hour of unfettered surfing, Chris was paddling back out along the southern boundary of the beach, an area characterized by large, volcanic rock formations, when movement to his right caught his eye. It took him several moments to understand what he was looking at when it finally dawned on him that the dark blob he'd just seen drop off the rocks into the water was a marine iguana.

Sitting up on his board, Chris watched as three more iguanas followed the first into the water. The fact that there were waves breaking with some force against the rocks did not seem to bother them at all. Their swimming, at least at the surface, was not particularly elegant, Chris noticed. They swam with their heads held just above the waterline, their massive tails propelling them forward.

"You coming over this way, dude?" he asked of the first iguana, which answered by submerging and disappearing from view.

Chris knew that the dives would not last long. The challenge for these incredible creatures was not the breath-holding required for these dives, but rather the rapid temperature loss. Like all of their terrestrial cousins, marine iguanas were ectotherms, meaning that they derived their heat from the surrounding environment. This was opposed to Chris himself, who, as an endoderm, generated his own heat internally.

After some time, Mac paddled over to see what was going on. "This is pretty cool," he offered. "But what's with all the sneezing?"

"These guys are herbivores," Chris explained why in between dives, the iguanas would periodically sneeze. "They are making dives to eat algae off the rocks."

"Okay," said Mac.

"Well, while eating the algae underwater, they ingest a fair amount of saltwater. Too much salt for their bodies, so they sneeze the salt out through their noses."

Mac watched an iguana swim past. "*That* is some wild stuff."

After half an hour watching the iguana show, during which time the four iguanas came very close to Chris and Mac, Chris realized that it was not likely to end anytime soon. So, they returned to the lineup to catch a few more waves. An hour later, he was beginning to feel the type of fatigue in his arms that only surfing could produce when he spotted two familiar faces standing at the water's edge.

Catching a wave in, Chris rode right up to the two figures, one of whom was still using a sling.

"Dr. Black!" observed Frank Donagan with his usual enthusiasm.

"You can't get rid of us," noted Hendrix.

Chris could see himself reflected in Hendrix's signature sunglasses. "I'm beginning to realize that. Are you here to surf?"

"Not exactly," explained Donagan. "We came for you."

"Oh?"

"There's an interesting little job in Israel, down in Eilat on the coast of the Red Sea, that I could use some help with."

"Oh?" Chris put down his board, grabbing the towel he'd hung on a nearby tree branch.

"It's a joint operation between the Israelis, the Jordanians, and the Egyptians to deploy a temporary undersea lab adjacent to one of the coral reefs in the area."

"I know Eilat well," said Chris, instantly considering the many possibilities provided by an endeavor. "There are some interesting things one could do with a lab like Poseidon off-shore there. The coral reefs are in pretty good shape, and the fish fauna is quite diverse. It's got many of the tropical Indo-Pacific species present."

Donagan and Hendrix shared a bemused glance as Chris held forth on the project's potential.

"There's also an interesting gradient of fishing pressure from the southern part of the Red Sea off Sharm El Sheikh in Egypt, where fishing is intense, to Eilat where there is greater overall protection. That could prove interesting."

Chris paused and then said, "But what kind of help are they looking for?"

"Therein lies the rub," explained Donagan. "As a truly international effort, no one wants to rely solely on the Israelis or either of the other two countries. We require a third party. That's where Hendrix and his capable team come in."

"Are you up for such a job already, Hendrix?" asked Chris, motioning to the sling with his hand.

Donagan clarified, "Oh, the work won't start for about three months, which should allow plenty of time for Mr. Hendrix here to fully recuperate."

"Okay," said Chris, pulling down the top of his wetsuit and wrapping himself in a towel.

"Talking with the organizers, Hendrix continued where Donovan had left off, "it is pretty clear that they don't have, how do I say this? A deep well of experience with saturation diving. You, on the other hand, do."

Mac walked up and leaned his board against the large volcanic boulders lining the shoreline. "What's up?"

Chris looked at Donagan, then at Hendrix, then turned to Mac and said, "How many clean pairs of underwear did you say you have in your suitcase?"

Acknowledgments

This book, like all of Chris Black's adventures, is very much a work of fiction. But like the other books, it is informed by reality, experiences I've had over the course of my career.

But I also get to work with amazing people, and their stories find their way into Chris's adventures as well. For instance, a version of the eco-terrorist attack happened to my colleague, Dr. Rick Starr. And the menacing presence lurking behind a sailboat in the wee hours of a transit across the South Pacific happened to my friend Frank Degnan. You'll have to ask both of them about the details of the real experiences.

I'd like to thank the many residents of the Galapagos Islands who helped make my two trips to the region extraordinary.

I'd also like to thank, once again, my team of manuscript reviewers, including Carrie Bretz, Peter Auster, Rick Starr and Andrew DeVogelaere. Their collective adventures would make Chris Black envious, and as serious readers I highly value their insights.

Finally, this book would literally not have happened were it not for the considerable editorial talents of Dr. Helga Schier, my editor at CamCat Publishing.

About the Author

Dr. James Lindholm is an author who dives deep for his inspiration. His novels stem from a foundation of direct, personal experience with the undersea world. He has lived underwater for multiple 10-day missions to the world's only undersea laboratory and has found himself alone on the seafloor staring into the eyes of a hungry great white shark.

He has drafted text for an executive order for the White House and has briefed members of the House and Senate on issues of marine science and policy. James Lindholm's diverse writing portfolio includes textbooks, peer-reviewed scientific journal articles, and action/adventure novels.

For more information, please visit www.jameslindholm.com.

Follow CamCat from undersea dives to high mountain climbs.

If you've enjoyed James Lindholm's Chris Black adventure series, you'll enjoy Mark Broe's *Temple of Conquest*.

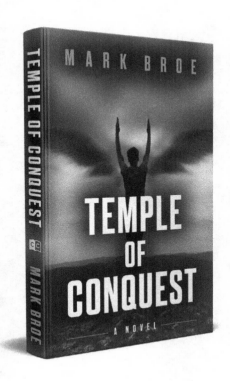

Hot, white slits of sunlight drifted up Telep's cheek as he lay in bed. The blinding light squeezed through the gaps in the wooden shutters covering his bedroom window. When the light finally reached his fluttering eyelids, he stirred and recoiled. Purpose and routine dragged his feet to the floor where he pulled on his climbing attire: thin woolens to increase maneuverability, a knit shirt that hugged his body tighter than the shapeless tunics that could snag a rock, and a pair of firm sandals that were closed at the toes and had extra straps extending up his calf. He'd had the same climbing garments for several solars now, and they had become worn and tight on his growing frame. His wool trousers barely extended past the calf. His toes had blisters from being forced into outgrown sandals, though he always seemed to stretch the leather a little bit more every time. His knit wool shirt had started off white, but solars of grazing rock faces had stained it a reddish brown. Every time he put it on, he pulled the fabric away from his chest to stretch it out a bit.

Out of the saltbox, he pulled two chops of lamb and put them on a thick slice of hard bread. Grabbing his large lumber satchel, he was almost out the door when he heard his parents descending the stairs. Both stood a head shorter than Telep, though his father sounded much larger the way he stomped down the steps. Both of them wore robes, his mother cinching hers, and his father making no such effort.

"What's the cargo this sun?" his father asked.

"More dark wood," Telep said.

"Alright. So, when will it be done?"

"The Temple of the Sky?" Telep asked the question even though he knew what his father meant.

"Yeah. You've taken so much lumber up there, can't it reach the sky yet?" His father crossed the kitchen and leaned on the saltbox to stretch his back. His mother followed behind impatiently.

"Did you get enough breakfast?" she asked, trying to lift the wooden hatch of the saltbox, which her husband's lean made impossible.

"Yes, Ma. I'm fine."

"When are you back?" his father groaned amid a deep stretch.

"Should be back tonight."

"Neil, would you move?" his mother pressed.

"No classes this sun?" his father asked, and then turned to his wife. "He said he ate, hun."

"Can you just stretch on the floor?" she shot, still pulling on the saltbox lid.

After a moment of silence, Neil laughed and grabbed his wife around the waist.

"You want to put me on the floor?"

She giggled.

"Yeah, I'll be back tonight," said Telep, turning out the door. The laughing got louder as he closed the door behind him.

Blue skies radiated overhead as he walked the main path to the wood stockade, which had been moved after the collapse of the North Rim. The collapse had slowed the transportation of raw materials on Eveloce, and Telep found himself busier than ever. He and Ell's father,

Caleb, were among the select few who were able to scale the South Rim with a decent payload of cargo.

Construction of the Temple of the Sky had slowed considerably with the supply of materials dropping off after the North Rim's collapse. Though most of Eveloce's habitants were skilled climbers, only the best were able to traverse the jagged vertical faces leading to the top tier crescent. This was where the highest elders and mountain elite resided. It was also where many of the most sacred temples were built.

Telep looked up to the top tier with admiration. To him it was something to strive for, something to idolize, a place embodying the pinnacle of human endeavor.

Even in his earliest memories, height had enthralled him. His mother liked to speak of his infancy when he would sit at the bottom of the stairs as if in a trance, his eyes fixed on the top step.

Telep couldn't deny that he found much of his identity in climbing. It made him valuable in Eveloce. It gave him a chance to advance his societal rank to top tier. And it was through climbing that he had met Ell, his love, the girl he wanted to hold until his last breath. Climbing put it all within his reach.

Looking up the path to the wood stockade, Telep saw the brawny silhouette of Caleb. This surprised him as he almost always reached the stockade first; something he did to show Caleb how responsible he was. He felt a kinship with Caleb because he was the only climber in Eveloce whose ability and zeal matched his own. They had been climbing partners for three solars and had grown very close. Looking at the sun's position over the mountain, he took a breath, confirming he was not late.

When he reached the stockade, he saw an inordinate amount of lumber behind Caleb, who waved him over with a smile. Usually there was just enough lumber for three or four stacks, an amount that he and Caleb could move in two sun's time, but he counted twenty-four stacks.

Only two were dark wood, he observed, one already loaded into Caleb's lumber satchel.

"Morning," Telep said.

"Hey." Caleb slapped him hard on the shoulder, and they walked over to the other stack of dark wood. "I learned something about you, Telep."

"Yeah?"

Caleb knelt next to his fully bundled satchel and started examining the straps. "Do you need silver? Does your family need silver?"

All flippancy faded from Telep's face. He always tried to present himself to Caleb as well-off and capable. After all, he was Ell's father.

"No, we are fine. Well, I mean we need it; we all work, but—"

"I mean are you struggling? Does your family have debts?" Caleb looked at him with concern.

Telep bit the inside of his lip hard. "No, we are fine. We're more than fine."

Caleb jiggled one of the straps on his satchel and started tightening it. "Why do you ask?"

"I spoke with Elder Anaea," Caleb said, standing up. Though he was a hand shorter than Telep, the power he asserted could intimidate a bear. "He tells me you have been bartering the price of the wood."

Telep looked down at the pile of dark wood, slung the leather satchel off his shoulder and knelt to start loading it. "We are fine."

"Okay." Taking a breath, Caleb knelt down to help load the satchel. "Listen, I know you can take care of yourself. I know you contribute to your family. And I don't doubt you could take care of Ell."

Telep stopped, a log mid-air in his hand, and looked up at Caleb as he continued.

"You know this landslide has been hard on everyone, the elders too. They are cut off. They used to get their supplies very cheap from the North Rim—"

"Anybody with a wheelbarrow could deliver on the North Rim."

Caleb grinned. He secured the last strap of his satchel, and they departed.

———————

The South Rim had several sections of vertical rock face, and each one needed precise planning and execution. If a climber didn't know where the next hold was, there would not be much time to find it considering the weight of the load was enough to peel even the strongest climbers off the wall. Relative to his weight, Telep had the strongest hands in Eveloce but with a full load, there were times when they burned with exhaustion.

Caleb and Telep climbed slowly and steadily, resting after each section of vertical rock.

The sky darkened. Black clouds enveloped the horizon. The dark wood grew heavier as they made their way up the South Rim. Calling it the "South Rim" made Caleb and Telep laugh because prior to the landslide, it was known as the "Southern Cliffs." It was scarcely travelled because of its extreme climbing difficulty.

Halfway up the third vertical face, they looked to the next landing. They named it "The Precipice of Perdition" because it came before the largest and most strenuous section of the climb.

Telep looked up at Caleb, about ten holds ahead of him. He stopped and took a deep breath. The strong aromatic scent of wood from his satchel permeated the air. He felt honored to be carrying dark wood to the top tier. It was a very rare wood used in the most sacred temples. While the other supplies could be lifted up the cliffs using hoists, the elders required dark wood to be carried by climbers so it remained connected to the people harnessing its power. It had a smooth texture but was dense and heavy. The bark was black; the wood, dark gray. It proved very difficult to burn, but when dark wood did ignite, it released an intoxicating fragrance so palpable that people spoke of tasting it rather than smelling it. A dark wood fire sent thick dark smoke high into the sky. It was said that, if set on the top tier's burning pyre, the smoke could be seen anywhere, from the seawall of the south to the lakes of the West Isles. Everyone in the world would be seeing the same thing.

Telep noticed the humidity rising. The rock face felt moist to his touch.

POP! The sound pierced the air.

"TELEP!"

His eyes shot up. Logs of dark wood plunged toward him. He leapt from the wall and grabbed for the safety line, kicking sideways at the rock, trying to evade the falling logs. He gripped it. A barrage of dark wood whipped past him. A strong WHACK from the descending lumber rang in his ears. His left hand jolted off the hemp rope which began burning through his right hand, unable to support the weight. He forced his hand back on the rope, trying to stop himself from sliding, but the weight of the cargo dragged him down. Tiny pieces of calloused skin clung to the rope as it passed through his hands. With a pained yell, he cocked his hands in different directions and ground to a halt.

Again, his gaze shot up. Caleb was falling, his outstretched hands searching for the safety line just out of reach. Telep froze in terror. He stuck out his left foot, hoping it could help in some way, but all he felt was a whoosh of air as Caleb flew past him. His eyes shivered in horror as they followed his mentor, his friend, Ell's father plunging toward the rocky ledge below. An image of Ell shot in his mind—she was smiling so big as she always did upon their return from a climb.

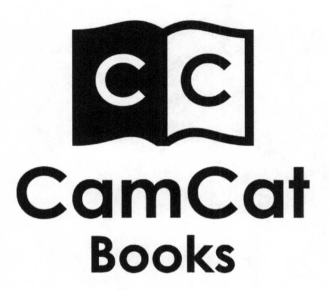

CamCat
Books

Visit Us Online for More Books to Live In:
camcatbooks.com

Follow Us:

CamCatBooks   @CamCatBooks   @CamCatBooks

Printed in the USA
CPSIA information can be obtained
at www.ICGtesting.com
LVHW091218081123
763026LV00003B/29/J